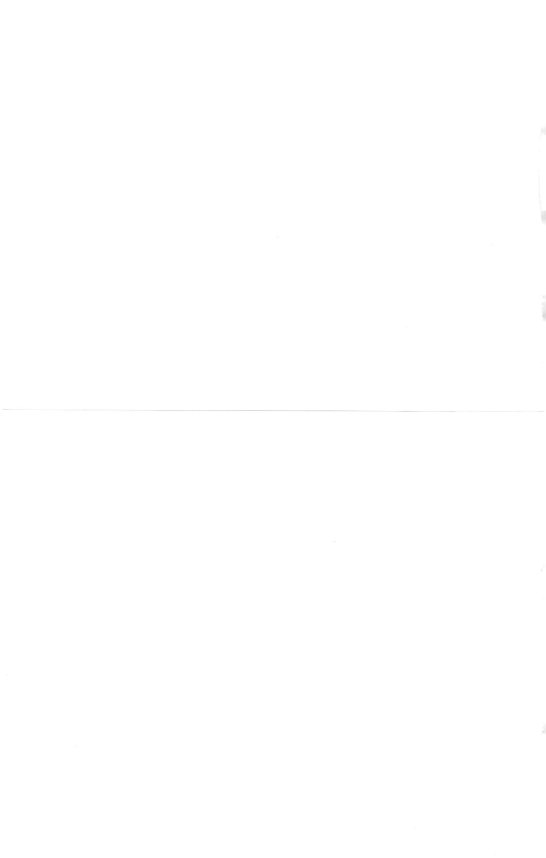

IN THE
HANDS
OF THE
SHADOW

C.JAY!

authorHOUSE®

AuthorHouse™
1663 Liberty Drive
Bloomington, IN 47403
www.authorhouse.com
Phone: 1-800-839-8640

Published by AuthorHouse   11/05/2012

ISBN: 978-1-4772-7161-2 (sc)
ISBN: 978-1-4772-7160-5 (hc)
ISBN: 978-1-4772-7159-9 (e)

Library of Congress Control Number: 2012917354

Chapter I

~⌒∿∧∿⌒~

IT WAS A good day. The birds sang as the sun shined in the skies over Watertown, New York. Aaron Williamson, a muscular, six-foot, three-inch bronze bomber, awakened to the sight of his beautiful girl friend, Laura Hinkley, still sleeping. He stepped out of bed carefully so as not to wake her. Aaron slipped into his robe and stepped over to the window. Looking out, Aaron saw the leaves gently swaying in the fall breeze. It looked exceptionally clear and crisp, Aaron's favorite kind of day. Turning to look back at the still sleeping Laura, a smile warmed Aaron's face. With sunlight casting a gentle gleam across her face, Laura's skin looked like soft down.

Aaron found himself suddenly aroused as Laura turned her shapely five-foot-six-inch frame and her shoulder-length hair fell softly across her face. She was practically purring when she released a sigh and brushed her hair away from her face. He shook himself and mused at his own vulnerability where Laura was concerned.

"I am one lucky man to have her in my life," he thought to himself as he headed towards the kitchen. He moved about quickly in the well appointed black and white kitchen while he prepared breakfast. Aaron gave the table a quick once-over making sure that the juice; muffin, strawberries, melon balls and grapes appeared appetizing. He placed a daisy in a single vase and set out the napkins and cutlery. Aaron headed back up the circular stairs of the duplex condominium into the master bedroom to find that Laura was still asleep. He bent over her to place a gentle kiss on her lips, and gently brushed her face. She finally responded to his caress and gave Aaron a big, sleepy smile.

"Hmm what time is it?" she asked sleepily. "It's ten o'clock, breakfast is ready and we have to get ready *if* we're going to leave by eleven forty-five. We don't want to spend too much time in here, because we might not make it out at all if we start" . . ." Aaron gave Laura a lascivious glance, only to get his hand smacked away.

Laura padded out of bed, kissed Aaron softly on the cheek, and went into the bathroom to shower. Quickly lathering and rinsing herself several times, she dried herself and headed downstairs to the kitchen where Aaron was waiting to have breakfast. She was wearing a short silk purple robe which complemented her red hair. Laura headed straight to Aaron, wrapped her arms around his neck and gently kissed his full lips. "Good morning, my life," she said. "Good morning, my love," he replied, returning her kiss. "I am loving everything in my view and viewing everything that love! In fact, I can't think of any other way that I would rather begin my day." He gazed hungrily into her eyes and wrapped his arms around her, lifting her slightly off the floor while his tongue probed her mouth. She was beginning to breathe deeply as she felt her insides warming; her body was rapidly heating up to Aaron's touch. They both pushed slowly apart and sat down to breakfast, still holding hands. "Aaron, how we ever get to leave this place is beyond me. I hope these feelings will always be as full of fire as they are now." "Laura, don't worry. As long as you keep loving me, my fire won't ever go out," he answered.

The two finally started breakfast, which they ate quickly. Afterwards, Aaron went into the bedroom to dress while Laura cleared the imported marble table and placed the dishes into the dishwasher. Once finished in the kitchen, Laura went back into the bedroom and began to dress herself.

Laura dressed quickly and, leaving Aaron in the bedroom, she decided to listen to some music while Aaron completed his grooming.

Walking into the living room, she flipped on the Spice Girls CD. As the pulsing rhythms of their hit song filled the air, Laura began to dance around the richly appointed room. The plush light gray Aubusson rug, midnight blue love seat and sofa, brass lamps, glass and brass accent tables were carefully selected for their quiet beauty. When Laura danced her way towards the African paintings and masks on the stark white walls, she noticed something on the floor in front of the door.

Cautiously, she walked over, picked it up and slowly opened the envelope. On the inside of the envelope was a card with what looked like a person's shadow. There were no other markings on the card. Not quite sure what to make of the card, or its implications, Laura decided to ask Aaron about it.

Laura ran quickly upstairs and headed into the bedroom where Aaron was slipping on an alligator belt. She asked, "Aaron, honey, this envelope was in the living room in front of the door. Someone must have slipped it under the door last night or earlier this morning. Were you expecting anything like this?"

"What's inside the envelope? What does it say?" he asked.

"It doesn't say anything. There's only some sort of shadow-like figure on a card," she answered.

"OKAY just a minute, let me finish brushing my hair and I'll check it out," he said, turning on the overhead lights and slipping over to the double dresser.

As he slowly brushed his hair, Laura watched Aaron's face. She saw what she thought was a look of wariness in his eyes. When he lifted up his head and brought his gaze to meet hers, he snapped on a brief smile and shrugged his shoulders.

Aaron took the envelope and went slowly downstairs to the living room as Laura followed. He sat down heavily on the sofa and opened the envelope with a decided air of resignation. As he looked at the figure of the shadow on the card, Laura knew without a doubt that the image was distressing to Aaron. His face went blank, his eyes seemed frozen, and that fake smile quickly faded.

Trying to sound as calm as she could, Laura asked, "What is it, honey? What's this all about? Who sent this card to you?"

"Aw . . . . It's really no big deal, baby. Don't worry about this because it's nothing that I can't handle."

But Laura KNEW that there was indeed something to worry about. Very few things really rattled Aaron, and whatever this card symbolized, she knew that it was trouble. She thought to herself, "Aaron never keeps secrets from me, but now suddenly, he's holding back." In the two years that they had been together, he had always seemed to be honest and above-board. She was certain that Aaron had some kind of problem because the appearance of the shadow on the card had instantaneously altered Aaron's personality. Laura began to feel her resolve welling up inside of her. She knew at that moment that she was damn well certain to find out exactly what the card meant.

As the day progressed, Aaron and Laura followed through on their original plans to lunch with their good friends, Stanley and Dawn. They even managed to find time for a relaxing walk through the town mall. In the mall, Laura tried to talk Aaron into going with her to the Blockbuster Video Store so that they could pick out a few movies together for the night. Aaron, however, had a different idea for that evening.

"Baby," he said, "you know, I do have to get up early in the morning. How about if we just go home after shopping, make love for the rest of the night and just pass out in each other's arms." He smiled one of his, 'I'm so cute' smiles, leaned down and kissed her on the lips.

When the two returned home, they did just as Aaron had suggested, making love long into the night. By the time they were ready for sleep, it was after ten-thirty. Aaron tossed and turned trying in vain to get comfortable, while Laura laid there thinking about the mysterious card. Each one thought the other to be asleep, but they were both worried about the card. Finally, around midnight, Laura was drifting off to a light fitful sleep when Aaron eased out of bed.

When Aaron finished dressing, he stood next to the bed. He watched Laura thoughtfully as she slept. A tear worked its way down his cheek. He thought to himself, "She is so beautiful. She is gentle, caring and smart, too. Why, why does she have to be put in danger because of my past? She really deserves a peaceful life. I don't know why they've come back, but my service to them is over and I will maintain a stable life for Laura and for myself!"

Aaron turned and quietly eased out of the bedroom to make his way quickly downstairs. He hurried towards the door, grabbed the keys to the Hummer from the rack and headed out towards the elevators.

Hearing the front door shut, Laura jumped out of bed and quickly changed. She slipped into her black cat suit and pulled her hair tightly into a baseball cap. Timing the elevators just right, she ran downstairs, grabbed the keys to the Eldorado and raced out into the hall to make her way down the stairs.

Laura peeked through the windows of the parked cars in the underground parking complex as she waited for Aaron to pull off in the truck. Before he turned the corner which led to the up ramp of the exit, Laura hopped into the Eldorado, started it up and followed the truck at an undetectable distance.

After he drove through Watertown, Aaron headed over to the interstate highway, driving down the entrance ramp which led onto the southbound interstate 81. As he drove, Aaron glanced at the card with the mysterious shadow and wondered again what they wanted from him. He searched his memory and began to understand that there was only one reason that he would have been contacted. Growing increasingly angry, Aaron shouted, "yeah, I DO know. I know just what these bastards want, and I do not want to be involved in their shit."

Driving at seventy-five miles per hour, Laura slowed and exited the interstate onto U.S. Highway 343. She could barely see the rear lights of the Hummer, but she continued to press on. She began to question things that she had never even thought about concerning Aaron. Things such as, where and how he had made enough money to open and operate two successful clubs and a thriving bar at the age of thirty-six.

During their eighteen-month relationship, the subject had never really come up. Laura had noted that Aaron was extremely focused for a man of his age. He was very frugal and he invested his money very carefully. Initially, she had believed that his seed money had come solely from hard work and perseverance. Yet, the more that Laura thought on the subject, she realized for the first time that she actually knew very little about Aaron's past. He was always closed about his past, but he was open to anything that concerned the two of them. The most important thing to Laura about Aaron was that he was tender and caring; she knew that he did indeed love her. It was this life that Laura would protect at any cost!

Laura strained to see the lights from the Hummer as Aaron turned rapidly off of the road to the left. She accelerated so she could keep Aaron's rear lights in sight, but when she sped up, she almost missed the sharp turn-off. After she slammed on the brakes, the car came to a screeching halt. Turning into a dirt road, Laura tried again to see the rear lights of the truck. Her stomach twisting in knots, she continued to drive down the dirt road with a sense of trepidation. She noticed the tall eerie stalks of corn against the dark night standing stark on either side of the road. She momentarily stopped the car to decide in which direction she should continue. She was out in the middle of nowhere and couldn't tell which way Aaron had traveled.

Before Laura had a chance to ease her foot off of the brakes, the passenger side of the door flew open and a large man loomed in at her. Laura became instantly hysterical. "Oh, my God! Get away from me!"

"Calm down," said the deep voice. "It's only me, Laura." Through her tears and her gasping breath she managed to focus in on the face of Aaron just before she passed out cold.

Aaron put the car in park and gently revived Laura, holding her closely as she came to with a roar. "Aaron, I want to know . . . and I want to know right now, just what in the hell is going on with you. Out of the clear blue sky we find this card with a shadow on it. You start sneaking around in the middle of the night out here in the Netherlands, and you have the temerity to tell me not to worry! Well, I am worried, Aaron in fact, I am good and worried. You have to tell me what we're involved in that can cause you to behave so erratically."

"Laura, I really wish that you hadn't followed me. There are lots of things in my past that I haven't told you about. Some of those things I wish I could just bury because I'm really not proud of them. They are dark things, Laura; things that I never wanted you to know about, things that I never wanted to touch your life. I don't even want to think about my past, much less to talk about it; but now, it seems to have come back to haunt me. This was simply a chapter in my life that I wanted to totally delete. Believe me, this is one of those situations that really would be better if left untold. For now, Laura, all I can do is ask you to rely on my love for you and to try to trust me to straighten out this crook in my road." Aaron choked these words out as he looked pleadingly into Laura's eyes.

"Laura, it's just too dangerous for you to even be out here with me now. I love you too much to risk your safety and I just couldn't handle anything happening to you because of me. In fact, I'd feel a lot better about this situation if you would just take the car and go home. This," he said as he held up the card with the shadow on it, "is nothing to be taken lightly. Please, Laura, go home and leave this matter to me," he pleaded.

"No, Aaron! I am coming with you. If you're into something that is so bad that you would go through all of this cloak and dagger business, then I will be by your side," she said with a tremulous conviction in her voice.

"Damn it," he said. "OKAY come with me and lock the doors. The Hummer is parked just off the road."

Aaron held Laura's hand as he led her through the cornfield to the truck. He hurried her into the truck and as soon as Aaron jumped in, he reached into the glove compartment then pulled out a Desert Eagle automatic handgun. "Here," he said, "take this and keep it close to you, and be prepared to blast anything that comes near you!" Then Aaron reached under his seat and pulled out a Nickel plated Desert Eagle 44. Magnum handgun.

"Aaron, just get this shit away from me, you know that I hate guns. I don't need it, that's why I got my black belt. And, anyway, why would I need such a big gun? What the hell am I going to do, blast a hole in the ozone layer?"

"Laura, please just do as I say for now. A lot of your questions are about to be answered," he said. Aaron started the truck and roared back onto the dirt road. He found it hard to see with regular car lights, so he switched to the high beams. After he did so, just ahead in the distance, they both noticed a steep drop in the road. He grabbed Laura's hand, shot her a glance and yelled, "OKAY, Laura, hold on! This is a pretty big drop off, but I think the Hummer can take it."

Aaron gunned the accelerator. With a thunderous roar, the Hummer tore over the drop clearing a ridge and slamming onto the ground.—They had just cleared a seven foot drop which ended in a circular clearing.—

Before Aaron or Laura ever had a chance to collect themselves, bright lights hit the battered truck from every direction. Blinded by the lights, the two heard a voice come at them from every direction over loud speakers which said, "Step out of the truck, Williamson." Still somewhat shaken, they were trying to find their legs when the voice repeated its demand even louder. Still unable to focus clearly, Aaron managed to help Laura and the two stumbled out of the truck. Neither of them could see anything, but Aaron did manage to make out a person coming towards them. Just before the figure closed in on them, he heard a familiar Korean female voice shout, "Turn off the lights now. I want him to see us."

After the lights went out, both of their eyes took a few seconds to adjust. Once they could clearly focus, they saw a raven haired Korean woman, standing a few feet away from them. Laura immediately looked up at Aaron as if to ask, "What's going on?" But in his eyes she saw a look of shock and disbelief.

The tension of that moment thickened in the silence until the smirking Korean woman said, "My, my, Aaron, it's been nearly two years. No hug, kiss or even a hello? Don't tell me you've forgotten my name already!" She was standing there with a smile on her lips, but her eyes held a steady daring gaze directed at Aaron.

Curiously, confusion and a rapidly growing annoyance raged within Laura. She remembered what Aaron had said to her a few moments earlier about all of her questions being answered in a few minutes. Yet, there were only questions heaped upon questions in her mind. Finally, she couldn't remain silent any longer. With her mounting anxiety coming to a boil, Laura had to speak. Shooting a look of burning intensity towards the woman, she turned to Aaron and said, "Aaron, who in the hell is this woman? And why does she keep looking at you like that?"

"Not now, Laura. This is not the time for questions."

"Yes, now, Aaron! Who is she and just what in the hell does she have to do with you?"

"Oh, Aaron," interjected the Korean woman as she sidled up to Aaron. "She is a feisty one, isn't she?"

Laura shot back, "Oh, don't worry, bitch, my bite is worse than my bark!" A slow, sly smile formed on the woman's lips as she sauntered towards Laura. As she drew closer to Laura, Laura suddenly realized that she was much taller than any other Asian woman she had ever seen before. She thought to herself, "Damn, this woman must be at least six feet tall." The woman stopped about three paces short of Laura and looked down into Laura's eyes as Aaron quickly stuck his arm out, forming a barrier across Laura's chest. Upon Aaron's intervention, the woman smiled smugly then said, "Since Aaron is being so rude, please allow me to introduce myself. My name is Yung Lee Kim. I used to be Aaron's lady, but that was then; now I am simply the MOTHER of his two-year-old son, Aaron Jr. And judging by the look on your face, you're not very happy to have the answer to the questions that you so rudely posed!"

Tears began to form in Laura's eyes, but before she had the chance to say anything, Aaron shouted to Yung Lee, "All right, enough of this. Yung Lee, why have you come here?"—

"Do you mean to tell me that you didn't know that it was me who slipped the card under your door? Oh Aaron, you're getting a little rusty in your old age," Yung Lee said.

Aaron returned, "I don't know what goes on while I'm sleeping, so I'm not rusty, just relaxing . . . and don't flatter yourself. Let me remind you that Yung Lee alone is hardly The Shadow!

Yung Lee replied, "OK If you *didn't* know that it was me who slipped the card under your door, then what made you come out to our cottage?" Aaron answered, "Did you think I would go over to North Korea? I knew that someone in the Shadow was attempting to contact me, but I didn't really care about who was trying to draw me out, only that it was the Shadow, and your house was the first place that came to find. Besides, none of this is important. Again, why has the Shadow contacted me? Just what do they want from me?"

Yung Lee's face faded into a serious scowl as she began to speak. "I didn't come to you for the Shadow, Aaron. Rather, I came to give you a warning about the Shadow. I know that you remember my brother, Alex Kim, Jr. Well, I thought you deserved to know that he is looking for you. He has not yet learned of your whereabouts, but he is very close to finding you. I have known for some time now where you were, I just didn't know that you had THIS in your new life", she said, pointing to Laura.

Laura's face flared to bright red as she gritted her teeth. She shoved Aaron's arm out of the way and stepped towards Yung Lee, looking directly up into her dark gaze. Laura stuck out her chest and growled, "I've had just about enough of you, Damn it! Aaron Williamson is a part of my life now, not yours. You've had your chance; now he's found a good woman and if you think that fact is going to change, I'm here to tell you that it's going to be changed over my dead body."

Yung Lee let out a maniacal wail of laughter, then stopped suddenly while looking at Laura and said, "Over your dead body, huh? Well, I think that expression has a nice ring to it."

Before things got out of hand, Aaron pulled Laura back towards him as he said, "Look, Yung Lee, Laura is an integral part of my life now and I won't stand for any harm coming to her. Now, what does your brother want from me?"

Yung Lee said," Well, Aaron, just for your information, it is Alex who is controlling the Shadow now. Alex wants you for a very important mission that he is planning and . . ." before she had the chance to finish her statement, Aaron grabbed her by the arm and vehemently replied, "I *am* no longer in the service of the Shadow! I am finished—do you hear me? Can't you understand that that part of my life is over and done with?"

Yung's face went blank as she stepped directly in front of Aaron and looked him dead in his eyes, 'Oh, yes, I do understand, Aaron. I understand all too well. However, since we have company," Yung nodded quickly in Laura's direction, "I suppose that I will have to speak with you again at another time since we obviously can't speak openly. I can see from your friend's reactions that you've told her nothing about your past or about us. Go for now, Aaron Williamson, but we will speak again!" Yung Lee stepped back slowly into thenight shadows, her gaze intense upon Aaron as she slipped from sight.

Laura, still shocked from the entire event, looked up into Aaron's face, "will you please explain to me what I've just been through?" she asked in a weak and weary voice.

"Come on, Laura, let's just get in the Hummer, and go back for the Caddy and I'll do my best to explain what's going on" Aaron said.

As they climbed into the Hummer and sat down in the seats, Laura was poked in her side by the Desert Eagle 44. She grabbed the gun, looked at it and suddenly slammed it on the dashboard. She was overcome with a wild outburst of emotions. Flinging her arms about, Laura started to scream. Tears were flooding her eyes and her breathing was coming in short hitching breaths. Aaron gently, yet firmly took hold of Laura in an attempt to soothe her.

"Honey, it'll be alright. I'm here with YOU now as I will always be. You're going to be alright, too, and so will we. Don't worry, you're safe with me now," Aaron said.

The tears continued to race down her face as she shook in Aaron's arms. All the while, her mind worked in over time as the events of what she had just been through finally set in. Laura began to slowly calm down enough for Aaron to pull off and drive to the other car parked back up on the dirt road. He stopped the truck quickly jumped out, grabbing a tow chain from the back. He hooked up the Eldorado, then got back into the truck.

Aaron looked over at Laura and took her hand to give her some measure of reassurance. He caressed her cheek as a tear ran down it and kissed the fingers upon which her tears had fallen.

"Honey, I told you that there are a lot of things about my past that I chose not to tell you," he began, but she cut him off.

"Why, Aaron? Why did I have to almost die to find out about your t?" she asked angrily.

"Laura, I am truly sorry about all of this. The way things came out, I never wanted you to find out like this. No matter what, I do love you very deeply and I do want you in my life, so please, try to be patient so that we can work this out," he said.

"Aaron, how in the world can I be sure that you love me when I don't even know if I can trust you? I've known you for two years now. After you opened your first club and hired me as your manager, we started dating. After another three months of constantly being together, me staying at your condo, me moving in with you, I thought I knew you. I have lived with you, worked with you, loved you, slept side by side with you for eighteen months. Now I find out from a homicidal Korean Amazon that wants to kill me, that you have a two-year-old son! How am I supposed to believe anything that you say, Aaron?" she shouted.

Aaron's shoulders slumped as he turned his face away, trying to hide the tears running from his eyes. In his mind he knew that he would have had to face this day sooner or later. At this moment he truly wished it could have been faced differently.

"Laura, I know what kind of doubts that you must be feeling at this point, but please, try to think of things another way. What would you have thought of me when I first met you if I told you that I was a retired assassin and a thief? Do you think that you would have been attracted to me if I had told you that I use to murder people for money? I was attracted to you from the moment that I laid eyes on you. I felt you in my spirit. I sensed then something very special in you. You were then and are now something very precious to me. Simply put, Laura, I love you. I just couldn't risk losing you. You have restored my humanity."

Laura immediately embraced him in a passionate hug and kiss. Both had tears in their eyes and love in their hearts. Laura knew at that moment that, if nothing else, what Aaron felt for her was real. She knew that their love would transcend any obstacle.

"Well, Laura," he said, I'll try to put things into a clearer perspective for you. "All right, Aaron, I'm listening, but please go slowly. This sounds as if it's going to become confusing," she said.

Aaron explained, "Ten years ago, when I was twenty-six years old, I was newly promoted to sergeant first class, the youngest ever promoted to that rank in the U.S. Army.

I was on patrol with my platoon in the demilitarized zone in South Korea. While on patrol, my driver, a private first class named Johnson, spotted a man in an ice covered pond just off the side of the road. I ordered the platoon to a halt, then a few soldiers and myself went over, jumped in and pulled the man to safety.

As it turned out, that man was Kim Alex, a fugitive from the South Korean government. He told me that for saving his life, he would forever be in my debt. He then offered me any amount of money if I would see him safely across the border. I provided the transportation for him. I didn't know who he was, I guess I just felt sorry for him. Hell, I figured since he had been chased by the South Korean police and fell into that pond, the poor guy had been through enough. When I dropped him off at the break in the fence, I gave him a little money. Kim Alex told Johnson and I that we would both be compensated for our deeds. What I didn't know was that Kim was, at that time, a high level figure in the North Korean underworld. Johnson and I soon found out just how high up Kim was in the underworld.

Aaron paused for a second to restart the Hummer as he gave Laura a chance to take in all of the information that he was giving her. He shifted into gear and slowly pulled off towing the Caddy over the bumpy dirt road.

"So how did you find out how high up this Kim was? What did he do for you? Did he give you something expensive?" she asked.

Aaron responded, "Alex did something that my limited experience and poor imagination would never have dreamed of. He sent me a deed to a mansion from the other side of the border. The messenger waltzed right into Camp Casey, straight into the barracks and knocked on my door. The mansion was in North Korea, about seventy-five miles from the border in the city of Kaesong. Johnson and I went to check it out for ourselves," he explained.

"So was the mansion what you expected? Was the place like some of the mansions on Lifestyles of the Rich and Famous?" she asked.

"Well, it was what I expected and a hell of a lot more. The place was amazing. It had marble tiles and gold fixtures, it even had Mediterranean style concrete outer walls. I swear, from the antique furniture to the original Michelangelo paintings and the swimming pool in the basement, that place blew me away. To tell you the truth, what I didn't expect was for Alex himself to be there waiting for us both to arrive. When we got there, he offered us both a place in his organization. He went on to tell us both that we would be generously remunerated and well cared for. Let me tell you," he said, "to a twenty-six-year-old from a poor family, this was like a tmas fantasy.

"And this 'place' in his organization, was as a paid Assassin? You mean that he just came right out and told you that you would become a murderer for him?" she asked with a note of contempt and disbelief in her voice.

"Well, things were a bit more complicated than that, but that was the basic idea. Just remember that I was young, poor and impressionable, and this man was rich and powerful and he as fanning all of this wealth in front of me. Wait just a minute, this is our turn off," he said as he turned the wheel then headed onto the off ramp. After he exited the interstate highway, they drove through the center of town. He went on to explain in detail some of the things that he and his friend, Johnson had done in the underworld organization called The Shadow.

When they pulled into the underground parking complex, Aaron realized at that point that he had lost all track of time. He looked at his watch, but when he did, he got a small surprise. "Oh, my God, do you know what time it is? It's two in the morning. Honey, I don't think that I'm going to make it when that alarm goes off in the morning, so if you would, would you do the book reviews for the clubs and the bar later this morning?" he asked as he put on a grin.

"No, Aaron, I won't go to the Underground, The Rock Place and AW's to review your manager's books. I'll do one and we can both review the other two, but I'm not going to do your work alone, not for your businesses," she said sternly.

Aaron turned off the ignition, pulled the keys out, then turned towards Laura as he began to speak. "Laura, I'm not asking you to do all of my work. Damn it, I just need some time to go over to my gym to work off some of my frustrations on the sandbag. I really need some time to think," he said.

"Oh, so this Yung Lee bitch or who ever, shows up and you just go to shit? It sounds to me like you still have feelings for her. Do you, Aaron? Do you still love her? And what's the deal with her age? She's at least ten years younger than you, and if you think back, you told me that I was the youngest woman that you ever had a relationship with.

Hell, I'm thirty, and I know that I have at least four or five years on her," she said

"Alright Laura, this is important to you, so I will tell you. When I joined The Shadow, Yung Lee was only sixteen years old. I found her to be very attractive, but she was too young for me. She grew up around her father's business and was all too familiar with killing people. In fact, her first job for The Shadow came about when she was just thirteen years old. Alex sent Yung Lee and her brother, Alex, Jr., who was only eleven years old himself, on a mission into the Philippines to kill a government official. She worked closely with Johnson. She and I trained intensely to maintain her black belt in Kung Fu. After I had known her for about two years, on her eighteenth birthday, she walked up to me, threw her arms around my neck and told me that she was in love with me. From that point on, we were together for six years. In that time span, I had made over Ten million American dollars. However, I was beginning to mature, and my feelings for her and my lifestyle had changed. I had developed a deep revulsion for the life I was living, as well as the people around me who could find no other way to solve their problems except through violence and death. The time finally came when I had to make a break from The Shadow in order to maintain my sanity. I went to Kim Alex, who fully understood. I made a complete exit from The Shadow, and I started my life over. I stopped killing people and made a brand new start. I was coming to a crossroads in my life when I met you, Laura. I didn't dare risk losing you, because you had brought a great measure of peace and comfort to my life. I Loved you then and I love you even more now. I'm just not willing to give up on us so easily, Laura. I won't risk losing you to The Shadow. Not for their money, not for Yung Lee or even a child

I believe she is lying about. Yung Lee was always headstrong and very calculating. I know she would go to great lengths to get what she wants, including spinning a horrific lie. Laura, there is nothing in this world that I know of that can make me risk losing what we have formed together," he said sincerely.

Laura countered slowly, "But, Aaron, if Yung Lee does have your son, what will that do to us? You know that I can never give you children. If Yung Lee is telling the truth, she will always have a special part of you that I can never hope to match. To be honest, just the thought of the two of you sharing a child makes me feel hopelessly lost and inadequate. No matter how close the two of us become, Aaron, I can never enlarge upon our love in that very special way. If Yung Lee does in fact have a son from you, I will try to develop a relationship with him. I will do whatever I can to help you and him. I do love you, Aaron, and even if Yung Lee does have your child, we can make it work."

Aaron responded, "Let me reassure you right now, that if there is a child, then I will do whatever I can to become a good father to him. Know that nothing and no one can come between you and I, not a son, not a woman, and especially not The Shadow. Understand, Laura, you are the woman that I have chosen to be in my life; It doesn't matter to me whether you can or cannot have children. Simply put, you are my life, and that's all I need you to know."

A wave of emotions swept over Laura as she reached out to Aaron, embracing him as they passionately kissed. Afterwards, they walked silently to the elevator bank, waiting for it to come to the lobby. As they waited, Aaron ran his long brown fingers through Laura's thick red locks. Looking deep into her ever changing hazel eyes, which were now a peaceful blue, he said "Think of things this way. We start over as of now. No more secrets. And speaking of now, I do still need you to cover for me just for today. Take care of this morning; I'll go around and do both clubs and the bar in the evening."

Laura answered with a smile, "I guess that I can go along with that, but you mentioned something earlier about frustrations that you need to work off? Well I have a sure fire way for you to work out a good amount of them with me."

Aaron gave no answer, but when the elevator arrived, the two stepped in and he immediately swept Laura into his embrace. He probed her mouth with his tongue and proceeded to strip off her clothes while gently planting kisses all over her. By the time the elevator reached their floor, the mirrors were totally steamed up. The pair left a trail of clothing leading up to the master bedroom, once in bed; Laura planted kisses slowly on Aaron, from his neck to his thigh and everywhere in between. Laura kissed away Aaron's frustrations, causing him to moan loudly as he pulled her up and gently planted his mouth on her upturned breast. Laura, too, cried out as she felt her loins overheating the moment that their two bodies met. As they locked bodies in a flowing of mutual rhythm, their eyes never left each other. Their pulsing bodies now increased their commitment to the enjoining until neither could hold back any longer. Aaron suddenly whispered in a hoarse rasping gasp, "Laura, I love you." With beads of perspiration dripping from her too hot body, Laura returned in whispers, "Me too, Aaron, me too!"

The room was now silent except for their labored breathing. They drifted off to a deep sleep. They slept locked in each other's arms until morning when Laura woke, showered, changed and headed out for her first review of the books.

CHAPTER II

⌐∿∧∼⌐

I T WAS BRIGHT and sunny late Monday morning, as Aaron lay asleep. He slept peacefully until the song of a sparrow chirping outside of his window awakened him. He rolled over to notice that Laura was gone and looked at the clock across the room to see how late in the morning it was: 11:45. He thought to himself; I would have slept into the afternoon if not for that fucking bird on the feeder that wouldn't shut up. I asked Laura nicely to take down the damn feeder, but no, she likes the pretty birds that come to feed in it.

Oh, well, he thought, he had more important things to worry about, such as Yung Lee and The Shadow looking for him. There was also the possibility of a child in North Korea that he might be father to. His future with Laura was very heavy on his mind and in his heart.

Time to stop woolgathering and face the day. He finally gathered all of his senses about himself. He used the firm springs of his specially made mattress to spring to his feet. Once he was upright, he dove over the side of the bed as if he were on a diving board and laid out into a summersault, landing on his feet in a shaky two-point stance. Aaron thought to himself: a little rusty, but I'm still the man of skill that I once was.

He walked into the bathroom and began to shave. The hot, steamy water felt good to him while it ran down his face and shoulders. As he enjoyed his shower, he began to sing his favorite reggae song, Genie in the Lamp, by the group Steel Pulse. Twenty minutes later, he got out and dried himself off.

Back into the bedroom, he dressed in his warm-up suit. He then proceeded into the kitchen where he fixed a bowl of his favorite breakfast cereal, Captain Crunch with Crunch Berries. Once he was finished, he washed the dishes then made his way down to the underground parking complex.

In the complex, he saw that Laura had taken the Hummer instead of the Eldorado. That small fact struck him as strange because he knew she didn't like driving the truck, she preferred the car. He thought to himself, I better call her once I get to the gym. He sat in the car, started it and pulled off toward the ramp which led up to the streets. He drove through the city square, into the center of town and proceeded to the outskirts of town to where his warehouse was located.

Upon arrival, he parked outside the warehouse. Stepping out of his car, he unlocked the doors to the huge three floor building. Walking in, he switched on the lights, walking past the huge Olympic sized swimming pool and the ten-person hot tub. He then moved into the rear of the building where there was a cargo elevator and stepped in.

He rode it past the second floor, where there was an indoor running track and exercise mats. Aaron finally reached the third floor. He moved the elevator switch to stop and walked onto the main exercise floor where he kept all of his personal work-out equipment, from free weights and nautilus machines to universal gym sets.

Before he began his workout session, he walked over to the wall phone and called Laura at his club, The Underground.

"Morning, baby, or should I say good afternoon," he said.

"Oh, so the sleepy-head is finally awake? You're bad, honey. I tried to kiss you this morning, but you wouldn't wake up," she answered.

"Sorry, I was out cold. Anyway, what's up with the Hummer? You hate driving that truck," he asked.

"I only drove it because I knew it would make you wonder if something was up and cause you to call me," she explained.

"I see. Well, as long as you're all right, I'll start my workout. Before I go, let me say that I love you and can't wait to be in your arms again," he said with compassion in his voice.

"I love you, too. I'll be over there after my regular time, 4:00 P.M. since somebody didn't check the books of his manager at the Rock Palace today. So . . . . how's your thinking been going on that other subject, or have you even started yet?" she asked.

"No, I've mainly had you on my mind for most of the morning. The question is how you are doing with all of this?" he asked.

"To tell you the truth, I think the whole situation stinks. The very thought of me not being able to give you a child, through no fault of my own, while another woman is the mother of your son—not daughter, but son—drives my blood to a raging boil. Anyway, don't get me to talking about this over the phone. If you're still there, I'll see you later, OKAY? Till then, remember that I love you," she said.

"I love you, too, honey, and come over as soon as you're finished. Tell Charlie I said 'good morning.' OKAY honey, love Ya," Aaron said as he hung up the phone.

While Aaron began his work-out in the warehouse, across town in the club, Laura began to check the financial books of the club manager. The manager of the club was a personal friend of theirs named Charlie, who stood by as she went through the book figures.

"Everything seems to be in order, Charlie," Laura said.

"Where's the boss man this afternoon? I thought that it was his turn to check The Underground's books today. You know, it's kind of an insult to get checked on every day if I'm supposed to be the one who handles the day to day operations," he said.

"Charlie, my business professor once told me that, trust given by a blind man is trust given by a fool. Aaron takes no risks and no chances.

Believe me, I know, because he used to check on me every day, bright and early every morning. Don't take it personally." she said.

"I won't. Why the sexy red dress, Laura? You have some place important to go after you leave here?" he asked.

"No, Charlie, I just wanted to look my best today. Besides, this old dress barely fits me anymore," she replied.

Laura knew deep in her mind that she was lying. The gorgeous silk dress she wore wasn't even six months old. The deep scarlet coloring matched perfectly with her hair. She wasn't a tall woman, but she added four inches to her height with a pair of red stilettos. Her small waist coupled with her ample bosom filled out the dress in just the right way. The sweetheart neckline added just the right amount of cleavage to the entire ensemble. Fitted to her shapely body, and against her slightly tanned white skin, the dress turned her into a sure fired knockout.

Laura was deep into the previous night's numbers as the front door of the club opened. She didn't pay any attention to who walked in. Charlie looked up and saw who entered; he asked Laura if she knew who the person. "Laura, do you know who this woman is that just walked in the door, because I have no idea," he said.

Laura took a quick glance, her temperature rising immediately. Yung Lee, she thought to herself, and the nerve she has to come here. She must have thought that Aaron was in here since the Hummer was parked outside.

When Yung Lee stepped into the light of the front area of the club to reveal her short red dress, Laura thought, she must know that red is Aaron's favorite color. Yung Lee was a tall woman who stood an awesome five feet, eleven inches in height. Her hair was a glossy jet black and styled into an elegant French braid, which hung over her athletically built body, down to the bottom of her back. Laura slowly looked her up and down as Yung Lee took her hair and flung it about.

The length of Yung Lee's hair especially angered her, recalling a remark Aaron made regarding her own shoulder length hair being a bit short. There was no doubt in Laura's mind: she hated everything about this woman who stood before her.

"I'm sorry," Laura said, "We're not open for business now. On your way out, the hours of operation are posted on the door."

"So cheerful in the morning, aren't we, Laura?" Yung replied.

"Look, It's bad enough that I have to be civil towards you because you and Aaron may have a son together, but don't push your luck" she snapped.

"I understand your hostility, your somewhat delicate situation. It's all clear to me now. You've been with Aaron for nearly two years now and have no baby. Well, I can certainly vouch for Aaron's fertility. Oh, my, if I were in your position, I'd hate me, too. Poor thing, you'll never know the joy of holding a baby that comes from the man you love. I understand the hate in your eyes, because you're merely half a woman. You will never experience the fullness of what real women go through," Yung Lee said.

Laura's face turned as red as her dress upon hearing what Yung Lee said to her. It angered her the way Yung had so quickly figured out her inability to conceive. Even more so, it felt as if Yung Lee looked deep inside and saw Laura's frustration and despair. In her anger, she also felt shame and embarrassment, as poor Charlie stood there with his mouth hanging open.

"Charlie, would you please go into the storeroom and recheck the inventory," Laura asked.

Yung Lee did all that she could to restrain herself from laughing. Deep inside, she reveled in the fact that what she said made Laura so angry. She looked at Laura's face as Charlie walked across the dance floor to the storeroom. Yung Lee noticed that her lip was quivering in an attempt to hold back her tears, but once the door to the storeroom closed, Laura's entire demeanor changed.

"Now you listen to me, you little bitch! I don't know what you want with or from Aaron and, to tell you the truth, I don't care! You may have had him once, but I've got him now! Aaron Williamson is my man and my life and I'll kill any fucking slope eyed bitch that would try to challenge me!" she screamed.

Until the "slope eyed bitch" comment, Yung Lee had maintained a smile on her face. Before Laura could finish her statement, Yung Lee abruptly reacted. In one lightning quick move, Yung Lee reached across the bar and grabbed Laura by the top of her dress. She then pulled from her purse a .357 hand gun, placed it to her temple and quietly said, "Now you listen to me, you red headed bitch! The only reason you're still alive is because I've allowed you to be. Never question or doubt that fact, you pathetic piece of nothing! I've passed up so many opportunities to kill you, that it's not even funny! So you had better speak to me with a little fucking respect, otherwise you and Aaron will be look very dead in your funeral shrouds. Do you understand me?" she screamed.

"Y—y—yes, I do," Laura stuttered. "That's, Yes, Kim Yung Lee," she said with a taunting grin. "Y-yes, Kim Yung Lee," she replied through her angry, shaken tears.

As Laura repeated Yung Lee's name, the storeroom door flew open and Charlie stepped out. Poor Charlie wasn't exactly the fear striking presence that Laura could have used at that moment. He was an older white man in his upper forties, standing only five feet, nine inches, and portly with a head of gray hair.

"What in the hell is going on out here? What's all the yelling about?" he demanded.

"Shut your fat fucking mouth and get your punk ass back into that damn room," Yung Lee shouted, pointing the gun in his direction. "Oh shit, OKAY" he said flatly, going back into the storeroom. After the door was fully closed, Yung Lee looked back at Laura, who was still in her grasp. She pulled Laura half way across the counter top of the bar.

"Don't get me wrong, Laura, I'm really a nice person. I don't enjoy going all loco on a bitch, but you earned this ass kicking! Oh my, look at me! I must seem all kinds of crazy to you right now. Here, let's put you down. By the way, for an off the rack dress, that's a really cute outfit you're wearing. Now, Miss Hinkley, where is Aaron today?" she asked.

Laura never answered Yung's question. Taking a closer look into Laura's face and how she seemed to stare off into space, she immediately knew that Laura was in shock. The very thought of a gun being placed against her temple must have tripped some sort of inner defense switch. Yung Lee thought to herself, "Humph, some assassin's woman you turned out to be. One gun to your head and you go into a little mental closet. Pathetic."

Finally, Yung got fed up with the look on Laura's face, so she simply turned and walked away. Once the front door closed, the storeroom door opened slightly. Charlie peeked through, and checked to make sure that Yung Lee had left. Certain she was gone, he fully opened the door and walked over to Laura; she still had the hundred-mile stare on her face.

Charlie called out her name, but he got no response. 'Damn,' he thought to himself, "What the hell do I do now?" "Laura! Laura, can you hear me? It's Charlie!" he shouted. He continued calling her name and shaking her for the next few minutes. He finally grew tired of yelling, grabbed a pitcher of water and splashed her with it. S P L A S H!

Charlie knew immediately that Laura had snapped out of her trance. She started looking wildly around the room. Once her eyes met with his, in the blink of an eye, she flew into a rage. She flung her arms and hands all about while she yelled the word 'NO' at the top of her lungs. Charlie stood watching in shock and was struck with indecision. Through this melodrama, the only thought that came to Charlie's mind was to bring Laura back to the here and now. He slapped her—S L A P! "Laura, snap out of it she's gone, OK? That bitch is gone," he said as he shook her by her arms.

Laura slowly came to her senses. "Thanks, Charlie, I think. I feel like I've been out of it for days," she said with a weary look in her eyes.

"I heard the front door close; then I came out. You were in never land for a few minutes. What happened out here? What did she do to you?" he asked.

"You know, Charlie, I don't know. For some reason, all I can remember is her grabbing me, then you splashing me. Oh, God, she must be going over to the warehouse to see Aaron. Give me the phone!" she said with renewed strength in her voice. Charlie handed the phone to her and she called the gym. She slammed the receiver down, picked it up again and pressed out the number for his cell phone.

"Damn it, Charlie! There's no answer. Aaron must be on a different floor," she said. She came from around the bar and headed to the front door. "Laura, where are you going?" he asked.

"To the gym. Aaron's gun is still in the Hummer. If she's over there, she's a dead slope," she said with hatred in her eyes.

"Laura," Charlie said as he walked over to her and placed his hand on her shoulder. "You've really been through a lot just now. I think that you should calm down and really think about things. That Asian woman seems like she doesn't play very many games, but when she does, they aren't kids' games. If you're set on facing her, then, I can't stop you, but please take a second to clear your head."

"You know, now that you mention it, I do feel a slight bit tired. Maybe I will lay down for a bit, Charlie, but if you would, could you please bring me a glass of brandy?" she asked.

As soon as he removed his hand from her shoulder and turned around towards the bar, Laura ran toward the front doors. She jumped into the Hummer, started it, and then pulled off. Charlie watched her drive off through the huge glass window. He continued to try to reach Aaron at the gym, but to no avail. The phone kept ringing and he kept trying the cell phone. He finally grew tired of dialing. Charlie quietly hung up the receiver, went to his knees and began to pray.

Driving through the center of town, Laura headed toward the industrial end of town where the gym was located. Once there, she turned off the truck, grabbed the gun and ran into the building. She looked around the first floor, in the pool and hot tub and saw the Aaron wasn't in sight.

She walked over to the elevator. Before she stepped into the car, she examined the gun to see if she could figure out how it worked. She quickly saw that it was on SAFE. She switched it to FIRE and stepped onto the lift. She moved the elevator car lever to RUN. On the way up, she began to flash back to the events that had just transpired between herself and Yung Lee. With the floor in full view, she saw Aaron down at the far end of the room. She ran off the lift with tears in her eyes toward him.

Aaron watched as she came closer, but didn't notice at first that she was carrying the gun in her right hand. Once he realized what she had in her hands, he knew that something was terribly wrong.

"Laura!" Aaron yelled. "What the hell are you doing with that? Why do you have the gun"? "Where is she, Aaron? Where is Kim Yung Lee?' she demanded.

"Laura, let's calm down and hand me the gun," he said softly.

"No. That insane Korean bitch has to die! I will not allow her to just waltz in and totally disrupt our lives, I won't, damn it!" she shouted.

"Laura, will you calm the fuck down and tell me what in the hell has happened that would have you so riled? I thought we had an understanding this morning."

"Okay, Aaron, here's what happened. Yung Lee yanked me over the counter top of the bar, placed a gun to my head and made me thank *her* for letting us live. That bitch was nuts! When she came to the club, she was looking for you. When she left the bar I thought she would have come here next," she explained.

"So what exactly were you going to do with the gun, Laura? I don't know if you've figured this out yet, but these are professional killers, Yung Lee especially. Believe me, I know, because I trained them. If she wanted either of us dead, we would have been long gone by now, so just you keep that in mind," he said in a calm voice. "You can't think that you can deal with them alone just because you have a gun!"

Her face turned red as she listened to Aaron talk about Yung Lee. Unconsciously, Laura had begun to slam the gun against her leg as she started to speak.

"You listen to me, Aaron! That bitch, and anyone else who gets in my way is going to die. No one threatens me and lives to tell about it. I don't give a damn if Steven Segal trained her ass, she's a dead woman walking! And don't you forget, she's not the only one who has a black belt. Today she caught me unaware, but I can guarantee you that shit will never happen again. The next time we meet, I'm going to try my best to make it her last."

"First of all Laura, if you truly intend to face her, you need to calm down and think clearly. Look at me, I'm pissed off like a motherfucker, *but* you don't see me flying off the handle, do you? The only way to deal with these people is to turn off your emotions. In this type of situation, feelings will get your ass killed QUICK FAST!" he said.

"Maybe you're right, maybe I do need to ease up a little," she said with a calm voice.

"Secondly, I need to show you how to use that thing. Be careful before you blow off one of your toes by beating it off of your leg one too many times" he said with a slight laugh in his voice.

"Damn it, Aaron, I do know how to use this thing. Just point and shoot. I'll blow out one of your windows if you don't believe me," she said as she turned toward the far side of the building and aimed the gun.

She pulled the trigger, but nothing happened. She pulled it again and again with the same results. Aaron stood up from the floor and sighed to himself. As he slipped on his shirt, Laura, in total frustration began to slap the top of the gun with her left hand as she shouted, "Work, damn it, work." Aaron shook his head as he walked toward her and gently took her left hand and looked at her with a smile.

"Please, allow me. Yeah, you've disengaged the safety, but without a round in the chamber, pulling the trigger won't do you any good. This is a Semi-automatic handgun. You simply slide this part back, let it go, and now you're ready to rock and *roll,*" he explained.

"So you mean that last night, if I would have had to use this thing, nothing would have happened?" she asked angrily.

"In this business, sometimes all you have to do is point a big gun at someone and they'll freeze in their tracks," he said.

"I'm glad I didn't have to find out the hard way who would have frozen and who wouldn't have. Are you done with your workout because, if you are, I'm ready to go home." she said.

"Yes, I'm ready. I did a lot of thinking about this bullshit. Come, follow me up to the locker room. While I was hitting the punching bag, I remembered my old friend down in New York City. Do you remember me telling you about my driver and me being offered a place in The Shadow? Well, Johnson goes by the name C.J. He dropped out of sight from The Shadow about two years before I did and relocated in New York City with a group of his own," he said.

"What does this group do, or should I even have to ask," she asked.

"They're a mercenary group named Infiltrate. Their cover is a non-profit organization known as The Street Foundation. They do a lot charity work. They help the homeless and hungry, children in need, battered spouses-anyone who genuinely needs a helping hand. Ironically, it's the perfect set-up for what they do, which is anything from industrial espionage to high-priced assassination. If you can pay their price, you can get anything done—guaranteed." he said.

He went on to explain about his friend C.J. and his group, Infiltrate, as he changed in the small locker room. Once he had completed changing, he and Laura walked over to the phone.

"So, what happens now? What's our next move going to be?" she asked.

"Well, my next move is going to be contacting C.J. He told me that if I ever needed him that he would have my *back*. AT this point, I surely can use his experience and his expertise. Here, hold this card for me, will ya, baby?" he asked. "Sure, give it to me," she said as he handed the card to her. While she held it up, he dialed the number; the phone rang twice before *a* woman answered the phone.

"Street Foundation information center; this is Tracy speaking. How may I help you?" the woman asked.

"Hello. This is Aaron Williamson. I would like to speak to Johnson," he said.

"Mr. Johnson is away on business at the moment. Shall I take a message, sir?" she asked.

"Yes tell him that Sarge called and it's very important that he calls me as soon as he possibly can" he said.

"I'll deliver this message personally. Does he have your number, sir?" she asked "Yes, he does, but I'm going to leave my pager number. Tell him to call me at home, and please, if there's no answer at my home number to be sure to page me. Thank you Tracy", he said as he hung up. "Come on Baby, let's go and take the Caddy back to the garage. I'm taking you to the pistol range so that you can get the feel of that gun you're holding" he said.

After they exited the building, Aaron jumped into the Hummer as Laura got into the Cadillac. They drove through the center of town, then down into the underground parking complex of their high rise. Laura parked the car as Aaron waited for her in the truck. After she locked and closed the door to the car, she jumped into the waiting Hummer. Aaron pulled off and headed toward the ramp, which led up to the streets. As they drove toward the interstate 81, Aaron looked at what she was wearing.

"By the way, honey, nice dress, although it looks too good for where we're going. You might think about putting on one of those coverall suits I have in the back. I've got a medium that should fit you nicely, or at least nice enough for where we're going," he said.

"Aaron, where do you want me to change, we're on the open highway?" she asked.

"I have to drive down the 342 state highway to get to the pistol range. Once we're on the highway, you should be able to change into the coveralls in the truck because hardly anyone travels down that road during the weekend," he explained.

"You really like my dress, though, baby?" she asked.

"Hell, yeah, honey, you look damn good in it," he shouted.

"I'm glad that bitch, Young Lee Kim, never made it over to the gym because she had on an even shorter red dress. It showed off even more leg and cleavage than mine! Anyway, what's her back story? I mean, I've never seen an Asian woman that tall" She said.—

"Yung Lee is half Caucasian American. Alex's wife was a six-foot, seven-inch basketball player who once played for a team in China. Needless to say, they looked strange together since Alex was only about five feet, four inches tall. If you asked me, she was only with the little bastard because he had money," he said.

"Now, I understand. Is her mother still alive?" she asked.

"No, she's been dead now for about six years. An underground Chinese clan placed a price on Alex's head. In an attempt to kill him, they blew up his limo with a rocket propelled grenade, or RPG. Only thing was, Alex's wife and youngest son, Kim David, were in the limo, not Alex.

Thanks to C.J. and me, Dragon Clan, including its hires, no longer exists. Alex wanted them to pay a heavy price for fucking with him and his family. He had us first kill the wives and children of the high commanders of the clan, then the clan members. The clan master was finally brought before Alex, about a year after Mrs. Kim and David had been killed. He was stripped of all his clothes, and Alex personally killed the Dragon clan master in front of the entire Shadow clan," he explained.

"In one year's time Aaron, how many people did you and this C.J. kill during that year!" she shouted.

"There were ten clan commanders under the clan master and each of them had a wife with no less than three children. Then, there were several members of the clan with families as well. It was a busy year for me and C.J. With us being Black and easily spotted, the only way we could kill them would be at night under the cover of darkness."

"Here's the turn-off onto route 342. Hop in the back and change into the coveralls. After you've changed, lift up the driver's side seat in the rear and hand me the other gun that looks like the one you have," he said. He turned off onto the ramp and headed onto the state highway 342.

Laura changed in the back of the truck as Aaron drove down the road. After she finished dressing, she lifted the back seat and saw no less than twenty different types of handguns under the seat. After a few seconds of searching, she finally found another Desert Eagle .44 handgun like the one she was holding.

"Aaron, how long have all of these guns been under this seat?" she asked with the sound of concern in her voice.

"Ever since you've known me. Hell, you hate this truck, though I don't know why, but I knew that you would never go under the seats because you hate driving it" he explained.

"Well, it's scary, but it does make sense. The question is, how many other secrets do you have hidden right under my nose?" she asked.

"I'll just say that there are many things in my past that have yet to be seen. The only way to let you fully know would be to sit you down one evening and tell you as much as I can stand to talk about, or as much as I think you can hear. But, remember, Laura, I'm not too thrilled about what I used to be."

"That's a scary answer if I ever heard one, and I think at this point there isn't too much I can't hear. Not to change subjects, but what time is it? I seem to have misplaced my watch and I'm a bit hungry," she said.

"It's 1:30. There's a little truck stop not far down the road that serves about the best lunch specials you could ever find anywhere. We can stop, sit and talk a while and have a great meal before we hit the range. This place is right on the same route," he said.

After driving for a short distance, Aaron turned into a truck stop on route 342 just outside of town. They went in and sat and ate for forty minutes before returning to the Hummer. Once they were in the truck, Aaron drove the long winding trails that led out to the range.

Aaron carefully showed Laura the many steps of firing the Desert Eagle .44. Soon afterward, Laura began to fire a few rounds down range from her .44. After he saw that she was comfortable with the big gun, he began to send rounds down range himself with the other .44. They continuously fired and reloaded again and again until very late into the evening. In total, they sent a total of one thousand rounds down range. As they did, Aaron took a few moments to watch her fire and saw the huge smile on her face, which ran from ear to ear. He heard her yell with each shot, "Get some, baby, get some."

Aaron looked at his Rolex sportsmen watch and realized that he had lost all track of time. It's late, he thought to himself, Damn, we've been out here a long time. "Baby, you ready to go, because it's 7:30, we've been here for hours" he asked.

"Damn, time flies when you're having fun. The question is: will you teach me how to use the other guns you have in the truck?" she asked, a slightly maniacal grin on her face.

"There's really not too much difference between hand guns when it comes to firing them. As I told you when we first started all there is to it really is point, aim and pull the trigger. Guns like the .38, .357, .44, and .22, and most revolvers only have six rounds or bullets. It's hard to find a silencer for them. Guns like the ones we fired here are called automatics because they have a recoil action, which chambers a round automatically. These guns are easy to find silencers for. Come on, let's head home. Did you remember how to clear that gun like I showed you?" he asked.

"Yes, baby, it's cleared. Now can we go? This suit is making my skin crawl," she said.

They both jumped into the truck and he pulled off. He drove up the winding trails, which led back to the U.S. highway. When they reached the road and were on their way, Laura began to change out of the coveralls. During the drive, she slowly slipped out of the suit. As she changed, he watched her through the corner of his eye. Laura also peeked at him from time to time to make sure that he was watching her. She made sure she slipped out of the suit very slowly and very seductively. She did everything she could, short of touching him, to turn him on. After she was out of the suit, she looked at him with a come-hither look in her eyes and licked her lips.

Aaron did all that he could to maintain his composure as he turned into the interstate highway. He knew what Laura was doing, but was powerless to fight what he felt inside. She held onto the roll bars as she felt the truck speed up. As they entered the highway, Laura still wiggled and gyrated her body. She saw from his heavy breathing that she had him exactly where she wanted him. Once he parked the truck in the underground parking complex, he reached over and pulled her towards him. They made hot and passionate love in the center of the truck. The threat of people walking past and seeing them added fuel to their raging wildfire. They steamed up the windows of the truck for the next hour.

Eventually, Aaron stuck his head out of the top of the truck to make sure that they were alone, and the way was clear. He saw no one around; he and Laura made a mad dash for the elevator. They were both holding their underwear and the guns that they had fired at the range. Once the elevator car arrived on the parking level, they stepped in, dropped their things and steamed the mirrors of the elevator.

The car reached their floor. They picked up their items and ran toward their condo door. After a few steps, Aaron stopped short and took hold of Laura's hand. She looked up at him as if to ask, 'what's wrong?'

"Aaron, What's happening?" she whispered as he stared at their door.

"Look at our door—it's open! I don't know about you, but I'm not expecting any company. Did you grab the other gun?" he asked her, as he shot a look of burning intensity toward the door.

"Yes, baby, I have it. *You* take the other one and we'll go in and see what the fuck is going on!" she replied. She slapped in a clip of ammo, pulled the slide back and gritted her teeth.

"Laura, stay out in the hall and don't come in until I tell you to come in. Give me your gun and I'll check this shit out," he said as he looked into her eyes.

"You can forget that! I'm in this with you 'til the end, damn it! You're the man I want to spend the rest of my life with and that means that I'm by your side in tough times like this. I'll kill anyone who fucks with us from now on," she said.

He looked into her eyes and saw the raw determination in them. From then on, he knew that whatever plans he made, he had to include her in them as well.

"OKAY, just keep behind me. Once we get into the front room, point your gun to the left and put your back against mine. You got that?" he asked.

She reached and took hold of his neck and kissed him on his lips. She looked into his eyes and saw a new strength that she had never seen before. From his strength, she felt empowered. With just one glance in Aaron's brown eyes, Laura was no longer afraid. She felt that, no matter what they may go up against, they were going to come out on top.

"Understood. I love you," she said.

"Love you. Let's move," he replied.

Aaron ran forward at full speed as he led Laura by the hand. He reached the door, kicked it in and saw that all of the lights in the condo were out. Still in mid stride, and based on pure instinct and memory of his furniture layout, Aaron turned his head and quietly told Laura, "Jump and roll honey!"—

Laura heard and understood just in time. She dove over the couch into a combat roll, then quickly up on her feet with her back against Aaron's. She swung the gun from left to right, but couldn't see anything in the darkness. Aaron reached back and took hold of her hand in an attempt to comfort her. She clamped down on his hand just as he figured she would. He slightly turned his hand, keeping his eyes down the sight post of his gun and giving her more instructions.

"Keep hold of my hand and keep quiet. Let your ears be your guide," he said.

They slowly made their way to the bedroom. They both heard a voice come from one of the dark corners say, "Jump on the big dude, I'll take the babe."

Before Aaron or Laura had the chance to brace for impact, bodies flew at them from all points. Laura went down with the first hit. Aaron managed better, recalling old techniques and training, dodging the person who flew at him. Listening to their footsteps, Aaron immediately knew there were five men, as well as one on the floor who fought with Laura. Another person stepped into Aaron's reach, but was knocked out with a lightning quick kick to his head. Aaron turned after the kick. In the blink of an eye he caught the other person's punch in midstream. He turned with the punch in the same direction it was thrown and flipped the man away from him. As Aaron prepared himself for another charge, he heard a familiar voice saying, "I see you haven't lost your touch, Sarge." Aaron immediately knew the person behind the voice. "C.J., is that you, ya young buck?" Aaron asked with a cheerful tone to his voice.

After Aaron's greeting, the lights clicked on to reveal his old friend, who stood in the corner of the living room with his back to the wall. C.J. *was* clad in an all black ninja type suit and mask. He stood an imposing six feet five inches tall and had black hair, which was cut into a box style. His eyes were black and bared the look of hardness in them.

"You've lost a bit of edge, old man. About six years ago, my men wouldn't have gotten close to you and survived. Still, though, it's good to see you again, Sarge. It's been a long time." C.J. said.

"It's good to see you again C.J. I take it that you got my message?" Aaron asked.

"Yeah, I did. That's why I rounded up my men and flew here in our private jet. Oh, yeah, please allow me to introduce the Sub-leaders of my group, Infiltrate. Please meet my number two man, code name Half, real name Anthony. My number three man, code name Dusty, real name Nigel. My number four man, code name Big Dog, real name Smitman; and my number five man, code name Sandman, real name Jose. Men, this is Sergeant First Class Aaron Williamson, the one I've told you all so much about," he said.

"A real honor gentlemen. Everybody, this is my lady, Laura. We live together and she knows just about everything there is to know about what's going on, from The Shadow and Yung Lee to your group," he said.

"So what's up, man? What's so important that would make Tracy tell me that you sounded worried about over the phone," C.J. asked.—

"Yung Lee has tracked me down. I've been out of The Shadow for about two years, now. She told me that her brother Kim Alex, Jr. is running The Shadow and is close to finding me," he explained.

"Damn, Sarge, I told you many years ago that that crazy bitch was trouble and that you shouldn't mess with her. Hell, Half has the same problem. He likes to mess with those Asian women, too," C.J. said. "So, what does that crazy bitch want, anyway? Knowing her, she didn't take kindly to Laura being in the picture, did she?" C.J. asked.

"No, she didn't. In fact, she mentioned something to the effect of being with Aaron over my dead body. Hell, just this morning, she pulled me over the counter top of our club, held a gun to my head and made me thank her for allowing me to live," Laura said.

"So, again, Sarge, what's the deal? Anything you need done, we'll do for you. You don't have to worry about supplies, transportation or communications. We've performed many services for industry giants. Infiltrate is totally mobile throughout the world. Airlines and rail companies provide us with transport. If you're thinking what I hope you're thinking, we can do this," C.J. said.

"I'm not interested in killing anyone any more, C.J. I'm not even sure if I'll need you for fire power for any of this bullshit. I just need to know that, if the time comes when I dial your number, I'll have a friend who has some back bone," Aaron said.

"Old friend, you need not ask. I and all of Infiltrate will be there for you when the chips are down. Whatever I can do for you, all you need do is ask. If it is within my power, consider it done. Here, take this number down. Pay close attention to this because it's a ten digit number that is only accessible by your cellular phone. I've got a few things worked out with AT&T, using one of their satellite and scramble codes. From now on, call that number; not only does it hook into my secured lines, it' also part of a beeper system which I always have on my person. If, for any reason, you have to call The Street Foundation, use the code words UPPER ROOM." C.J. said.

"Okay, what's the number C.J.?" Aaron asked with a smile on his face. In spite of the current situation, he was impressed with the younger man's resources.

"(718) 6784771440. If there's no answer within five rings, the beeper system will kick in. Where will you be tomorrow during the latter part of the day?" asked C.J.

"He'll probably be at his bar, AW's by five or six. He's going to check on all of his manager's books in the morning!" Laura spoke up, and said with authority.

"Well, there you have it C.J. I guess I'll be at work for most of the day." said Aaron sarcastically.

"Okay, good, I have all of your business phone numbers. I'll try call you when we get back to the city. Again, Sarge, if you need anything, call me as soon as you can," he said as he and his group walked out of the front door.

Before C.J. could walk out of the door, Aaron walked over to him and embraced him in a fierce hug. The young man gave his Sarge a look that said that everything was going to be all right. After they were done, Aaron walked back over to where Laura was still standing with the gun in *her* hand. She shook her head as she ran her fingers through his hair. She looked him in his eyes and smiled. She said, "Well, honey, if this keeps up, by the time I'm thirty, I'll have nothing but gray hair."

"This isn't anything! Baby why do you think I dropped out of The Shadow? There were times when C.J. and I were the most hunted men in the Far East. Every underworld clan in that region had people after our heads. They feared us because they knew that we were good at what we did, which was killing their men. In fact, all of The Shadow members were trained to be killing machines. That's why we were hells own killing group!", he said with a touch of nostalgia. He had a look of melancholy in his eyes.

"You sound like you're starting to miss those days. I'm still having trouble imagining you as a killer for hire. You're so sweet and lovable. I can't reconcile the image of the brutal killer you were with the gentle man I know you to be. I mean, baby, you're my teddy bear. Please, Aaron, promise me that no matter what happens, you won't go back to that life," she pleaded.

"I promise, Laura. I promise you that my killing days are over. I have a life with you and that's all I need. Come, I need to show you something," he said.

"What, Aaron, what is it now? You've shown me so much in the past twenty-four hours," she said.

He took her by the hand and led her to the closet next to the master bedroom. He opened the door and popped the ceiling of the closet open. He reached into the opening, pulled down a large, flat case with a handle. He blew off the dust and gently set the case down flat on its back. Laura looked on with a puzzled look on her face. She saw that there was a crucifix on a gold chain wrapped around the case, which went through its handle.

"This was my baby when I was in The Shadow. You're looking at the case of the most powerful sniper rifle in the world. In this case is my personally tailored Beret light 50-caliber sniper rifle. One of its bullets is as long as your hand and, with its sights in line, I can hit a dime from two miles away. Normally, when I used this rifle on someone, they couldn't hear it as it was fired, because they're so far away. It's specially designed for almost silent firing. I want you to know there were only three of these specially made rifles in the world and I, personally, destroyed the other two," he said with definite pride in his voice.

Laura's eyes were as wide as half dollars. "So, baby, when do I get to learn how to use it?" she asked.

Aaron was quiet for a moment. "You don't. The crucifix and the gold chain is my seal. See how I've wrapped it so that it's through the handle? That's my constant reminder of my new life without the killing in it. When we started dating, I sealed this case and I don't ever want to open it again," he said.

"In that case, what are we going to do about The Shadow? If we're not going to kill them, what are we going to do?" she asked.

"Well, to tell you the truth, I don't know. Right now, it's almost 10:30, and I need to get in the whirlpool and get some sleep, especially since I'm doing all of the work tomorrow," he said.

"Okay, Sarge. Take a bath and get some sleep. Is that all you're going to take tonight?" she asked with a knowing smile and a devilish look in her eyes.

"Yes, honey, that little scuffle with C.J.'s men took me right out of the mood. I'll make it up to you in the morning, Promise. I'll make it worth your wait," he said, smiling.

"The hell you will because I'm sleeping in 'til afternoon. That's not to say that I wouldn't mind having a bite of you for lunch." she said, with yet another devilish look on her face.

The rest of the evening passed without further incident. They showered together, washed each other down and then soaked in the whirlpool. In the tub, they relaxed in the hot pulsing waters of the Jacuzzi. Done with their bath, they dried themselves off and went into the master bedroom, where they changed for bed. Aaron slipped into his spandex shorts and Laura put on her purple night gown. They kissed good night, wished each other sweet dreams and cuddled up for the night. In his sleep, Aaron tossed and turned. Nightmares of his past life and of the violent things that he had done to the many faceless victims had resurfaced to haunt his dreams again. After a while, Laura hugged him from behind as he finally settled into a deep sleep. When the alarm sounded at 8:45 the next morning, Aaron quickly shut it off so it wouldn't wake Laura.

Aaron took a second to gather himself before he stepped into his shower shoes and threw on his robe. He showered for fifteen minutes, dried himself and returned to the bedroom, where he dressed himself in a pair of black dress slacks and white collarless shirt. He stepped into a pair of black leather and suede Italian loafers. After he was completely dressed, he walked over to the mirror to check his appearance. "Damn," he thought to himself, "thirty-six years old and I still don't look a day over twenty-five. Not too bad!

He walked down the long hall into the kitchen. He prepared a bowl of cereal for himself, and, after he finished his bowl of Captain Crunch, he went back into the bedroom for the last time of the morning. He took a second to watch Laura as she slept peacefully. He thought to himself, "Even in her sleep, without any makeup and bed head, she is still the most beautiful woman in the world!" He walked over to the bed, kissed her on her forehead, and then headed for the front door.

He grabbed the keys to the Eldorado and made his way to the elevators. He drove the Eldorado across town, heading for his rock and roll club, The Rock Palace. When he reached the club, he parked outside and walked into the club, where his manager and personal friend, Stanley, sat with the financial books of the club.

"Good morning, boss. I see you're up and about early this morning. Yesterday, Laura was by when I thought you were going to be in," Stanley said.

"Well, Stan, every once in a while you have to take a break, so I put Laura out to work while I chilled for most of the day," he said.

"Well, sir, the books are here and ready with last night's figures in them," he said as he slid the books over to Aaron.

He sat across the table from Stanley as he went over the book figures with his calculator. Before he began, he looked at Stan to see if he showed any sign of knowing what had transpired between Laura and Yung Lee at the Underground.

Stanley was a young man, only twenty-four years. He stood five feet eleven inches tall, weighed one hundred sixty-five pounds, and was athletically fit. When Aaron opened his rock club, he wanted a young college graduate with a sense of what a rock crowd wanted in a club. Stanley applied for the job and was hired immediately.

As they worked, the phone in the manager's office rang. Aaron looked at Stanley as if to tell him to go and answer it. Stan walked into the office and spoke on the phone for a few seconds. He came out and told Aaron that it was for him. Aaron had a puzzled look on his face as he stood up and walked into the office.

"This is Aaron. How can I help you?' he asked.

"Hello, handsome. Mind if I talk dirty to you this morning?" the voice asked.

"Laura, I thought you were going to get some sleep this morning. I didn't wake you when I left, did I, love?" he asked.

"No, baby, I just woke up and decided to call and tell you that I love you very much and hope that I can have a bite of you for lunch," she said.

"Oh, yeah, honey, you can count on that. You're always my favorite meal of the day," he replied.

"Good then I'll have *you* . . . I mean, I'll see you for lunch" she said, with a throaty chuckle.

"Yeah, I'll have both of those. Talk to you then; love ya, honey," he said as he hung up the phone.

Aaron had his back to the door as he spoke to Laura. When he turned to place the receiver back on its hook, he looked up to see Yung Lee standing in the doorway. She was wearing a skin tight, candy apple red, sleeveless patent leather cat suit. The front had a zipper, running the entire length of the suit, pulled down just far enough to expose the top part of her cleavage. She had her long jet black hair down over one of her breasts. She moistened her bright red, full lips before she began to speak.

"Good morning, Mr. Williamson. I see you're out early this morning. You're looking mighty fine in those slacks I bought for you a few years back," she said in a slow and sexy voice.

His eyes grew wide as a child's on Christmas morning as he looked at her from head to toe. He remembered the outfit she was wearing because he was the one who thought that it would look good on her when he bought it. He was at a loss for words for a couple of seconds, as he watched her walk over to the desk and slide across the top of it.

"What the fuck are you doing here, Yung? And what in the hell were you thinking pulling a fucking gun on Laura yesterday?" he asked angrily.

"I'm not here to talk about Little Miss Laura, Daddy! I'm here to talk about you and me. In fact, I've come here to do your body good like milk," she said, lying flat on her back with her head towards him.—

"Thanks, but no thanks, Yung. I've had my milk for the day. Now what do you want, I've got work to do," he said with a flat tone in his voice.

"I want you; don't you want me? Remember, Aaron, we were together for six years. I know when you're turned on. Remember what happens when I do this?" She ran her fingers through her hair and moaned the word "Daddy" as she licked her lips.

Aaron bit his lip as he tried to fight his body's reaction. He started to regain his control and calm down, but Yung knew Aaron very well. She grabbed his hand and led it to her left breast, making him pinch her nipple. She knew then that his body was under her spell and when she looked in his eyes, she saw he knew too. She whispered, "You remember this, Daddy. It was your favorite toy. Take me, Daddy, take me to that special place where only you could ever take me," she said as she zipped her suit all the way down and slid his hand into her panties.

As his hand touched her hot wet cleft, Laura's face flashed before his mind's eye. He suddenly remembered what they had together and what she meant to him; it was like a bucket of cold water thrown in his face. He removed his hand, and then pulled away from her grip. He started towards the door. Yung angrily sprang to her feet in one single bound. She used her extensive Kung Fu training, came off of the desk into an end over end flip and landed on her six inch heels, right in front of the office door.

As she caught him in her arms, she thought, 'this next move will take the fight right out of him'. She raised her knee and gently rubbed it against his genitals. It didn't quite work out that way. Aaron roughly pushed her away. He said, "You know something, Yung. I left The Shadow because I wanted to stop killing people. I left you because of your devious nature, which eventually would have gotten me killed. To tell you the truth, I don't think there is a child. I know you, Yung, and if I had a child, he would have been right here. You only said that to get Laura upset and to deceive me, but I know better. It's what my gut tells me. I have a damn good woman in my life now, and I won't fuck that up for a cheap quickie with you so go, Yung. Go back to your brother and tell him that all bets are off, and if I see hint of any member of The Shadow, I'll exterminate them all. And by the way, Yung, it was your right tit that was my favorite one. You must be talking about some other fuck you've had since you lost the best."

As Aaron spoke to her, his words seemed to hit her like cold, hard steel. With each word said, she slowly moved her head back and gasped in shock. She was silently crying before he finished his statement. When he was through, she replied, "I see that you're serious about your Laura. I don't really want to come between what you have with her. Seems as though I can't. She's a lucky woman. You do have a child, and I'll mail you pictures. For old times' sake, if it wouldn't be too much to ask, could I have a hug before I go? I'm leaving the country tonight. I have a feeling that I'll never see you again. When you left The Shadow, you left me too, and you didn't even say 'goodbye.' I miss you so much, and I'd like to hold you just once more. Is that too much to ask, Aaron?" she said with a sad and defeated look in her eyes.

Remembering their shared past, he couldn't refuse. He thought to himself, "One hug, what harm could come from that," so he walked up to her and embraced her body in a hug. As let go of her, he felt a sharp pain in his side. He felt what seemed to him like a pinprick of some sort. He tried to push her away as he began to feel faint. He looked at her as she looked back at him and coldly smiled. He tried to speak, but she pushed him down onto the desk, and said, "Save your strength, Daddy, you're going to need it because, when you wake up, your life might not ever be the same."

As he slipped off into a deep sleep, the last thing he remembered seeing was Yung Lee, atop him with a switchblade in her hand. After he went under from the sedative, Yung pulled his pants off and saw his monogrammed underwear with the words "Laura's toy" in cursive. She clicked open her blade and began to cut up his boxers. "Isn't that fucking cute. You have your bitch's name across your dick. Too bad, Daddy, I'm going to have to cut that shit off."

She pulled a small bottle from her purse and sprayed a scent around the room, and wet the destroyed boxers with it as well. When she was done with the room, it looked and smelled as if there had been a very heated sex session going on for hours.

Yung slowly left Aaron's office. As she was leaving she thought, "Not quite what I had in mind, but still, it's enough to get things really started." Afterwards, she zipped up her cat suit and walked out of the club. She was gone, just as quickly as she had appeared. Aaron slept on peacefully into the early afternoon.

Chapter III

THE SUN WAS shining high in the sky early Tuesday afternoon, as Aaron slept peacefully his office at The Rock Palace. He slept until he was awoken by the ringing of the phone. He quickly gathered himself then answered it on the fourth ring.

"Rock Palace, Aaron speaking."

"Hello, remember me, the woman waiting at home for you to come taste her for lunch?" Laura asked with a touch of anger in her voice.

"Damn baby, I'm sorry. I must have fallen asleep while I was looking over these figures from last night." He quickly said trying to hide the embarrassment in his voice.

"Aaron, is something wrong? It's not like you to fall asleep like this while at work. It's 1:00 in the afternoon and you haven't been to either of your other businesses yet. Are you feeling alright?" She asked with a deep concern in her voice.

"No honey I'm fine. I just dozed off for a minute, that's all. I'll hurry up and get finished, so I can have a bite of you for dinner", he stammered. As he was on the phone, he took a look around the office. It looked and smelled as if some seriously hard love making had happened. After he hung up, he leaned back into his seat, still feeling the effects of the sedative Yung Lee had stuck him with, and quickly fell asleep. He slept very briefly, for about 15 minutes. This time he wasn't woken by the ring of the phone but by the tapping on his forehead from Laura.

Half dressed and the strong reek of sex in the air, Aaron jumped to his feet. He opened his eyes and saw her standing over him. As far as she was concerned, he didn't need to say a word. The look of guilt in his eyes told the entire story.

She looked over the desk to find his ripped boxer shorts next to the switchblade with Yung Lee's name engraved on its blade. She grabbed the blade as she looked into Aaron's eye, saying . . . "I figured something was wrong when you didn't come home for lunch, but I didn't think you were fucking that bitch Yung Lee!!", shouting as her face turned bright red with anger.

"This is a setup! I was drugged, let me explain . . ." he said but she cut him off. "I don't want to hear it Aaron! You put your dick in that slope eyed slut . . . how the hell how do you think I feel? Look at yourself. You still have her pussy juice crusted on your dick! How fucking stupid do you think I am? My God Aaron, you were going to fuck her then come home and make love to me?"

"Laura it's not like that. Yung Lee stuck me with a needle that knocked me out" . . . he said as she cut him off again and said . . ." Enough, you're lying Aaron!" She threw the blade onto the desk and slapped him as hard as she could.

He fell back into the chair and clenched his fist. He ran his knuckles across his top lip, wiping away the blood that ran from his nose. She reared back for another swing, but before she made contact with his face, he caught her by the wrist. He spun her around and roughly sat her down between his legs.

"Now you listen to me. I can see what you think happened in here today, and that's why you hit me, but I'll be damned if you're just going to hammer away at me while I just sit here and take it. Fuck no, not me, not ever! Yung Lee stuck me with a needle and knocked me out. While I was out she must have ripped off my clothes and sprayed something to make it smell like sex. I know all of this looks fucked up, and I'm not sure I would believe it either if our roles were reversed. I know the past few days have been rough and my creditability with you *isn't* the best it's been, but I'm asking you to stand by me. Don't pull away from me-Yung Lee wants us apart.

After he finished speaking, he stood her up then let her go. He hated that Yung Lee had caused her so much pain. She turned to look him in his eyes with her tear filled ones. She took a deep breath, and sniffled as she held out her chest. "Aaron I not sure if I can believe you. You have lied to me about your past because you thought that I would leave you. How do I know you're not lying now? You must admit, this sounds pretty farfetched, even for you! I'm going home to be alone and think about all of this. I'm probably the world's biggest idiot, but I love you very deeply, that's why this hurts so much. I hate not knowing if I can trust you and I don't know if I'll ever be able to again."

Aaron looked down at her, and then said . . . "I love you too Laura. If you can't believe anything else, believe that, and know that I would do anything for you."

"I'm leaving now Aaron, please don't come home until late tonight", she replied as she turned and walked out of the office.

He watched as she walked away, waving at Stanley as she passed him on her way out. Just then it dawned on him that, Stanley was here the whole time. Through all that had happened Aaron completely forgot about him being in the club. He thought to himself: all this time he was out there, he knew Yung Lee came in here and he had to have heard some of what happened in this office. He could have at the very least warned me that Laura was on her way into the club. Gritting his teeth, he said . . . "Stanley, why didn't you warn me that Laura was on her way in to see me?"

"Boss that crazy broad who was here earlier put her gun to my head and told me not to wake you up or else she'd kill me when I went home. She said that she'd be watching me and I didn't want to be shot, so I let you sleep. Shit, that bitch almost shot poor Charlie yesterday at the Underground; I wasn't going to fuck with her under any circumstances. Sorry boss.

"Well how the fuck did you find that out? I didn't think you knew anything thing about that based on your facial expressions this morning."

"Do you think for one minute that your managers don't talk to one another? I found out about yesterday's incident from Rob, who only knew because he was told by Charlie right after it happened", he said with a slight laugh.

"Well thanks a lot then Stan. Not only did you leave me out on a limb with Yung lee, but you sold me out with Laura as well. If you weren't such a good manager, I'd fire your ass on the spot. How much more do you know about what's going on?" He asked with a serious look on his face.

"I only know what Rob told me over the phone, but I've been able to piece a few things together myself. From what you've said about your past being filled with a lot of darkness, I figure this Yung Lee chic is either coming after you because you owe her money, or because she has your kid."

"Well regardless Stan, it's not important anymore. In fact, the less you know, the safer you'll be. Tell me, do you still have the shotgun and pistols behind the bar?" he asked with a flat look in his eyes.

"Yeah, they're still there. I've never had a need for them thank God. After Rob told me what happened at the Underground, I went to the gun shop across the square and brought extra ammo for all the guns. Three boxes for the shotgun and six for the pistols. I'm not going to have a need for them, am I boss?" He asked with a concerned face.

"Hopefully not, but if you have to pop some caps in someone's ass, don't sweat it. I can handle the Watertown cops," he said through a fake smile.

"Well boss now that you got your excitement for today with that Yung Lee and Ms. Laura, the figures from last night are still waiting" he said with a childish grin.

"Fuck it; if it's not there, it's just not there. I'll try again tomorrow morning, but for right now I'm heading over to AW's. Once I'm done, I'll peek my head in here tonight to say 'what's up' to all the rockers." He turned and walked toward the front door.

Aaron walked up the stairs leading out of the club onto the sidewalk when he noticed Laura had taken the car instead of the truck. As soon as he sat in Hummer and started it, his cellular phone rang. As he pulled into traffic, he let it ring twice then answered it.

"This is Aaron. Go ahead."

"Sarge it's me, CJ. What's up?"

"Nothing man, just dealing with this fucked up situation", he said with a touch of sadness in his voice.

"What's wrong Sarge, did you fuck something up?" He asked through a laughing voice.

"Thanks a lot, old buddy! That bitch Yung Lee drugged me with some kind of sedative. She made the office of my club look and smell like I fucked her all morning. Laura walked into that office and saw my boxer shorts all cut up next to Yung Lee's engraved blade, and she freaked. Hell, I can't even go home right now because of this bullshit."

"Well Sarge, I told you years ago not to fuck with that crazy bitch, didn't I? Shit, you know how I feel about that 'other' shit! I still say the darker the berry, the sweeter the juice. It's ok to slide them the pole, but don't catch a case—fuck that," he said proudly.

"Well thank you, oh wise one! Listen, I've just parked in the bar parking lot and have to go inside. How about I give you a call a little later?"

"Negative, Sarge. I've got a mission to go on with Infiltrate tonight I'm coordinating the transportation." He answered quickly.

"How long will you be out of the net? I mean, what if something comes up and I need to reach you?" he asked with obvious concern in his voice.

"Just call the Upper Room if things get bad, Sarge. Besides, we'll be closer than you think because our theater of operations is not very far from Watertown. Worse comes to worse, our SP time is set for 2230, so it's going to be awhile before we head out."

"That's a Roger CJ. Good luck on your mission tonight and don't *forget* to be careful" he said, terminating the call.

Aaron cut the ignition, then hopped out and walked into his bar, AW's. Sitting by the end of the bar, waited his manager and personal friend, Robert. A well-built, 32 year old black man, he stood six feet tall. He kept his hair in locks and usually had a cigar in his mouth whenever Aaron saw him. As Aaron walked in, Robert stood to his feet and extended his hand in a handshake. After they exchanged greetings, the two men sat down at the bar. Robert asked . . . "What's up Boss? I thought you were going to be in earlier. What's going on?"

"Nothing and everything all at the same time Rob. Let me ask you something. What do you know about what happened at the Underground yesterday?" he asked with a serious look on his face.

"Well boss, Charlie called me right after Laura left yesterday. He told me everything that he saw and I told Stanley, who I guess told you. Is it that important, what we know or don't know? I mean really Aaron, what's important right now for you is to get back in good graces with Laura" he said with a touch of compassion in his voice.

"Stanley told you about that already? Shit, Do I have any loyalty in my organization?" he asked, slightly disturbed.

"We're loyal, but we also talk amongst ourselves of the events of the work day. We wouldn't be effective managers if we didn't communicate with each other. Who can tell what may or may not affect each business? Hell, Stan called me right after he saw the office door close when you were at the Rock Palace", said Rob, speaking through a bold voice and smile on his face.

"I'm glad that I didn't install those video cameras like I started too. By now, my life would have been on sale to some video store. Listen Rob, these are very trying times for me right now and I don't want my managers talking behind my back like a bunch of little girls, understood?" he said, looking directly into Rob's eyes.

"Alright, you're the Boss. Here are the figures from last night", he said as he slid the book across the counter top of the bar.

"I'll go in the office and look these over. Look here, if anybody comes in looking for me, I'm not to be disturbed under any circumstances—got it Rob?"

"Got it Boss, whatever you say", he answered flatly.

Aaron picked up the books and walked into the office, closing the door behind him. He pulled out his calculator and slowly went over the receipts and cash totals. He took his time going through the books. All in all, he took a total of three hours. Satisfied, he walked out of the office, turned out the lights, placing the books on the bar. He looked at Rob and said . . . "Everything seems in order with the books. Is the stock up to standard?"

"Yes, the bar tenders took the bar backs shopping yesterday and completely refilled the liquor store room and freezer", he answered quickly.

"Ok then. I'll see you tonight when I make my rounds", he said as he walked out of the front door, then onto the sidewalk.

He hopped into the truck, started it and pulled off. He drove through the center of town, heading down Washington Street where the Underground was located. He parked outside it once he reached the parking lot. After he turned off the truck, he walked down the stairs that led into the front door, then went, shutting the door behind him.

On the inside, he saw Charlie sitting behind the bar, which was next to the dance floor. As Aaron walked toward him . . . What's up Chuck? How are you doing this afternoon?"

"I'm making it, all things considered. How's Laura doing from yesterday? That shit scared the hell out of me, so I know she must still be pretty shaken up", he stammered.

"She's doing fine. The whole thing tired her out quite a bit though, so she's home resting up right now. In fact slide me the books so I can go into the office and get started. I'll be on the phone with Laura as I go over the books, so if anyone comes in looking for me, I'm not to be disturbed under any circumstances. Understand Charlie?" He asked.

"Understood Boss, please tell Laura I said sorry about yesterday when I acted like such a pussy." he said as he lowered his head in shame.

Aaron patted him on the shoulder and gave him a reassuring look. He picked up the book, then walked into the office and went to work.

After a short while, he took a break and picked up the phone to call Laura at the Condo. She answered after the second ring.

"Hello" she said. "It's me, how are you doing?" He asked with concern in his voice.

"Aaron I'm so not in the mood to talk to you right now." she said with coldness in her voice.

"Laura, I know all of this is fucked up right now, but let me try to explain. Yung Lee tried to seduce me, but when she realized it wouldn't work, she injected me with some sort of sedative. She set up the whole scene to look as if we fucked all afternoon. Think about it for a moment. You were meant to find me in a compromising position. A rather ingenious way to divide and conquer. Remember when I told you that I left the Shadow? Well I left her, too—purposefully. She is very conniving and controlling, just like The Shadow. I still don't want that life, I want the life we have together. Please, I love you, and I'm trying to apologize, can't you meet me half way?" he asked.

"Aaron I really don't know whether to cry or spit right now. She tried to seduce you? You didn't respond? Well it looked like at least a few inches of you responded very well! Maybe it was a setup. How the fuck am I supposed to feel about that? How would you feel if it were you hearing this bullshit? I don't think you would want to talk to me right now. Talking is the last thing that I feel like doing, I feel like beating the shit out of you and that little slope eyed bitch! All of this pain and anger lies on your shoulders!" she said, with real frost in her voice.

"Well fuck it then Laura. I'm not going to kiss your ass or bend over backwards trying to make things right when it seems like you're not even interested in trying. Tell you what Ms Laura, I'll stay here and close the club. Then I'm coming home whether you're in the mood or not!" he replied as he angrily broke the call.

In a fit of rage, he swept everything off the desk. He silently shed tears of anger and frustration. He placed his head in his hands as he thought of how fucked his life had become. He thought long and hard about how he could make things right. After a few minutes of soul searching, he finally regained his composure. Aaron came to the conclusion that for the moment, it was all out of his hands. He realized that these event and changes was meant to happen. For some reason it wasn't yet clear to his eyes, but time would bring the solutions to his problems.

He wiped his face and went back to his work on the book figures and totals. As he had done at the Rock Palace, he took his time in going over the figures. Just in the interest of consuming time, he went through the book for a second time. This time around, he took a total of four to go over and recheck to club's book. When he finished, he walked back into the main room of the club where Charlie was standing with a smile on his face.

"Oh my god, he's alive, he's alive! Everything ok Boss?" Charlie asked with laugh.

"Everything's in order Charlie, I just took my time going through all of the figures. Damn, it's going on nine o'clock. I hadn't realized that it was this late", he said with a stunned look on his face.

"Yeah Aaron, you were in there for a long time. The DJ's are in the booth already; you going to hang out with us tonight? It's been awhile since you've graced us with your presence", he said jokingly.

"Why the hell not Chuck, the night is young and I'm in the mood to have some fun. But damn Chuck, it's been so long, I don't even remember what tonight is or what type of crowd will be in."

"Only the best night of the week: tonight is ladies night! In about an hour we'll start to see our first guests for the evening. You see, the bouncers are on their way in the door, which means it's not long till show time at The Underground", he said with an explosion of enthusiasm in his voice.

"Well hell Chuck, I'll do something to help. I don't want to just feel like a third wheel or something. This is going to be just like the old days when I first opened this place. Remember, you and me behind the bar, how we use to keep the drinks flowing? I think it's time for them to get another taste of that Chuck, you and me once again at the bar. Hot damn ladies, look out!" he yelled out with excitement.

As the night progressed, Aaron helped Charlie and the other bartenders set up for the night as he counted the money in the register and made sure all of the liquor bottles were filled. By ten o'clock, the doors to the club were opened for business as the first ladies made their way in. Aaron looked out of the front windows at the long line of people, mostly women, waiting to come in and have a good time. When the bouncers let the crowd in, one of the first women to come in was an old friend of Aaron's named Regina. She made her way over to the bar as soon as she recognized him.

She was a short, barely 5'3", shapely woman, her hair a rich honey blond color, which perfectly matched her almond skin tone. As she walked over to him, she began to smile as she spoke . . . "I see you finally got permission from your keeper to come out and party with us crazy people. How have you been man, it's been a long time since the last time you were out and about!"

"What's up Regina, it has been a long time since we've talked. I don't know about that keeper stuff, but it is good to see you again. How is your man Ricky doing, I haven't seen him around town in months", he asked with a large smile.

"Damn Aaron, it has been a long time since we talked! I've been single for almost six months now. See what happens when you stay home with your woman, you miss out on the entire goings on in this beautiful city. Hell I told you when you first opened this club that I'd be the one who would bring you back to the sister girls, and I'm not a quitter", she said as she ran her fingers across his lips.

They continued to talk and reminisce of old times as the action in the club began picked up and the night progressed. Across town, Laura slept quietly. In her dreams she dreamt of how happy Aaron made her. She also dreamt of the day when Aaron would finally ask for her hand in marriage.

She slept on until the slamming of the front door awakened her. She woke up thinking that it had to be Aaron coming home to make up with her, and she was very ready making up. She slipped out of her nightgown and sprang out of bed, as she went running into the hallway. As she ran through the bedroom door, she shouted loudly, "I forgive you honey, I forgive you", but she suddenly stopped cold. Almost shocked by sight of the person standing there, she stopped in mid stride and fell back on her ass. Deep in her mind, she knew that this person had to be the Shadow's Master standing there before her. Covered from his mask to his feet in all black, he was an imposing and fearful figure.

Her heart felt as if it was in her throat. She had no words to say, and as she sat on the carpeted floor in her birthday suit, she realized her situation was gravely serious. The masked person looked down at her and in a scratchy Korean accented voice said . . . "You may forgive Williamson, but we will never forgive him for his betrayal. With you in his life now, he's not the same man he was. The Shadow was his life and now it appears you are, so as the Master I must ensure that there are no other distractions in my family. Little white girl, you are that distraction". Laura began to tremble with the thoughts of implied violence running wild through her mind.

As he spoke on of her demise, she noticed her Desert Eagle sitting on the table by the door. She carefully watched his movements. She saw that he had no knowledge of the guns' presence. After he finished his speech, he asked her what she thought about her soon coming execution, but she never answered.

In her mind, she prayed that her silence would somehow draw him closer so she would have a clear run at the gun. After a few seconds of silence, her plan worked. Shadow Master started slowly walking towards her, dramatically cracking his knuckles.

When he reached her, he bent down to grab her but before he had the chance to react, she kicked her leg up as hard as she could. The surprise blow caught him square in the face and knocked him back onto his ass next to the wall as she sprang to her feet and sprinted toward to table.

Diving at the table, she grabbed the gun, then quickly spun in his direction and pointed it at him. Before she had the chance to pull the trigger, the front door flew open as two heavily muscled Korean men jumped on her, knocking the gun out of her hands. She struggled but was over powered by the two huge men. They held her upside down her ankles while the Shadow Master walked over to her. He was still a little woozy form her kick and the bump against the floor, but when he looked at her held by his men, he smiled and said . . . "Let her down and place her on her feet. You dare kick me in the face you white bitch. This will teach you some respect!" he shouted as he kicked her in her stomach then against the head.

Laura dropped to her knees and cried out in pain as she held her stomach and head. They all watched her while she laid there on the floor in agony. The Shadow master wiped away the blood that ran from his nose, reached down and grabbed her by her hair then dragged her to the center of the room. After he lifted her up to her feet, he snapped into a round-house kick and struck her in the face. The force of the impact sent her flying back into the wall, knocking her mercifully unconscious.

The Master stood looking down at her as the other two men walked over to his side. They both had black tattoos on the backs of their hands of a man's shadow with white eyes. The taller of the two men began to speak as they watched Laura lie on the floor.

"What do we do with her, Master?" he asked flatly in Korean.

"Take her to the van and tie her up. After that, I want you to show Mr. Williamson what I think of his business establishments" he answered with hatred in his voice.

"Shall we kill him and his staff Master?" the taller man asked.

"If Williamson opposes the will of the Shadow, if he opposes my will and refuses to come before me freely, then you will bring his head to me in a box", he ordered. The shorter of the two walked over to the couch, flipped it upside down and left The Shadow's signature calling card on it. They both trashed the condo before carrying Laura down to the van. Once she was tied into place, the men vanished into the night.

Meanwhile at the club, Aaron spoke on with his friend Regina. He really relaxed and enjoyed himself, as they talked and laughed for what seemed to be hours until he received a call from Stanly over at the Rock Palace. He screamed hysterically over the phone as Aaron heard sounds of gunfire and people screaming in the background.

Before Stanley had the chance to say anything else, the phone line went dead.

Aaron slammed down the phone. Frantic, he ran across the dance floor, parting the crowd then running up the stairs to the street where he jumped into his Hummer. He started the truck, shifting into gear and screeching off toward his club across town. As he roared through the center of town, he pulled out his Desert Eagle and sat it on his lap. He took a second to look in the glove compartment, pulling out six clips of rounds for the huge handgun. The ammo he pulled out were specially made clips. Each one held 10 .44 caliber bullets with armor piercing tips. As he reached the club, he drove up onto the sidewalk, bringing the truck to a screeching halt as he hopped out with his gun in hand, the extra clips stuffed into his belt.

Aaron took a few moments to carefully case the situation. He ran into the club through one of the shot out windows, noticing all of the bodies on the dance floor. He called out Stanley's name as he stepped over the bodies, but heard no answer to his calls. The smell of heavy metallic smell of blood filled the air as he moved closer to the bar. The odor brought back several vivid and violent memories of killings from his past which seemed to flash across his mind's eye with every step he took. As he walked closer to the bar, he saw what he thought at first to be a rug thrown over the charred body of his friend Stanly.

As he pulled the rug completely away, he knew immediately what happened to him. Acid attack, he thought to himself. Rage filled his mind as he thought of his young friend's wasted life. Wrapped in the moment, he lowered his head into his hands and quietly sobbed.

With his head bowed and his gun by his side, he heard footsteps from one of the darkened corners of the room. He listened closely without turning or showing sign of discovery as the person drew nearer. Aaron gathered a bearing on who was trying to sneak up on him. From his steps, Aaron was able to gather that it was a male about 185LB5 and, not very tall.

He listened, hearing the footsteps draw closer and closer. With the intruder's every step, Aaron shifted his weight onto his right leg as smoothly as possible. He didn't want the other man to know that he was aware of his approach. Once the man was in range, Aaron snapped into a whipping roundhouse kick, striking the man across the jaw, sending him to the floor.

When he recovered from his kick, he looked down at the man and immediately recognized him. Lee, he thought to himself, a member of the Shadow and one of his former students. In the back of his mind he knew it was time for him to show Lee just how much he still had to learn from the master!

Aaron jumped back into a defensive stance. "That was the move of an amateur Lee. I thought I taught you to never go in alone, especially when facing a master." A voice rang out from another dark corner of the room and said, "He didn't Williamson, you're just so old, you didn't hear my footsteps like you should have", the man said as Aaron heard the hammer of a gun being pulled back.

He also knew the other man behind the voice. This was a person who in the past he considered a friend. The man was a young Korean named Wang, who was also part of the Shadow. Aaron recalled several missions in the past where Wang was right alongside him as one of his best students.

He looked at Wang, who had him in the sights of his 45CAL. auto handgun and braced himself for his next move. Through the darkness Aaron saw the whites of Wang's eyes and spat before he began to speak.

"You're good Wang, and Lee, you're not bad yourself, but you both picked the wrong night to fuck with a brother from Brooklyn"! He said as he jumped into a back flip. Before Wang had the chance to pull his trigger, while still in mid flip, Aaron managed to get off one shot at Wang. He missed, but he caused Wang to pull his gun down and seek cover behind the bar. He landed on his feet, and ran out of the club onto the streets of Watertown at top speed. Wang ran over to Lee and grabbed him off the floor as they both took after Aaron.

They jumped through the window and looked down the street to see Aaron turn into an alley just down the block. Wang grabbed Lee by the shirt and snarled "Come on" as they took off after him. As they reached the alley, Lee pulled his .45 from his belt and held it at the ready.

They walked down the alley for a few steps and heard Aaron's voice, which seemed to shout out from every direction . . . "Is this the best you two can do? If you can do any better or have more, I have time, I'll wait!!"

"Yeah Williamson, there's a lot more! I'm going to kill you then fuck your bitch doggy style!" Lee replied angrily.

Aaron sprang to his feet from behind one of the dumpsters in the alley. He shouted out as he fired his gun, "I don't think so, you pussy!"

He fired off three shots in one fluid motion. The shots hit their intended target, striking Lee in between the eyes, in his heart and finally in his dick. Lee's lifeless body flopped to the sidewalk as the remains of his brains oozed down the wall of the alley. Wang ducked after the first shot was fired and tried hopelessly to draw a bead on Aaron as he fired off the last two shots. After the shots were on their way, Aaron jumped from behind the dumpster and disappeared further down the alley.

Wang looked down at his friend's lifeless body on the sidewalk. He looked up and shouted out, "It's you and me Williamson, you and me, you fucking traitor."

He ran deeper into the alley, coming up on an intersection in the middle of the block. The streets of Watertown's business district were basically quartered so that the owners would have a back alley to store garbage for pick up. Wang reached the middle of the intersection. "Aaron! Aaron! Come face me like a man! You killed Lee with a pussy's way out; face me so that I can bring your head back before the Shadow Master", he shouted.

"What makes you think that you can take me, Wang? You're not even good enough to go off by yourself and make a hit without some help from someone like me, so what makes you think you can kill me?" Aaron asked, his voice seemingly coming out at him from every direction and every darkened corner.

Wang held his gun up with both hands as he searched for Aaron. He was driven by his pride, but deep inside, he knew he was no match for Aaron. When he took a step the clinking noise of the coins in his pocket echoed off the walls. He tried to steady himself as he noticed the tremble in his step. He saw a movement out of the corner of his eye, and spun in its direction, letting off two quick shots. Wang shouted . . . "I've got you now mother fucker, now I'm the best there is!"

Even before he finished speaking he realized that he had shot at nothing more than a shadow on the wall. Looking about, he quickly spun in the direction the light was coming from. He looked up and saw Aaron looking down at him, his gun with its hammer pulled back. He stood on the steps of one of the back doors in the alley.

Aaron coldly smiled as Wang's eyes met his, and he saw the fear in them. The fact that Wang stood there trembling softened his heart none as he called out to him, "So you're the best now Wang? I think not. In fact, I know not!" When he saw Wang blink, he lowered his gun and shot Wang's gun out of his hand. He threw his own to the sidewalk and said . . . "Wang, this is how it ends for you, getting stomped by a Brother just before I stain my hands with your blood", punching him in his jaw.

Just as he felt Aaron's blow, he rolled with it springing into a leg sweep, which took Aaron off his feet and sent him crashing down to the sidewalk. As Aaron went down, he quickly jumped atop him and punched him in his jaw repeatedly. Wang yelled "THIS IS FOR THE SHADOW! THIS IS FOR ALEX KIM! And this one is for Lee!" missing his last punch. Pushing him away, Aaron quickly sprung to his feet and snapped into a low spinning kick, which struck Wang across his eyes with pinpoint accuracy. After he recovered his stance, he grabbed Wang and body slammed him onto the sidewalk, and he crashed down with a sickening thud.

He looked into Wang's blood shot eyes and gritted his teeth, tasting the bitterness of revenge and hatred. As Wang trembled helplessly, Aaron repeated his earlier statement, "I told you that this was the wrong night to mess with a black man from Brooklyn, but it was even worse for you and Lee to fuck with *THIS* black man from Brooklyn!", as he stomped down on Wang's neck.

Crushing his windpipe and major blood vessels, Wang's body flopped under his foot for a few seconds as he drowned in his own blood. Moments after the deadly strike, Wang's body lay lifeless, in a pool of bright red blood.

As Aaron walked over to retrieve his gun, he noticed the blood stains on the white portions of his shoes. The sight of the stains brought violent flash backs of vicious killings which he had orchestrated. He remembered the faces of the people in their final moments of life as he snuffed their lives out like candles. After a few minutes of stillness in his remembrance, he shook his head and walked away.

Once he reached his truck, he looked up in the distance and suddenly realized the lights to his condo were out. Laura's face raced across his eyes. Only one thing ran through his mind—she was home alone without his protection.

He quickly jumped into the Hummer, started it then pulled off. He picked up his cellular and tapped out the ten digit number to Infiltrate's secured lines. As he drove, Tracy answered the phone, using her Infiltrate code name . . . "Upper Room, Chipmunk speaking", she said.

"This is Aaron, you know, Sarge. I have a situation up here that needs immediate attention, A.S.A.P!" he shouted. "Calm down Sarge, I've been briefed on your situation and help is near. I'll patch you through to #1 right now, so please hold" she replied as he heard a few clicks over the line.

After a short wait, the next voice he heard was that of CJ's. In the background he heard the sounds of chopper blades cutting through the air as CJ spoke to him. "This is #1 Sarge, what's up?"

"I just got into a fire fight with some of the Shadow. Do you remember Wang and that kid Lee? Well, I just had to smoke one while I killed the other one with my bare hands. I'm down the street from my place and the lights to my condo are out. I know that Laura would be up by now, so I'm sure something's not right. Alex Jr. knew that Wang and Lee wouldn't have stood a chance against me so he probably left some men at my house. All I need is some backup. I'm good, but outmanned. I can't just go into a situation where an unknown number of enemies is waiting for me. Time flies CJ, how fast can you and your people get here?" he asked flat out.

You're in luck Sarge; we're on our way to Fort Drum on a mission as we speak. We're only a few minutes out from your location in our special ops Chinooks choppers. I'll detour over to your building and hot rope my men onto your roof in about two minutes. Worry not old friend, we're twenty men deep and have two gun truck Hummers with us. We'll take care of any problem that you might have down there."

"Good then I'm going to take the underground parking complex and we'll meet up at my place, Sarge out."

"We're changing course now, talk to you in your building. Be careful and watch your targets once you get onto the upper floors."

After CJ ended his call with Aaron, he undid his straps, jumped to his feet and ran to the cockpit of the helicopter. He told the pilot about the change in mission and where to go. The pilot swerved the bird in the direction of Aaron's Watertown high-rise. As they skimmed over the rooftops at 130MPH, CJ spoke to the men of Infiltrate. "Ok men this is the new situation. We've changed course and are in route to Sarge's building. Some of you met him yesterday, but that's not important right now. This is a hot rope drop onto a roof in a possible hot situation. Once we're down, I want every floor cleared of any opposing forces. The ones we're looking for wear black hoods and most of them are Korean. Its two minutes and counting before the drop so let's look alive once we hit that roof. Good luck men, let's do this." They all checked their weapons and chambered a round.

They undid their straps and stood to their feet as the chopper sliced through the night skies. Aaron moved with stealthy through the streets toward his building. As he maneuvered along using cover and concealment techniques learned in his early years in the ARMY, he heard the blades of the chopper cutting through the air as they swung into position over his building. The sight of the two huge 45-foot long, 18foot wide helicopters left him in a temporary state of awe as he watched the birds move effortlessly before his eyes. Supported by their twin counter rotating horizontal rotor blades, CJ's chopper dropped its 3000lb capacity rear ramp as Aaron saw several ropes string down from the bird to the top of his roof.

Before the first man slid down the rope, the second chopper moved into over watching position, hovering slightly higher and away from the building. Automatic gun fire began to hit the fist chopper's armored bottom and rear ramp. CJ pulled Half back in the nick of time before the Shadow's men walked their gunfire onto the opening of the rear of the bird.

The pilot of the second bird swooped down as he ordered his door gunner to open fire on the men on the roof. He dipped down below the roof top and swung around to the opposite side of the building. As the chopper reached the rear of the tower, the pilot jerked up on the helicopter's elevator contra stick and raised the bird up until it was level with the rooftop. Once the chopper stopped moving, the door gunner opened fire on the men. Those men were faced away from the second chopper, firing up at the other bird as it pulled away higher into the sky.

Once the gunner opened fire with his eight rotating barrel machine gun, the night turned into day as the tracer rounds lit up skies. The rounds came out of the gun at over five hundred rounds per minute, so when the water fall of glowing bullets stopped flowing, there were no noticeable signs of human remains left on the roof. When the shooting stopped, the pilot radioed to the first chopper that the roof was cleared for a tailgate landing.

That meant that the chopper could hover with its ramp dropped onto the roof so that the men could run out instead of sliding down the rope from 150 feet up. Once in position, CJ and his men ran onto the roof wearing night vision goggles, and entered the building. As they moved deeper inside, CJ looked back at his men and gave them the signal to switch from safety to firing position on their 9mm silent firing assault rifles.

As Aaron waited in the garage, he tried to see if there was any movement in the complex. He was unable tell because of the power outage. He held his gun up at the ready in case one of the Shadow ran out into the lights of the street. He thought for sure that he'd see some action on the ground as the shots rang out from the roof. He finally swallowed in a deep breath and rose to his feet as he readied himself for total darkness combat.

While he moved slowly down the ramp into the complex under the building, infiltrate slowly descended deeper into the upper floors of the high rise. Half led his group as they moved down the stairway floor by floor. CJ and half kept in close contact through their boom mike communicator headsets as they crept along. CJ ordered them into a staggered formation with no less than five meters between one another, but once Big dog brought his up the rear of the formation and entered the building, and saw the staircase setup; he let CJ know how he felt as he said.

"1 it's 4 I don' like this at all. This staircase is the perfect set up for an ambush." He said as CJ cut him off.

"Keep that shit quiet and keep a watch on our six alright. We've done this shit before, just whatever jumps out at us, kill it. Understood?" He said. "1 it's 5, where the hell are all of the other people that lived in this building? This whole situation smells like a setup." Sand man said.

"Now that you mention it, someone would have been looking out of their window when those fools started firing at us form the roof. 5 take your squad and give me a recon of this floor. Everyone else, rally on number ~ position. 2 give us your location over the net." He ordered

"This is 2, I've stopped on the 15th floor. Number 1, these landings aren't very big, and if the entire group rallies on me, then we'll be too bunched up for firing just in case we're engaged upon. Let me take my squad to the 11th floor and do a recon?" He asked.

"That's a roger, but watch out for the Sarge. I believe he's taking the stairs up and you and your squad need to watch you're targeting." He said as he signed out.

After CJ completed his instructions, Half and Sandman took their four man fire squads to their designated floors. Each leader had three men charged to their squad on this mission. Their communicator headsets were specially made with multi frequency capability, so the leaders could all talk on one secured frequency, while each group had their own internal secured frequency. Even the way they spoke into the boom mikes was special since they used a very low monotone voice and not a whisper when they spoke because, if they whispered into the mike, the air sound would distort the sound over the net.

While group 2 reconned the 11th and group 3 reconned the 16th, Aaron moved along through the underground parking complex as he moved along ever so slowly toward the generator room. With his gun at the ready, deep in his mind he knew the he was going to encounter some of the shadow sooner or later and he felt a fire fight coming up soon deep in his gut.

As he walked along, he closed his eyes so that he would be totally dependent on his ears, reaching the door of the generator room, he opened the door, walked inside and felt around for the power lever and once he found it, he moved it to it's on position. Once the generator got up to speed, most of the lights slowly began to come on.

This presented an even larger problem for him in that he could use the cover darkness for his movement. but he said fuck it to himself and placed his back against the wall next to the door. In one lighting quick motion, Aaron grabbed and opened the door. As it swung open, from the corner of his eye, he saw a flash and moved his arm back just in time as shot gun shells flew in and struck the generator, sending the entire building back into darkness.

He tried to calm himself as his heart rate rose with a sudden rush of adrenaline. After the shots were fired and the generator stopped working, the only thing that he could hear was his own heartbeat. He had to regain his composure; he had no idea of how many bodies he was dealing with. He recalled some of his old martial arts training, breathing in deeply and concentrating on slowing his heart beat. Now calm and with a clearer head, he heard footsteps shuffling around in the parking complex.

Through the darkness, he heard three pair of footsteps moving toward the door. He listened closer and even began to hear them breathing as they closed in on the doorway. He heard the cocking action of a shotgun, the slide track of a 45-auto handgun being pulled back and the bolt of a fully automatic machinegun snap forward into firing position.

Going over the layout of the complex in his mind, he remembered there was a staircase entrance only a few steps to the left of the room he was in. He knew that the only chance he had was to take out the person who had the shot gun and wound the person with the automatic rifle, if not kill him. He wondered how he was going to get through this situation, when suddenly an idea came to him.

Reaching into his belt, he grabbed a bullet out of one of the clips he had stuffed in it and threw it against the generator in hopes that one of the persons come toward the room had an itchy trigger finger. His plan worked as the man who carried the shotgun, fired off a shot that lit up the entire room with sparks off of the generator.

As the sparks still danced about the floor, Aaron rolled toward the doorway and fired off one shot. The blast struck the man in the center of his chest as the round blew a hole through his back. After he fired the single shot, he dove out of the doorway to his left as the other two men opened fire into the room. He knew full that if he fired off just one shot, it would cause the other two men to open fire, making them light up the complex. The machine gun lit up the area with a strange strobe light effect, which made him slightly dizzy as he fired off his gun and missed.

Once the two saw the white flash from his gun, they turned and fired in that direction, while Aaron ran behind one of the concrete pillars that supported the building's weight. He kicked off his shoes and pulled off his socks as the men bounced bullets off of the pillar. He again wondered, how the hell was he going to get out of this as he counted the number of rounds they fired. I've counted at least thirty shots fired already from that machine gun, and as soon as he thought that, the gunner ran out of bullets.

He listened and bit his lip as he thought, this is it, I live or I die, but no matter what, this is the time. He jumped out from behind the pillar and opened fire while he was in the air, parallel to the ground, catching the machine gunner first in his head then in his chest. He rolled on the floor to his feet and waited for the last one to fire. Seeing the flash of the man's gun, he opened fire and killed the gunman on the spot. After the shooting, he turned and ran toward the staircase, then began his slow climb up to the 12th floor.

While he dealt with his attackers in the underground complex, on the upper floors of the building, Half and Sandman ran into some problems of their own. As they maneuvered their squads on the 11th and 16th floors, the sudden glare from the white lights instantly blinded them.

When the lights clicked on squad 2 was in the middle of the hallway as the four-man team attempted to check out each condo on that floor. The sudden rush of light caused their night vision goggles to turn bright green. Half jerked his sights off as his men did the same, but once they regained their regular sight, the lights again went dark. The door at the end of the hallway swung open. Half heard the sliding action of an automatic bolt being pulled back. It was a sound that he was all to used to hearing. He yelled into his boom mic telling his team to hit the floor, but was too late as the heavy machine gun opened fire on the squad. As he dropped to the floor, he watched the tracer rounds fly over his head, hearing one of his men scream out in agony as the round passed through his abdomen. Half ordered: "Open fire, repeat open fire—the gun flash is the target"! He fired his own sub machine gun, but didn't see who or what returned fire. They hit someone, because suddenly the enemy fire stopped.

When the shots stopped, he jumped to his feet as he put his night sights back on. Half ran over to his fallen team member, but was too late, for he was already dead. When he switched to the leaders frequency, he heard the leader of the 5th squad, speaking to CJ saying . . ."#1 I'm telling you man, this building is a done deal. There's no living person on this floor besides the 5th squad and if you ask me, I say this entire building is a wash! We should get the fuck out of here before we lose some of our own." he said as Half cut in on the conversation.

"#1 it's #2, and #5 things are worse than that already. I've lost our squads' special ops man. Didn't you all hear when we took on fire down here?" he asked with an angered voice.

"No we didn't. The fact that you took on a gunner and we didn't hear shit explains how the Shadow took out the residents of this high rise. The walls even in the hallways must be insulated. What's the situation like down there now? What kind of hardware did you encounter, and how many were there?" Sand Man asked.

"There was only one man with an M60 machine gun. I sent my other two men in for a recon of that condo where the fire came from, but all they were able to find was the one Korean gunner and two gutted bodies. I don't like this shit #1, someone knew that this floor would be checked and set up an ambush. This entire building could be a death trap and I can't even imagine what the hell is in the Sarge's condo on the 12th, but I know that it can't be nice. We still have a mission to do and our repel master is dead, damn it! How much more do we have to lose in order to help out your friend, #1?" Half asked angrily through his gritted teeth.

CJ was silent for a few moments before he began his slow, thoughtful response. "#2 Aaron Williams is my friend and he has saved my ass more times than I can even remember. His loyalty to me has never been in question, and I know that what I do for him, he would do for me. The risks we take during any mission are no different than the risks we take now, only now it's about honor and friendship instead of money. I expect and will accept no less than the very best you have to give; if I called on him, he would do no less than his best for us. Let us all not forget that if it hadn't been for him and his training, which in turn I used to form us, we would not exist, nor would we make the money that we make today. You accepted the possibility of loss when you became a part of Infiltrate, don't bitch up now!

Now I want Sarge's condo on the 12th floor stormed and cleared. #4 take your squad back up onto the roof and drop the ropes out of the choppers down in front of the condo windows, make sure they're secure. #2 and #5 move your squads to the 13th and use the ropes to assault the condo from the outside and watch your targets; #2 and I will be going in directly through the front door. Everyone on line with the instructions?"

"1 it's 2, 1 copy and am in route to your location."

"1 it's 3, roger we're in route."

"1 this is 4, I read your last. We're in motion to ours." The Big Dog answered with a bold and proud voice.

"1, 5, we're moving." Sand man simply replied.

While CJ's men shifted into their positions, Aaron made his way upstairs, reaching the 9th floor and hearing a sound which caused him to pull out his gun and hold it at the ready. As he was in his defensive stance, he carefully changed the clip in his gun for a full one and waited for any sign of movement. He knew full well that Infiltrate was in the building, but had no idea of what they might have been wearing or where they may have been.

He ran past the 10th floor and once he reached the 11th.

He saw a man through the darkness, dressed in all black from head to toe holding a gun in his hand. He jumped up and grabbed the man by his mouth and placed his gun to his head and said . . . "Take it easy kid," he said in a low voice "You've got five seconds to say who you're with or else your head becomes wall splatter!"

Before the man had the chance to speak, someone reached from behind Aaron and grabbed his wrist and began to speak to him very calmly, telling him to take a chill and to ease up because they were on his side. Aaron looked around to see the person who was speaking to him as the man said . . . "I don't know if you remember my face from yesterday, but I'm #2. Half from Infiltrate. If you'll come with me I'll take you to CJ who is on the 12th floor waiting for my squad. He told us you might take the stairs and that we should be on the lookout for you. And I'd appreciate it if you'd let my trooper go and take your gun away from his head. I've already lost one tonight and I don't want to lose another. Here, these night sights will help you see a lot better. I'll give you a hand if you can't figure them out?" Half said as he offered Aaron some help.

"I trained your #1 on these sights when he first joined the ARMY. So what's the plan, Half?" he asked as he turned toward him with the sights on.

"We're going to hook back up with #1's squad. Once all of the groups are set, we're going to do a front and rear spear head assault to your condo. In case you forgot from your old ARMY days, you and I are going to be going in through the front door" he said with a touch of sarcasm in his voice.

"Listen up young buck! Before we go through this door, you and I need to set something straight. I've forgotten more shit than you'll ever know and what I do remember is more than enough to whip your punk ass. And in case you forgot, I trained your trainer when you were still suckin' your mama's tit, so you better show me a little fucking respect!" Aaron said sternly as he pulled the 12th floor door open.

As he walked onto the floor, he passed by the men of the first squad then knelt down beside CJ. Half took a knee behind the both of them as Aaron looked at CJ and said." I know she's not in there, but I have to make sure for myself. I have to." He said with conviction in his voice.

CJ moved his group into position and held his hand above his head. When his men saw him raise his hand up, they crouched into the ready position and waited for the signal to move forward. Giving them the order to move by swinging his hand forward, in one lighting quick movement, the men ran forward and kicked in the front door, while the 3rd and 4th squads simultaneously crashed through the windows in the rear bedroom. Once Half, Dusty and Big Dog met up with each other in the front room, they radioed out to CJ, telling him that the condo was cleared. They found no sign of The Shadow. Aaron stepped in the door and saw how trashed the front room was. He dropped down to his knees desolate and furious.

CJ made a brief effort to console him, but it did no good, for all of the men in the room felt the pure rage which rolled off from his heart. After a few seconds, Aaron sprang to his feet then ran toward the closet as CJ and the others followed. As CJ ran behind him, he yelled at him and asked what the hell he was doing, but Aaron never answered.

He just swung open the closet door then punched the fake ceiling to the side. He pulled down the sniper rifle case then popped the rosary that was wrapped around it. While CJ and the others watched, he changed into his old Shadow suit, and quickly assembled his huge rifle. He looked at CJ and said simply "I'm back".

CJ said "Sarge, I know you're in a world of hurt right now, but I still have a mission to complete and my time is running out."

"One more thing CJ, just one more favor. Since Alex Jr. is calling the shots, he must have known Yung Lee was in the States. He might go after her while she's at her house that's out past the corn field. If I'm right, Laura should still be there with them. There's not much time, so what's up CJ, am I good for one more?" Aaron asked as he placed his hand on CJ's shoulder and looked directly into his eyes.

"God damn it #1," Half shouted, "We don't have any time left. The target will not be there in the morning and will be gone for six months. If we don't do it tonight, we'll be out 12 million dollars!"

"#3 and #4 take yours and the rest of the second squad to the roof and prepare for immediate dust off. Half, you wait here. Move out", CJ ordered as the men began to clear out of the room.

Once they were all gone from the room, and down the hall out of sight and earshot, CJ turned toward Half and began to speak while Aaron stood there, watched and listened.

"Anthony, we've been friends for a long time, but you're my second in command!! I lead Infiltrate and the Street Foundation. There will be no questions—Don't you ever question me in front of the men Anthony, EVER! I know about our mission, I negotiated the deal, remember? I've never led us on a failed mission because of this man here-my friend. We'll make our money tonight Anthony, but first we will help Aaron out as much as we can. Now gentlemen, let's go to the birds on the roof, we have a house to storm."

CJ walked behind Half and Aaron up to the roof where the men of Infiltrate awaited them in the choppers, blades turning. Assured that everyone was present and accounted for, CJ radioed the pilot, Mr. Bob and gave him the order to dust off. Bob radioed to the second chopper pilot and told him what the situation was and where they were flying to next.

The pilot in the other bird was his seventeen year old son Rick. Bob gave him special instructions on how he wanted him to fly, being that they might be flying into a hot zone. He told Rick to move over to left rear side of Bobs' bird and to stay in a cover formation. He then explained to Rick what had to be done concerning a hot zone drop. Bob had well over 10,000 hours of combat interdiction missions under his belt from the combination of Desert Storm and the Panama war. Rick was a good pilot even though he was only seventeen, but he listened to his father very closely when it came to these types of missions.

The choppers quickly reached Young Lee's house out past the cornfield. Bob dropped the rear ramp and the men in the rear of his bird sprang the 150-foot ropes out of the back. This time the ropes hit the top of the house and no gunfire was seen from the ground. CJ gave his men the signal to repel down onto the roof.

Prior to their arrival at the house, both pilots engaged their rotor blade sound dampening system. This system used wide band ultra sonic sound waves that concealed the heavy sounds the chopper blades created as they sliced through the air. Any one more than five feet away from the bird heard no sound from the choppers as they hovered over the huge three-story house.

Not one to miss the action, Aaron assisted the men with their riggings. To CJ's surprise, Aaron retained most of his air assault and air born training through the years, and when the signal was given for the men to repel down onto the roof, Aaron was one of the first men down the rope with the second squad.

Seconds after the first member of Infiltrate had reached the roof, the chopper was empty and the men were ready the storm the house.

Sarge slid open one of the windows as Big Dog jumped through and cleared the room. He radioed back to CJ that the room was clear. CJ ordered all of his leaders into the house as they took the third floor of the house and had it cleared in less than ten seconds.

Moving on to the second floor, Half took his squad and cleared that floor with nothing to report. CJ himself, not liking what he was seeing ordered a force rally on the ground floor. After he radioed his orders to his group leaders, they all moved their men onto the first floor and quickly rallied around CJ. Dusty reached the ground floor first and reported all clear, then set his men in a perimeter defense by all the windows in the front room of the house. After all of the men in the squads were in the room, CJ spoke with his leaders and Aaron on what was going on.

"We've gone through every room and nothing's here. Send the 3rd squad down to give the basement the once over, but other than that, this place is a wash", he said with his palms held out before him.

"#1 this whole scene is a wash if you ask me. I think we should get the hell out of here and take care of our business like we came up here to do in the first place." Big Dog blurted out.

"Dusty take your squad down to the basement and give me a recon by the numbers. If there's anything down there, let me know about it ASAP" CJ ordered as #3 moved his squad toward the basement.

When the point man opened the door which led down to the basement, Dusty spoke to his group. He guided them through the darkness and ordering them into a two by two cover formation as they slowly made their descent. Through his night sights, the point man, Johnson, saw a beam of infra red light that ran across the bottom of the staircase-a trip wire.

Johnson warned Dusty of the light beam's location and its position as he stepped over it. Dusty in turn instructed all of his squad not to break the light beam. Sixty seconds after Johnson had stepped onto the basement floor, the entire 3rd. squad took up covering positions as Dusty moved forward through the large basement. After a quick search, Dusty ordered his men to look inside all of the closets, which lined the basement walls.

Immediately after #3 ordered his men into a room to room, or a closet to closet search, Johnson opened one of the closet doors and saw what appeared to be a bomb inside it. His body stiff with fear, he radioed Dusty a quick sit rep.

"#3, its Johnson. I've come across an unknown explosive device. It has a digital screen, but it's not powered right now", he said with a shaky voice.

"Don't move Johnson, I'm on my way over to your location. Everyone else, regroup with the main body upstairs. Now move!" He ordered as the other men ran toward the staircase.

In a blind rush of fear, the other two men ran up the stairs. The first man remembered the light beam that was running across the staircase, but the second man didn't. He tripped the beam as he ran up the stairs. It was connected to the bomb in the closet; the digital screen lit up on the device with the number sixty and began a countdown.

Johnson ran upstairs and yelled out to Dusty in a loud voice, "The bomb is active! Everyone clear the hell out!" Dusty followed Johnson, yelling over his mike to CJ about the bomb count down. As he reached the ground floor, he saw the last man run out of the front door. CJ told him to hurry as he saw Dusty jump out of the door, across the huge wraparound porch.

Once his feet touched the ground outside the house, CJ and the others all saw Dusty disappear in the white flash of light of the bomb's detonation. He was sent flying across the clearing by the sheer force of the explosion. After the debris stopped flying, the team quickly jumped to their feet and gathered themselves, as they began to look around at the complete destruction of the structure they narrowly escaped. CJ shouted out for everyone to begin the gruesome search for Dusty. After a couple of minutes of them sifting through the rubble, Half and his squad came across Dusty. Half yelled to CJ as the other two men lifted and picked through the wreckage to reach him.

Surprisingly, he was dazed and a bit cut up but relatively unscathed. The dark look on his face told the whole story of the mood that he was in as CJ and the others rushed over to him. After he dusted himself off, he slowly walked over to CJ and gave him a venomous look. "CJ I almost bought it in there just now—and for what? Because one of your old pals has lost his piece of pussy and don't know where to find it? That's it with this friend bullshit, we've helped enough—it's time for us to make our fuckin' money!"

CJ held his head down, feeling the weight of everyone's staring eyes pressing upon him. He took in a deep breath then lifted his head, his clear eyes meeting with Dusty's blood shot eyes. In that moment of pause, even the crickets seemed to quiet their chirping as everyone waited for his response.

Deep in his heart he knew where poor Laura had been taken and that her time was limited, but he also felt the pulse of his men. His crew of mercenaries, banded together in the pursuit of financial gain, all bruised and battered. He then sadly looked at Aaron in apology for what was coming. Sarge already knew what was coming, for he too felt the tenseness in the air. CJ looked up at the hovering choppers and began to speak as the men of Infiltrate all began to cheer.

"Bird one, this is #1. Prepare for landing and immediate dust off. It's time for our original mission", he said with conviction in his voice.

As the choppers landed, CJ walked over to Aaron. "Ok Sarge this is it, a favor for a favor. My repel master is dead. No one else on this team has the experience for what this mission calls for, and I'm now down a few men. In other words Aaron, I need you".

"CJ you know as well as I do where Laura is on her way to. I have to follow and save her before it's too late . . .". CJ cut him off . . . "Look here Sarge, I need your sling loading expertise and there's a lot of money riding on this. Help me out with my operation, and we'll help you out with whatever you need. Is it a deal Sarge?" he asked as he extended his hand out toward him.

Aaron took hold of his outstretched hand and asked . . . "Do you know what you're committing your group to? You hardly got them to help me out with this and what I need is going to be ten times worse than the little shit that happened tonight."

"Sarge this is what's going to happen. You're going to go in chopper 2 with Half, and he'll fill you in on the details of the mission. Once you've acquired the target, you'll take it to the port of Ogdensburg where a Canadian ship will be waiting for the drop. After that we'll meet up back at Watertown International Airport and head back to HQ in New York. Once we're in the Big Apple we'll discuss what our next move will be. Let me worry about my men, because when the chips are down, you'll see what's what about them" CJ said with a ferocious smile on his face.

Aaron replied "Damn I hate it when you smile like that. It always means trouble for me. Alright, I'm in. The other chopper is down, so I'll see you out side of Watertown". He ran over to the rear ramp of the bird and quickly stepped on.

After the rear ramp closed on chopper 2, Half handed Aaron a radio headset and motioned for him to put it over his head. Once he had the set in place and mike by his mouth, Half began to speak to him as the chopper lifted off.

"I've already spoken to CJ and he briefed me on what your purpose is on this mission. First off, let me explain my behavior back on the staircase. The man in my group who was killed was a good friend. We all know the risks we take on these missions, but we're just that good that we don't expect to not come back. CJ trained us all very well, but since he got it from you, I guess that means I owe you an apology and my respect.

Now that that's out of the way, our target is an Avenger Humm-Vee. The cables are all here, but I can't make heads or tails of them. I'm sure that you can, right?" he asked.

"Shit, it won't even take three minutes to hook on and get the hell off the fort. My question is what is chopper l's target since they have two Hummers with them?" Aaron asked.

"That part is a little trickier than ours. Do you know what a Singar radio is?"

"Yeah, but those were old before CJ and I got out of the ARMY. They do something to the radio frequencies when they transmit which make them totally secured and coded." Aaron quickly replied.

"Well soon after the Singars were in use in the armed forces, the government shared them with their allies. They shared only because there was a new radio under development that was not only secured and coded, but had the capability to listen in on the Singar's transmission as it cracked its code. There's only one unit in the ARMY with those radios in their vehicles and that's the 3/17th CAV unit. Our buyer wants all of them for study. That's the target for chopper 1" Half explained.

"That's it? What's so tricky about that? Hell with four squads of men with bolt cutters, it shouldn't take more than thirty minutes to get in and out."

"What you don't know is that the air Cav is in night gunnery tonight. Once we're on the Fort's radar, it's only going to take about ten minutes to get their Apaches armed and in the air. Hell we have the easy mission, that's why the kid flying the bird is with us and not with the others."

"Wait a minute, if you know that the Apaches are out and armed, why didn't you all plan this for another night?" Aaron asked with a sense of urgency in his voice.

"It's now or never. The entire Cav unit will be in the deserts of California in less than 24 hours. Not to mention that our buyer was able to schedule the boat for tonight only. There's no way around it, we have to do this tonight."

Aaron shook his head as he walked over to the bag with the slings in it. He unzipped the bag and assembled the men, handing each of them a huge Q-tip shaped device called a reach pendant. He explained what each of them would be doing and showed them how to hook on to the Humm-Vee once they reached the target drop. He walked forward into the cockpit, and quickly instructed the pilot what he wanted him to do once they reached their location.

Streaking across the land at 500 feet, Bob radioed to his son and told him to follow his lead. He dipped the nose of his chopper then swung over the road that led up to Fort Drum. Both birds skimmed over the road at just under 15 feet when Bob took his chopper to its maximum speed of 200 mph, while Rick did the same.

Seconds after they flew past the empty guard post on the main gate of the Fort, Bob radioed to Rick again. "This is it son! Once we rise up, we'll have only 10 minutes to be out of here. Good luck and see you at the rendezvous point. On my command now son—BREAK!" He pulled up on his elevator control stick and banked right.

Rick did the same, banking left. In seconds he flew in over the target and used a maneuver called aerodynamic breaking. He brought his bird from 200MPH to a halt in two seconds flat, a technique he managed without killing everyone in the bird.

Instead of going out of the back of the chopper, Aaron had the second squad go out of the right side door and hop down on top of the Avenger. During the frantic flight, he had the men string out the slings so that each man was able to grab two separate reach pendants of different slings as they jumped out.

Half and his partner hooked on to the Avenger's front bumper rings, then clamped the pendants onto the front hooks of the chopper. Aaron and his partner did the same with the rear truck bumper rings, clamping onto the rear hooks of the chopper. The entire process was executed in 45 seconds from start to finish. Now done, Half and his two men climbed back into the hovering bird.

Aaron himself stayed on the hood of the Avenger and told Rick to fly over to the other group. As they lifted off, Aaron explained to Half why he wanted to be dropped off with the others, . . . "Half, CJ and the others are going to need as much help as they can get. I figure that you can handle unhooking the truck once you get there."

"You got It Sarge. Hang on, we're almost there. Tell CJ I said not to lose too much time on this one; there's many other missions if we can't pull this one off completely."

Rick swung in over the motor pool and brought the chopper to a hover just five feet above the ground, and Aaron jumped down. As he ran clear, Rick pulled his bird with Half, the second squad and the Avenger Humm-Vee off into the night air disappearing from sight.

Aaron quickly ran over to the line of hardtop Humm-Vee's that had the new radios in them. He knew they had to be where the radios were, because of all of the men running around them. From the distance, he tried to see if he could spot CJ, but had no luck; instead he saw Big Dog getting out of one of the trucks with a pair of bolt cutters. He ran over to him and both men stepped into the next truck.

"Where's CJ at Big Dog?"

"He and one of the door gunners will be here in just a second with our two hummers. What are you doing here? CJ said that you'd be going with Half and his squad to the ship for the drop off."

"I'm here to help where I can. After Half explained this shit to me, I knew that you guys could use all the help that you could get."

Three minutes after Aaron arrived in the motor pool, CJ and one of the door gunners crashed through the back gate. Working at a fast pace, Dusty, Big Dog, Sandman and Aaron had the men place the radios on the hoods of the lined up trucks. CJ pulled up to the front of the trucks. One of the men from the third squad opened the backs of the two Hummers and began to load the radios. Each truck took a load of eleven new radios.

After they were done with the loading, CJ had each Hummer filled to capacity with squad members. He headed back and the rest of the men followed to the open field, where Bob was waiting with his rotors turning. While CJ and Aaron were on their way back to the chopper, Bob radioed #1 with an important message saying . . ." #1 this is Big Bird, I've got three in bound bogies, 5 mikes out. What's your position, over?"

"Big Bird its #1, I'm in route to yours, E.T.A. one mike. How copy?"

"Ok, my crew chief sees your markers across the field. This shit is going to be close 'cause those birds are moving in fast. Big Bird out", Bob said with a rushed tone in his voice.

After Bob's transmission ended, Aaron turned to CJ and asked . . . "If we're already at the bird, what's going to take so long? Why is this going to be so close?"

"You'll see Sarge, these Hummers are already a tight fit. The fuel cells are located on the sides. Going up the ramp into the chopper, we have to move slowly or it's kiss your ass goodbye!"

Driving up the ramp very slowly, CJ drove his truck back as far as he could go. Lacking the experience of driving a seven foot wide truck, the door gunner had to be ground guided up the ramp on to the chopper, causing the rest of the men to have to go in through the side door. By the time the last man was in, the crew chief in saw the Apaches streaking over the tree line of the field.

He radioed to Bob, who already knew from his cockpit radar of the Apaches approach. As he heard the direction from which the attack helicopters were coming, he used an old maneuver called the corkscrew to get the jump on them.

He jerked on the thrust control and turned in a counter clock wise motion 180 degrees, then flew under the Apaches as they went over him in the air. Bob was a well-seasoned pilot and knew that the only chance he stood against the world's best attack helicopter was to use his knowledge of the terrain to his advantage. He knew that his chopper was faster than theirs even though he carried a heavy equipment load. He also knew that in a high-speed chase, most attack pilots suffered from the same ill-advised problem of becoming fixated on the target during flight.

Remembering the different cuts and valleys of upstate NY's foot hills, Bob swung down into a winding valley and disappeared before the Apache pilot's eyes. All three attack choppers came to a halt as the lead bird climbed to three thousand feet, spotting the Infiltrate bird weaving through the valley. Maintaining his over watching position, he radioed to his fellow pilots and directed them to the Infiltrate choppers' location. The crew chief of the chopper looked out of the rear window and saw the two heavily armed attack helicopters swing in behind them as he radioed a sit rep to Bob.

"Bob, I've got two birds at our six o'clock. How copy?" he screamed into his mike.

"What's their formation and distance? Are they missile or gun range away?" Bob asked in a very calm voice.

"They're high off our six and closing into gun range. We've only got seconds before they draw a bead on us."

"Don't worry. I'll take us down to ten feet above the ground and fly right under the wires at Glens Pass. With their gun sights on and the pilots watching my flight lights in the valley, they'll never see what's coming. Tell everyone back there to hold on, I'm cranking her up as I do the left to right thing."

The two Apaches closed in on the weaving chopper as the gunner of the forward attack bird opened fire with his 30>Th1 machine gun. He fired in an attempt to control the movements of the running chopper, but had little success. Both attack birds flew along just as Bob said they would with a high angle of attack in a standard lead chopper, left wing man flight attack formation.

Seeing through his enhanced PVS-7 night sights, Bob and his co-pilot saw the high-tension wires as he flew through the valley toward Glens Pass. He stopped weaving from left to right and increased his speed to 170MPH as he dropped in altitude to only ten feet above the Black River, which ran the entire length of the valley. Even though he saw a sharp turn ahead right after the wires, he knew he had to make it seem as if he were trying to escape or the pilots wouldn't follow with the same intensity.

Closing in on the chopper both Apache gunners drew a bead, placing their targeting cross hairs right on the Infiltrate bird. As he flew under the wires, his swirling blades cleared them by just eight feet. He really knew what he was doing because the first Apache never stood a chance. It slammed into the high-tension wires doing better than 170MPH. The pilot of the following bird saw his lead wing man burst into flames as the night turned into day. He tried to bank off, but was too late. He also flew into the huge steel frame that held up the wires and instantly went up in a ball of fire.

Bob knew he wasn't completely out of the woods because he remembered there were three birds on his radar. He made the sharp turn and brought his chopper to a complete stop behind a cut in the hill. He took a chance, hoping that the sight of seeing both of his fellow pilots and gunners go up in flames would have caused him to go into a dive from his over watching position.

His gamble paid off, because the last Apache dove at the valley gaining speeds in excess of over 200MPH. In his dive the gunner began to pepper the area with machine gun fire, but missed the target due to its position in the cut. From the direction of the tracer rounds, Bob knew that the last Apache was going to fly straight over his position. He told his left side door gunners to be prepared to open fire on his command. And when the attack helicopter flew just five feet above his blades, he quickly pulled on his thrust control and rose up behind it as he gave his door gunners the command to open fire.

The first few shots missed, but once both of the gunners quickly walked their tracer rounds onto the unsuspecting war bird, they fully lit up the skies. Hitting first the tail rotor then its' fuel cell, both gunners caused the Apache to erupt into flames. Seeing the final war bird go down, Bob told CJ that they were on their way into Canada to the drop off point.

Aaron looked at CJ as he asked . . . "Are all of your missions so eventful?"

"Hell no! This one tonight wasn't shit because my heart isn't even beating hard."

"You mean this was calm? My God, I hate to think of what's in store for the immediate future."

"Welcome back to the old days Sarge! First things first, I need to set things up back home because if you're talking about what I thing you are, then I should get things rolling right now", he said as he pulled out his cellular phone and tapped out the ten digit code to his headquarters.

"Chip monk, it's #1. I'm en route to my drop off point. I want you to get our chopper transport ready for immediate departure. I'm sending Half back in bird #2. When he gets there, tell him that we're going to need all the necessary gear for a North Korean Hop".

"#1 is this going to be a full force hop, I mean damn, North Korea. That's a pretty heavy place. I guess that this is to do with the Sarge?"

"Not over the line, I'll fill you in once we get back. I have an ETA, at home base in five hours. Have control waiting."

"That's a will call #1, I'm on it", she said as she hangs up her phone.

After the line cleared, CJ called up Half and instructed him to return to head-quarters after they refueled at the airport. Half didn't bother asking questions because he knew he would receive a full brief once he touched base with CJ and they were together in NYC.

Bob flew into Canada's capitol city of Ottawa and landed on a skyscraper. CJ and his men off loaded the radios onto the roof. Once all of the radios were lined up, a man dressed in a long black coat walked up to CJ and handed him three suit cases filled with Canadian money. Big Dog, Dusty and Sandman each grabbed a case and counted the money then gave CJ the ok sign. There were no words exchanged between CJ and the man in the black coat, which struck Aaron as a bit odd. Well, he thought to himself, I figures that's how he liked doing business.

With the transaction having been completed, CJ waved his hand in the air in a circular motion and all of his men boarded the chopper. Seconds later they were airborne and inbound for the US. Bob stopped at Watertown and completely refueled his cells. Four and a half hours later, Bob touched down at LaGuardia airport in NYC where Half waited for them with a huge black ten-wheeled truck. Rick was also there waiting. He and Half boarded onto the chopper as the others climbed into the truck.

CJ told Bob and Rick to get some rest because there was a lot of work ahead. When everyone was aboard the truck, Half pulled off while Dusty and Sandman followed in the two Hummers. Aaron and CJ rode up front with Half in the cab as they drove down into a huge sewer opening. Aaron asked . . . "CJ why the hell are we going into a sewer, what's going on?"

"We take this way from the airport because it's the easiest way to reach the abandoned subway tunnels. We never use the streets to reach Infiltrate headquarters, not ever. Now that I think of it, Half call control" CJ said.

"Control its #2, deactivate grids 1 to 20 and open the LaGuardia entrance. How copy, over?"

"#2 this is control, grids 1 to 20 deactivated and LaGuardia entrance is opening. Welcome back guys. Control out."

As they drove along, Aaron saw the floor of the tunnel open into a down ramp. It was a tight fit for the truck, but Half forged ahead.

Minutes went by in the darkness of the old subway tunnel. CJ looked at Aaron after he noticed him yawning. "You'll stay at my place tonight Sarge. I'm sure my wife won't mind if I put you up in my guest room. Just don't wake her up or we'll both be sleeping in the hall. Get a good night's sleep if you can because I'm setting role call for the upcoming mission for 12 noon, and there's a lot to be done before we're ready" he said.

Thirty minutes later Half drove up a ramp into an underground parking complex where Aaron saw several different types of vehicles, trucks, motorcycles and ATVs parked. He followed as CJ led him to an elevator. He noticed there were eleven floors in the building. CJ pressed the top floor button and the other men pressed their respective buttons. Slowly but surely, Aaron and CJ were the last two on the elevator.

Once they reached the 11th floor, CJ led him to the end of a long hallway. There were no other doors on that floor. The building appeared to be an apartment building, but as CJ slowly opened his door, he saw that CJ's place completely surrounded the hallway, taking up the entire top floor.

CJ helped Aaron settle in, getting him a towel and washcloth, and a robe with slippers. Soon afterward, CJ went to bed as Aaron did the same. Before he went to sleep, he set the alarm clock for twenty minutes after 11AM. He finally settled into bed and slipped off into a deep sleep.

Chapter IV

⌒~∿~⌒

The RAIN FELL over New York City at 10:20AM that Wednesday morning as Aaron laid in bed in a deep sleep. Normally a light sleeper, this morning he was dead to the world as the door to the guest room opened. He was suddenly ripped from his slumber not by the sound of the alarm going off, but by the feeling of cold, hard steel pressed against his nostril. He opened his eyes to the sight of the one eyed stare of a .357 handgun. At the other end of it, he saw a light skinned black woman dressed in a green robe bearing down on him.

His sight was still slightly blurry from the deep sleep that he was in, so he couldn't really make out her face, but once she began to speak, he woke up quickly . . .

"You have only five seconds to explain who you are and what you're doing on my floor—and four of those have already passed," she said as she pulled the hammer of the gun back into firing position.

"Hey, hey hold on now, I'm Aaron Williamson and I came in with CJ last night," he explained in a calming voice.

"Oh, The Sarge. My husband spoke about you. I'm sorry about the gun. I'm just not used to anyone other than Anthony or the others being up here and even then they don't usually stay in my guest room. Let me introduce myself. My name is Dee—Dee Johnson, pleased to meet you," as she slipped the gun into her robe pocket.

"Well Mrs. Dee-Dee I'm pleased to meet you too. Is CJ up yet?"

"No he's still asleep on the other side of the floor. I just looked in on him before I stepped into this room. He doesn't like to wake me up when he comes in late; sometimes I can be a bit of a bitch when I get roused from a good sleep."

"No, I never would have guessed that," he said with a mild touch of sarcasm in his voice.

"Well Tracy's told me that Chris has a meeting scheduled for noon today, so he won't be awake for another hour or so. Being that you're already up because of me, how about you take a shower while I make you some breakfast, alright?" she asked with a smile.

"That sounds great, and besides, my mother told me long ago, never argue with a woman who has a gun" he said through a slight laugh.

Dee-Dee left and went into the huge white tiled kitchen, while Aaron went into the bathroom and showered. He admired the fine décor of the bathroom. Both the walls and floor were done in white marble with deep green veining, while the shower doors were made of bottle green glass. There were four separate massaging shower heads, and a wooden bench to sit on. As he walked up to the counter, he watched himself in the incredibly large mirror while he dried himself.

Once he was finished drying off, he wrapped himself in the robe CJ left for him and opened the bathroom door. He heard loud music coming from the living room. He thought to himself: Damn, I wonder how much it must have cost to sound proof all of the walls like this. He walked back into the guest room, dressed himself in the black sweat suit that CJ had also provided for him then found his way into the kitchen.

The aroma of sausages and pancakes could be smelled throughout the house and when he walked up to the long glass dining table with elephant tusk legs, Dee-Dee had his plate of food waiting for him.

"I see that you're finally done. Chris told me that you always took your time showering and doing your hair. In fact, whenever I take long to get ready for anything, he always tells me that I'm moving like the Sarge," she said in a bright and cheerful voice.

"Well, I guess it's better to be talked about than to be forgotten. Wow, these sure are good pancakes you've made. Hell my girl Laura barely knows how to turn on the stove much less fix a meal that doesn't have a box with instructions," he said with food in his mouth.

"Good, I see you two have met. Good morning honey." CJ said as he walked into the kitchen and kissed Dee-Dee on the cheek.

"Good morning Chris. You should have left me a note or something; I almost shot the Sarge when I walked into the guest room. You know that I'm not used to anybody staying up here."

"I'm sorry Dee, but you know I wasn't going to come in and wake you up, damn that. Baby when you get woke up before 9AM, I swear the dragon comes out in you."

"Man CJ, I never thought I'd live to see the day when you became domesticated. Oh Dee-Dee let me tell you, CJ use to be the biggest dog on two legs . . ." Aaron said as CJ cut him off . . . "Hey, hey that's enough of that now Sarge. My baby doesn't need to know my ancient history."

"Well since you're up, I take it that Sarge's being here is not a good thing? I mean, hell you never have back to back pre hop assembly meetings. What's going on?" she asked as she looked into his eyes.

"You're right, his being here in most definitely not a good thing. Remember me telling you about how I got started in this business, dealing with the Shadow and all that? Well the Sarge took a little longer to catch on but he finally left them two years after I did. They've returned and are after him, and have taken his girl. He and I both know that there's only one place that they could have taken her . . ." Dee-Dee cut him off.

"Korea, you're going to North Korea? CJ it's going to take a full group force hop to get this shit done. I know Aaron's your boy and all and that you and he go way back, but think baby, you're talking about a country with closed borders and all the funky shit that goes with that."

"Your wife knows about your group of friends and everything?" he asked CJ with a look of surprise on his face.

"Yeah Sarge, Dee-Dee knows all about Infiltrate," he said as he turned back toward Aaron. He took Dee-Dee by the hand and looked her square in the eyes. "Think of things this way baby. The Shadow is after Aaron. If we don't put an end to them, then who knows how long it would be before they came after me through you like they did with the Sarge. That's a risk that I can't afford to take. If something were to ever happen to you, my world would cease to exist."

"I understand, but I'm coming with you on this one. If this is as bad as you say then I want to be by your side every step of the way watching your back. If something were to happen to you, then MY world would cease to exist," Dee-Dee said with strength in her voice.

"Hell no, no way, no how, Not happening Dee! I'd never forgive myself if anything were to happen to you. You know this is what I do and I'm damn good at it. I'm not saying that you can't handle yourself, but on this trip only my best men, who've proven themselves under fire will go with me. Only the best stand a chance of coming back from North Korea safe and sound."

"Chris, do you remember the last time I was on a mission with you? We stole the blue prints of that fighter jet from Rockwell International. Do I need to remind you of the sabotage we did in that East German

Chemical Plant? Or the bridge we brought down in Helsinki? I know we're not going after the 11 herbs and spices for Kentucky Fried or the secret formula for Coca-Cola! I know what we're going up against. You know I've been in several of your training classes with your men concerning interdiction missions. You know I'm good, not to mention that you promised me that I'd go with you on the next mission. Well guess what—this is the next mission" she said with an ear to ear smile.

"I know I promised you, but the answer is still no! Still, I give you my word as your husband that once we're back from this hop, you'll go on the very next mission no matter where or what it is. That I promise."

"Alright damn it, but you just make sure that you come back from over there if you don't want to face my wrath! Now go take a shower and brush your teeth. I'd kiss you, but your breath is a little tart right now. Go on, I'll keep the Sarge company while you shower and freshen up."

CJ showered while Aaron and Dee-Dee continued their conversation. Soon afterward, CJ rejoined them in the kitchen. Dee-Dee had his breakfast waiting when he reached the table. Before he sat down she wrapped her arms around his neck, kissed him deeply and said "much better."

"Sarge, where do you think your girlfriend is in North Korea?" Dee-Dee asked.

"There are several places that they could have taken her, but I personally think that Laura has been taken back to the Shadow's head quarters in the city of Kaesong," Aaron replied.

"Yeah, I agree. I think Alex Jr. is trying to play his cards on this one and get you into country. I'm thinking that he figures that if he holds her, then you'll do whatever he wants," CJ said.

"Well then boys, there is only one course of action for you both, that being to take them down and make sure that they stay down. There is no other way, at least that's how I see it," she said with a hard look in her eyes.

"You know something, now that I think about things, don't you two think that you speak a little too open and freely about the things that your group does? Aren't you worried about being bugged by the government or some other agency?" Aaron asked.

"No I don't worry about talking about Infiltrate. This is what the code word UPPER ROOM refers to," CJ said as Dee-Dee cut in on him. "You see Sarge, anything above the ninth floor is part of the UPPER ROOM. All of the floors above the ninth are continuously and automatically checked, searched and scanned for listening devices" she said as CJ cut back in over her.

"In fact Sarge, from the ninth to eleventh floor, radio waves of any sort can't get through and including TV waves. All of our secured satellite lines are constantly monitored by operations control. In our control center, our computer gear is top of the line equipment, a lot of which not even our government or any other has or knows about."

"Well excuse the fuck out of me-I stand corrected! Dee-Dee that was a wonderful meal. I must let Laura meet you so she can see that food is cooked not only in the microwave, but also on a stove top," Aaron said with a laugh in his voice.

"And if you're ready Sarge, we've got a meeting to attend. I'll explain what's going to happen at this meeting on our way down into Infiltrate Headquarters," CJ said as he and Aaron both stood away from the table and made their way toward the front door.

Shortly thereafter, he followed CJ into the elevator down the hall. Even though the numbers on the panel read from ground floor up to the eleventh floor, he and CJ rode down for several seconds past the ground floor. Once the doors opened, Aaron looked down what appeared to be a long dark hallway. After only a few steps down the hall, CJ pressed a button on the wall and a section of the neighboring wall slid over to reveal a small auditorium filled with the members of Infiltrate.

On the small stage at the head of the auditorium, Half sat along with the others group leaders. When he saw CJ and Aaron walk through the entrance, he stood to his feet and called the men to order. They all went to their feet as CJ and Aaron walked toward the stage. CJ seated himself, and all of the men sat back in their seats.

Half began . . . "Men this pre hop assembly meeting has been called because of a great threat that threatens our very existence. This threat that I speak of, isn't any one person, but an entire force of men. They are a group, much like us only twenty times worse! Only as an absolute last resort do we kill, but they kill for the sport of it. This group of men calls themselves The Shadow. Their leader is a young man by the name of Alex Kim Jr. This isn't going to be like anything we've faced before and because of that, #1 has placed all other Infiltrate operations on hold. Men, there is a snake who is trying to bite and kill us. There's only one way to kill this snake, that being to cut off its head then destroy its body. Now the question is: who's with #1 and his group leaders on this ultimate hop? Let him stand and be heard!!" he shouted. In a thunderous show of support, all of the men in the room jumped to their feet and began to shout out: "I'm in, take me!"

After a few moments, CJ stood to his feet and held up his arms as he slowly quieted the men down and began to speak.

"My men, my brave men! You all know how I started in this thing we call a business and where we got our start from. This is Aaron Williamson, The Sarge I've spoken so much about. Some of us have wives and families upstairs in our totally secured building and would do just about anything to protect them from harm. Well my friend's beloved has been taken by The Shadow. There is only one way to make sure that what has happened to our friend The Sarge doesn't happen to us. There is only one answer and that is to destroy The Shadow and this man you all see above me. He's the last in his blood line and when we kill him, The Shadow will cease to exist," he said as Half flashed pictures showing Alex Jr. in his younger days as one of Aaron's students.

The men began to speak amongst themselves as the pictures flashed by. CJ clapped his hands together and quieted the room down once more. He had Half turn on the lights and he began to speak again.

"Half, how long until our birds are boxed and ready for flight?"

"Three hours #1. Bob and his crew are working as fast as they can," he quickly answered.

"There it is men. We have four and a half hours before the SP time and I need thirty good men, fifteen per chopper for this North Korean hop. This isn't like our other missions; this is by voluntary basis because there's no money waiting for us at the completion of this hop. If you wish to go, the group leaders will be walking around gathering names. If you're chosen, you will need to have your gear and yourself at our hanger at Kennedy International Airport in four hours. That's all for now gentlemen. For those of you who will stay behind, I'll need you to run the different shops at the Street Foundation."

After he finished speaking, the men stood to their feet as they began to chant the word "Hop". Once the chanting started, CJ took a few steps back then turned to Aaron and told him to watch. He ran forward at top speed and dove over the edge of the small stage onto the outstretched arms of his men. He body surfed the crowd until he reached the middle of the room where he was stood straight up, still supported by his men.

As he reached the center of the room, the men chanted the word "Hop" louder and faster and once their words reached deafening levels, CJ again raised his hands to quiet them for his last statement.

"In the Bible it is written that the family that prays together, stays together. Well in our case my brothers, when we fight together, we stay together! That's our business-fighting! In three hours, fifty eight minutes let's go and handle 'da family business!'" he shouted. The crowd went wild as they again began to chant the word "Hop" at the top of their lungs. After seeing CJ brought down to his feet, Half signaled the other group leaders off stage for them to begin gathering names. As they went into the crowd CJ made his way back toward the stage and told Aaron to follow him out.

They exited the auditorium through a side door which led back into the dark hallway, leading to the elevator. Aaron noticed that there were no call buttons to signal the car. He turned toward CJ and saw him reaching into his shirt to pull out an odd shaped key. CJ walked over to a solid square black glass panel on the wall next to the doors of the elevator, where he placed his right hand against it.

Aaron saw the square light up around CJ's hand. A small section of the concrete wall slid back and over to expose a keyhole which looked like the fit to CJ's key. He stuck the key in the hole and turned, and a few seconds passed before the door of the elevator car opened.

Aaron stepped on first as CJ removed his key from the hole. He placed it back around his neck then stepped onto the car. He pressed a button and the car moved, but not up or down. Aaron noticed that the car moved to the left at a moderate speed. He turned to CJ with a puzzled look on his face . . . "OK time out now CJ, how is all of this possible? I mean from your choppers, vehicles, over two hundred men and this incredible building, not to mention your weapons, the government should be all over you like white on rice. You know I'm not easily impressed, but this whole set up is blowing my mind!"

"Sarge hold on, we're about to go up. Most of our missions are for multi-national corporations. It's rare that Infiltrate is directly paid for our hops, but instead our clients make a sizable donation to the Street Foundation as payment for services rendered. Don't get me wrong, we've been investigated several times by the I.R.S. and F.B.I. Hell they just show up on any occasion with a general search warrant and tear up the Street Foundation, but nothing Infiltrate does is done in our Street Foundation building. We're almost there; we'll continue this conversation in my office. Please Sarge, allow me to show you my Street Foundation," he said. The doors of the elevator opened while bright white light poured into the car.

When the doors were fully opened, Aaron looked out to see a huge open area with a large table under a curved glass roof. CJ led him around the extremely large complex which made up the Street Foundation's building. As they walked, CJ lead him to a gym which was filled with children and teenagers who were playing team sports such as volleyball and basketball. The kids all greeted CJ with a hearty "Good Afternoon".

In another part of the building, next to the gym, Dee-Dee was teaching ballet to a group of young girls and teenagers. CJ and Aaron quietly stepped into the mirrored room. Dee-Dee smiled as she stopped the class and told them to greet their visitors. The girls giggled and said hello. Afterwards, she resumed her instruction.

CJ led Aaron past the tables where the kids ate their lunches, to a circular wall. Once they were around it, Aaron saw a sign with the word 'auditorium' above a set of doors. Next to the sign, there was a pair of lights, one green the other red. The red one was lit while the green one was out. When he saw this, he turned toward CJ as if to ask him what the deal with the lights were, but before he had the chance to speak, CJ simply said. "Once we're in my office Sarge."

They followed the circular wall until they were in the front of the building. There in a booth marked 'information center' sat CJ's secretary, Tracy. She looked up at CJ as he walked toward her with Aaron one step behind. She smiled as she said . . . "Oh this must be The Mr. Williamson, Mr. Johnson?"

"Yes this is. Aaron, this is the world's best secretary, the one you spoke to over the phone," he said.

"I recognize the voice. I must say that you're even lovelier in person than I imagined, Tracy."

Blushing from Aaron's comment, she replied "Why thank you Mr. Williamson. Mr. Johnson, there are no messages for you today. There's fresh coffee in your office which I just made."

"Ok, how about you come into my office after you turn on the answering machines? There are some things we need to go over in my UPPER ROOM?"

"I got it boss, I'll be right in," she quickly said as she switched on her answering machines and followed them into the office.

Once she stepped through the door to the office, CJ shut it behind her and flipped a switch on the wall next to the door. Aaron saw that there were no lights that came on, but he did notice his chain being pulled from around his neck to the wall. He leaned back into his chair, and then laughed as he clapped his hands and after a few chuckles, he calmed himself. He looked back at CJ and Tracy as they appeared to be waiting on him for silence.

"You ok Sarge? I should have warned you about the magnetic field before I turned it on. That's what the green and red lights are for. They indicate the magnetic field engagement, making the room fully secure from stealth listening devices. Tracy, have the travel plans been arranged?"

"Everything is on line. The Teckzue Corporation has provided the use of their hangar at Kennedy International Airport and one of their condor transport planes. I spoke with Bob a few minutes ago and he said that once you're on the ground overseas, he believes that he and his crew can have the birds in the air in seven hours," Tracy replied.

"Now for the million dollar question: was Mr. Fushang able to file us a phony flight plan sending us into North Korea?" CJ asked with his fingers crossed.

"That's our only problem. Mr. Fushang informed me that he could either send you into China or into Seoul, South Korea, but North Korea was totally out of the question. Any and everything that lands in North Korea is thoroughly searched. He said that you'd never make it in by plane. If you ask me, I think you should fly into China, and then go across the border; North Korea's northern borders are still open with China, but that's your call boss."

"No Tracy, You're right. I think we should travel into China first. Being that we'll have seven hours worth of down time, that should give us enough time to sneak in and do a recon of the Shadow's HQ and get a gauge on their current man power. OK Tracy, call Fushang and tell him to make the China arrangements. Transfer any funds necessary for this hop then let me know when everything is set and on line," he ordered.

"I'm on it boss, I'll let you know in a few," she said as she opened the door and walked back toward her desk.

"This may seem like a dumb question, but what does the magnetic field do exactly?" Aaron asked with a puzzled look on his face.

"This field blocks all forms of listening signals. I like to be careful because the F.B.I. was here only a week ago and I'm sure they tried to leave a few bugs around. After they left, I had the place swept and found thirty such devices they thought were carefully hidden. My security does daily sweeps of the building in the mornings, but this magnetic field makes me feel a lot better. Hell all of this slight trouble with the Feds came about because of this little weasel we did a corporate frame job for. We set up his Boss to take a fall but once the heat got turned up he buckled under the pressure and mentioned Infiltrate. Luckily he was seen to before things got out of hand but some damage was done none the less. Sage you listening?"

"Fuck it's no use, no matter how hard I try; I can't get Laura's face out of my mind. God if I could at least hear her voice, I'd be somewhat relieved. I know, no matter what, Alex Kim Jr is mine." He said with the bitter taste of revenge in his mouth.

"You got it Sarge, and rest assure, as I live and breath, right here and now, the shadow will go down for the count. You remember the now deceased Dragon clan right; well this shit is on the same level. They killed my girl and we burned them down so will it be the Shadow's fate after we get there again." He said with the look of intensity in his eyes.

"Wait a minute, your girl CJ? Oh my god, you were fucking Mrs. Kim! Fuck it all makes sense now. That's why she always wanted you to be her escort where ever she went. Damn, if it would not have been for me needing you for that run we made into South Korea, you would have been killed in that Limo when the rocket hit it." He said

"That's right, but now that you know let me tell you that she and I started our affair about three months after we joined the Shadow. Don't tell Dee-Dee about this, because as far as she is concerned, I've never been with a white woman and there's no need for her to know any different." He quickly snapped.

"Hey CJ, I'd never do anything like that to you because I wouldn't like it if you told Laura about all that I had done over there in Korea. I wonder CJ, is she alright, where is she. Later on, I'm going to call my clubs and the bar and let them know some of what's going on and see of the Shadow has left any messages. But for now tell me how all of this got started, from this building with its horizontal sliding elevators, to your UPPER ROOM and all of your contacts?" He asked.

"Now that's a long story Sarge, but since we have a little time till Tracy's off our lines, I'll start off from the beginning. Think back to around the time when I left the Shadow. Do you remember that kid at the Hundi motors in Soul we didn't kill, but were supposing to?" He asked.

"Yeah, the young American named Topher Stevens. I remember him, hell how could I forget, he cried like a bitch when you held the gun to his head. What does he have to do with all of this?"

"After we let him go, he fled into China and became an executive in the Teckzue corporation transportation division. Back four years ago, they were the largest suppliers of frozen foods to China town here in the city and still are today. One day about four years ago when I was in the city with Dee-Dee, I ran into Stevens and he freaked out.

He was scared shitless, but eventually I calmed him down, but that was already after he had broken down right in front of my back then girlfriend in broad daylight on a public street. I was the owner and general manager of the McDonalds on 14th street in Manhattan back then and not even three day after I had ran into Stevens, did he walk into my restaurant. He asked if he could speak with me in my office alone in a shaky voice and once we were behind closed doors, he asked if I was still with the Shadow. When I told him that I hadn't been with them in the past few years and had no intentions of ever working for them again he asked if I was doing any contract work. I told him no: but that's when he handed me a picture of a man he wanted killed in his corporation. In fact, that was the fastest Hundred thousand dollars, I had ever made just for killing someone's boss, because the man I killed was the vice president of the Teckzue International Corporation and Stevens was next in line for the job. Shortly afterward, I received several similar offers from many different people. I mean executives who wanted their bosses to disappear in companies and corporations such as, AT&T, General Electric, IBM and even Pam Am airlines. Soon after that I started the Street Foundation as a front for all of the money I was receiving. I hand gathered my leaders, trained them as assassins and over the years, we have expanded to the 200 hundred man operation that you see here today. This building and where we live, comes compliments of a Japanese corporation named Toshoka. After a job involving us breaking into Norfolk, VA and steeling the plans to a top secret sonar jamming device, they built these buildings and supplied us with our computer gear as payment. Every few months or so, they refit out gear just to make sure that our systems are better and safer than the CIA's who's tried to Infiltrate us already. They have an idea of who Infiltrate is, but they will never place their fingers on us or who we really are." He explained.

"What makes you so sure CJ? I mean you guys have Hummers with gun mounts, choppers with registration numbers and a Russian transport plane that flies out of major airports. "He blurted out.

"You don't understand Sarge. Infiltrate is only a name we go by. None of the vehicles are our, nor the choppers, weapons or even this building. When we get paid for our missions, most of the money is wired into the street foundation which makes for a tax deduction for our clients. Sarge, we're a world class assassination and theft organization that on paper looks totally legal "he explained.

"Damn CJ what did you just say? I'm sorry, I just thought about Laura again. I was trying to keep her out of my mind at least until we were on the plane on our way over there. I just can't get her out of mind CJ, I can't." He said as he placed his head in his hands.

CJ walked over to him as he placed his hands on his shoulder. When he did this, he looked down at him as he told him that he had his back and as for Laura, he reassured him that they would get her back alive and well as they made those responsible pay dearly.

As He began to speak about Laura with CJ, at that exact moment across the international dateline, somewhere in North Korea, a small leer jet landed on a lonely airstrip under the dusk skies. Near the end of the long strip of runway, waited a Land Rover—Range Rover sport utility truck with its engine running.

Once the jet taxied over to the truck, its front side door opened as a set of stairs flipped out and extended to the pavement. After the doors opened, two men with Shadow uniforms stepped out to make sure that the cost was clear, and when they were positive that all was safe, out stepped the Master of the Shadow Clan.

As he stepped down the stairs another member of the Clan's members pulled Laura out of the plane as she was masked and gagged, with her hands bounded to her back. Their were a pair of leg irons around her ankles which cut into them with every step that she took, which sent excruciating pain through her legs that caused her to cry out in agony.

They all piled into the Rover as the Shadow master told him to drive in Korean. The ride was a long and Bumpy one for Laura who was thrown into the rear of the truck with her hands still tied to the rear of her back. After two and a half hours of continuous off road driving, the truck finally stopped to her relief as she heard someone in what she had assumed was Korean and felt someone's hand grab the chain between her legs.

The man drug her across the floor of the truck, them draped her over his shoulder as she heard what seemed to her to be several men shouting as she was brought into a building. She had no idea of her where about, but for some strange reason, deep in her mind, she knew that she wasn't in New York any longer as she thought to herself; everyone is speaking Korean around me, I must have been brought to some location in Korea.

The man grabbed her blind fold off to expose her eyes to the light of the room she was in, which blinded her for a few seconds. After her sight returned to normal she saw the Shadow master as he sat behind a desk while he motioned to the man standing over her as he removed her gage while he said. "Sorry about the rough treatment Ms. Hinkley. I know my men can be a hit over bearing at times but then again, I do still feel the effects of your kick. If anything girl, thank your god that you are still alive because, anyone else would surely have died of course."

"Why have you brought me here? And for that matter, where is here?" She demanded.

"Oh Ms. Hinkley, so now you are in a position to demand answers are you? As far as the rest of the western world is concerned, you are nowhere. You are in the worst place any westerner could ever find themselves, Square in the middle of my headquarters, where I am Master!" He shouted.

"When Aaron finds me, which he will, he's going to kill you and when he does I'm going to be there watching." She said as she looked directly at the mask he was wearing with the look of determination in her eyes.

After her statement was completed, the Shadow master stood to his feet, walked over to her as he placed his mask against her face and took hold of her shoulders as he said . . ." The last thing I would think that you would hope for Miss Hinkley is for Mr. Williamson to find you here because, you see my dear woman, this is my headquarters. I and the entire Shadow are hoping that Aaron Williamson does make it here, for when he is before my eyes, then and only then will he choose what is truly in his heart and not what is in yours."

"No matter what you might think, our love is stronger than anything you could ever offer him. He'll kill you for this and you know this as well. Just like you were saying on the plane ride over here; No one in your organization is actually a match him in a one on one confrontation." She said with a touch of pride in her voice.

"But you see Miss Hinkley; the Shadow is more than one man! We are a force of many and together are we strong! Now, you mentioned something about this love between Williamson and yourself being so strong. Well as I understand things, he was recently unfaithful to you with the lovely Yung-Lee Kim. The question you should ask your self is, if he didn't tell you about her and as soon as she showed up, he made love with her, then where is his heart truly?" He said as he watched her break down into teas.

She cried for only a few seconds though, for once she really thought about what this person had just said, anger and hatred filled her mind and heart as she looked up at him and said . . ." Aaron may have fucked that bitch you call a sister, but it's just as any dog does, when it finds a place where several other dogs have pissed on, it feels free to relieve itself in that same place. That being the case in all, I don't blame Aaron for relieving himself in your sister!"

Her words struck just as hard as she had hoped as she heard him sigh from behind his mask. She was happy that she had pissed him off although, she didn't expect what was to come, for in one lighting quick motion, he reared back and slapped her as hard as he could. The impact from the hit against her face while she was tied in the chair caused her flip out over onto the floor on her side as the shadow master stood over her.

He reached into his back robe pocket and pulled out a 357 handgun as he said . . . "The only reason that you're still alive, white bitch is because I allow you to be. For such insolence I should blow you head off, but I need you alive as bate for Mr. Williamson. You see Mrs. Hinkley, once Aaron is in this country, it will be my turn to play with Laura's toy." He said as he looked over to his two men and told them in Korean to take her away.

After they heard this, the two men yanked Laura off of the floor then stood her to her feet as they walked her over the door of the room, where they gagged her with a sock and duck tape. Once her mouth was fully gagged, both of the men drug her down a dimly lit hallway which led away from the office.

While she was in their arms, she felt a bit of a chill from the draft in the hallway as well as tried from her long journey across the ocean. In her mind, she thought long and hard on what the shadow master had just said to her. She knew that there was something not right about him, and his entire plan didn't make any sense to her as well, but felt deep in her heart that some way, somehow, once she was reunited with Aaron, everything was going to turn out right.

The two men dragged her along by the arms slowly, but surely reached the end of the seemly endless hallway where Laura saw a flight of stairs. Walking up the stairs towards her, she saw a woman wearing a black hooded cape, garment which covered her entire body. The hood covered most of the woman's face and the shadows from the lights in the hallway concealed the portion of her face that the hood left exposed.

The reason Laura knew that the person who stood to the top of the stairs was a woman, was because, she heard a woman's voice speaking Korean to the two men who held her by her arms. As she spoke to the two men, they stood aura to her feet and moved her over, placing her back against the wall. Both men as they held her in place by her arms, bowed their heads as the hooded woman passed, closely followed by two other Korean well built men.

Once the staircase was cleared, the two men resumed their journey with Laura down into the lower reaches of the building. As they carried her down the long flight of stairs, in her mind, she pondered the many possibilities of the woman's identity. Deep in her mind, she had a feeling that she was definitely going to see that very same woman again.

While the two men brought her into the basement, back inside the office, the other two Korean men waited as the hooded woman spoke with the Shadow master in Korean. In the office, while spoke, she slowly removed the hood from atop her head and after the formal greetings were out of the way, the black haired, black eyed colored woman spoke freely . . . "Enough with these pleasantries! My father,

Kim-Ill Song is not pleased with your organization! I understand that my father's younger brother, your father, Alex Kim died four months ago and that you might still be experiencing problems with controlling your men cousin, but never the less, my father is still not happy. All of your operations from selling opium to the United States and guns to the Philippines communist resistance, to your prostitution houses in South Korean have and are experiencing major drops in profits which means my father is experiencing those same profits loses himself! What seems to be the problem Master of the Shadow clan?" she asked with anger in her voice.

"Since word of my father's death leaked out of your office to the rest of the Eastern world, compounded by their knowledge of Williamson's betrayal, I've slowly began to lose my strong hold of fear over my operations. When Williamson disappeared, my father was still feared from his younger days, but being that he's no longer here and my men are now are not as highly trained as they were when Williamson was here, my people aren't working as hard." He explained back in Korean.

"I trust that you know my being here means the worst? Kim-Ill sent me here to ensure, everything is in place back on track. I know of your plans concerning Mrs. Hinkley and luring Williamson into country. My father is not pleased with this plan. He wants Williamson killed and I agree with him. I don't believe that he will kill the president of South Korea for us and furthermore, if we can't turn to your organization which we supply and depend on for such missions; then what do we need you for cousin?" She asked as she crossed her arms.

"You listen to me Lyn Ty Kim, we've done more for your father, my uncle than you'll ever do, or for that matter, hope to do. I respect your wishes, but your wishes or opinion means nothing to me Lyn-Ty!" The shadow master said as Lyn-Ty ran around the desk grabbed him by his arm and said . . .

"Don't move! Someone else said that very same statement to me ten years ago when Williamson and his nigger friend Johnson joined the Shadow and it wasn't Alex Jr. Who are you under this mask? If you as much as flinch, you die." She said as she pulled a Gluck 10MM large hand gun from behind her cape, and then placed it to his head. Lyn-Ty was very athletically built. Through her skin tight black spandex bodysuit, showed her hard lines from years of weight lifting and countless hours of martial art training. She stood an even eleven five feet, six inches in height and weighed a lean 118 pounds. Her black colored eyes bared the look of hardness in them and matched her long black hair which was braided into two thick braids that ran down to the bottom of her butt. As she moved her hand toward the Shadow Master's darkly shaded, glass mask, he tried to shift away but Lyn shoved the gun into his chest and gritted her teeth as she told him not to move while she proceeded to remove the glass mask. Once the mask was off, Lyn dropped the gun on to the desk as the look of shock and surprise swept across her face, her mouth dropped open in disbelieve as she took in the sight of the person who sat in the chair before her.

From the inner depts. of her existence, she experienced pure and unbridled rage as she thought of all that was happening before her eyes and in one blind out lash of anger, she grabbed the person out of the seat then slammed them down onto the desk. In her mind, she couldn't believe who was behind the mask and in a way, she didn't wish to accept it, but had no choice.

As she looked into the person's eyes, which she had done on so many occasion, she broke down and said in Korean . . . "I'll not even ask where he is, or what has happened to Alex Jr! The important thing for now is make sure that my father doesn't find out about this, for he'd kill you for this the second he found out! How many of your men know about this?" She asked.

"None they think that I'm Alex Jr under this mask." The person answered in the same scratchy voice.

Lyn looked at this person as they spoke and noticed a small box under their chin then immediately thought to herself, that box must vibrate the vocal cords just enough to disguise their voice.

"Put this back on," She said as she handed the mask back the person without saying their name, "You know several of your men are from uncles Alex's time and are still very old fashioned. How are you going to pull this off without them and my father finding out about who you are under that mask?" She asked as the Shadow master slid the mask back into place.

"I never change in or out of this outfit unless I'm alone. I've ordered my men to capture Aaron when he goes to his mansion, which he will." The Shadow master explained.

"How are you so sure?" She asked . . . "He's like no other westerner I've ever known or seen. I understand that you'd be better suited to make a guess of his actions, but really, are you sure you're not to close emotionally on this one to really make the right choice?"

"I know he'll go to his mansion. He's a man of some principals. Technically it's still his, but since he's left, ~ done some remodeling to the inner structure. Aaron Williamson won't even realize he's walking into a trap until it's too late. You'll know if he's with us or not because if he refuses, I'll personally bring his head before your father."

"This better work, master of the shadow, for if it doesn't; Williamson's head won't be the only one before my father's feet. You know you're going to have to be on hand so that everything works out either way." She said.

"Worry not (Noona); I'll get to the mansion long before my men get there, so they'll have no idea of what's going on."

"I hope for your sake, things work as you've planed. Remember, barring what I've seen in this office today, I am my father's eyes." She said in Korean as she turned and walked back around the desk.

The Shadow Master watched her walk over to the blue high back leather chair, as she put on her black cape with hood; he sat behind the huge pure oak wood desk, which was covered on its sides with detailed carvings and Korean symbol writings. When Lyn-Ty fully covered her head, she turned and bid the Shadow master farewell in their language and said that she'd be watching. The person behind the desk returned her farewell and also told her to watch and lean as everything happened.

With their goodbyes completed, Lyn-Ty turned opened the door where she saw her two huge body guards waiting for her. The Shadow master watched her and the two men walk slowly down the long dimly lit hallway until they were out of sight.

As she made her way out of the Shadow's HQs, at that exact moment back across the international dateline, Aaron spoke on the secured phone lines at the Street Foundation to a shaken up Charlie. Poor Chuck took the news of his friends death very hard, but that wasn't the only thing that bothered him, He was shaken because of all that had happened in the past 48 hours, from a gun being pulled on Laura in the Underground and his almost being shot, to the vicious and brutal way Stanly had been murdered. Aaron on the line tried to console him, but wasn't doing a very good job of it . . . "Chuck listen to me! If would have been there, they would have killed you as well. This may sound fucked up, but I'm glad you weren't there." He said.

"No, matter what you say, I still feel like shit and what do you mean they would have killed me as well? Don't you forget I did three years in Vietnam? I would have shot those bastards just like I did with those pajamas wearing Gooks!" He snapped.

"Ok old timer, ok sorry if I under estimated you. I wasn't trying to take anything away from you. How are you holding up otherwise, and how is Rob with all of this?" He asked "Rob's really not doing so well. When I spoke to him on the phone this morning, he was all broken up. I admit that I shed a tear or two, but Robert and Stanly were best friends. It's going to take a while for Rob to get over this. As for me, it's just like it was in the war after I saw a lot of my friends die before my eyes. The gloom comes over you for a while but, then it passes. He answered.

"I hear that Chuck. Look, I want you two to keep the Bar and club closed for a few days. I'm as you've probably already have guessed, I'm not in town. I'll not go into all the details, but rest assured, the people responsible for this will pay dearly for what they've done. If the police ask any questions or want to speak to me, tell them to contact my lawyer."

As Charlie spoke on with Aaron, CJ looked at his watch as he saw that it was time for his leaders meeting in the Infiltrate conference room, He waved his hands in order to catch Aaron's attention and once he looked over at him, he signaled to him telling him that it was time for them to go. Aaron got the message as he told Charlie, who was still talking that it was time for him to go for now.

"Yeah alright Chuck, you take care as well and make sure that you get some rest. I'm out of here, bye." He said as he hung up the phone.

"He tried to talk your ear off didn't he?" CJ asked jokingly.

"Hell yeah he did. Charlie is cool and all, but sometimes that old fool can talk you to death if you let him." He said.

"Well Serge, if you'll come with me please, we have a strike force to assemble."

Aaron followed CJ out of the office as they walked toward Tracy's desk. CJ nodded his head to her as he told her, he'd be a meeting for the next hour or so and after that quick stop, they continued around the huge circular auditorium where CJ quickly stopped to grab a few papers and envelops out of one of the smaller offices.

After the short stop, CJ led Aaron to a staircase across from the room where Dee-Dee taught ballet and closed the door behind the Sarge. Once he did that, he pulled out his odd shaped key from around his neck, and then plugged it into a keyhole which was located just six inches above the floor on the wall next to the door. Once he removed it without turning it, Aaron saw a section of the cinder block wall pull back then slide over to the right to reveal a downward circular metal staircase. CJ told him to follow him and to keep close until they had reached the first landing.

After they walked down for a few steps, the section of wall which had opened for them, slid back into place and send them into complete darkness for a few seconds, until tiny blue lights lit up along the wall in a straight line. All, was quiet as Aaron heard their footsteps on the steel staircase echo off of the concrete walls that surrounded them. No words were spoken until they both heard a deep male voice which rang out from below them, that ordered them to advance and be recognized.

CJ grabbed Aaron by the wrist and told him to follow him as he said . . . "Number one, with 1. 3, 2, 7, 6, code for today." He said as they reached the landing where Aaron saw a very large built man dressed in a black uniform like the one he had seen CJ wearing.

"#1, who's this person and are the others leaders expecting him?" The large man asked

"This is the Sarge I've talked about and yes the other leaders are expecting him Mr. Thompson."

"You got it then #1. You know the way." He said as he pushed a button on his black radio box and spoke into his head set as he said . . . "Control its Big T, deactivate Head Quarters defense grid and give me a push over the net once we're active again."

"Head Quarters grid deactivated Big T. Tell #1 that everyone's waiting on him and the Sarge in the leader's room." The person in the control room replied.

"#1, its all clear for you and the Sarge. Just poke your head in control when you pass by on your way into the leader's room. Oh yeah, #1 Pope said that everyone's waiting on you."

"That's a roger Big T, come on Sarge, follow me." He said as he walked down further on the circular staircase with Aaron right on his heels.

They walked down for a short while this time around as they reached the bottom of the staircase where Aaron saw an open door which looked like a vault door with sliding steel bars and all. CJ walk through it As Aaron followed into a long hallway which was illuminated by the exact blue lights that were in the stairwell, and after a few steps down the hall, CJ turned into the first room on the left as Aaron followed.

In the room sat a young man, who appeared to Aaron to be in his mid twenties in front of a wall of monitor screens. CJ walked up and tapped the young man on his shoulders and motioned with his hands, telling the seated person to remove his ear phones and once he did, CJ began to speak to him.

"Sarge, this is Pope. He's the one who was in control last night when we came in. Pope, this is the Sarge I've talked so much about."

"Oh shit, this is him! Man, I heard that you are thee badest mother fucker in the world." He said

"I'm not that good, although I am nice with my gun skills." Aaron said with a slight laugh.

"#1 they're all waiting on you, ya know." Pope said.

"How many times have I set meetings and had to wait on them, especially Big dog and his women. By the way Pope, why does my control center smell like indo? I know I like to hit the bud every once and a while, but damn Pope, when I opened the door, the smoke poured out like milk." He said.

"Aw man, shit you know I gotta have my Buda man. I'm good though, everything's lock down and I'm in control of all of the grids man."

"I know; you know that I'm just fuck'en with you anyways. Alright I'm out." He said as he led Aaron back into the hallway.

As they stepped out of the control center, they both heard Pope call to Big T over the radio and as he told him that he was reactivating Headquarters defense grid and once he did, in the hall, Aaron and CJ saw the huge steel door close under its own power and lock. After that CJ tapped him on his shoulder as he told him to come on.

Walking to the end of the hallway, Aaron saw another hallway which extended to the Left and down that one, he saw other doors to rooms, but that didn't travel down it, for their door was the last one on the first hallway, which was marked, leader's room.

When CJ opened the door, inside, they saw the other leaders of Infiltrate, all seated around a round table. On top of this table, there were several small TV like screens which sat to the right hand side of each leader's position. After the door opened, the four seated men all looked up as CJ and Aaron walked in and took their seats.

"It's about god damn time #1, we've all been in here for the last 20 minutes!" Big dog shouted.

"Yeah, yeah, yeah, The Sarge had some business details to work out over the phone, so we took a little longer. Besides, how many times have we waited on you Big dog, with you and your chasing all of your women, huh?" CJ asked as he switched on his screen.

"I told you before CJ, the women chase after me, I don't go after them. When you have so many girls blowing up your pager all the tie needing this good dick, it's hard to be on time, but in your case, you're married and we're going to get the Sarge's girl, so there's no excuse." Big dog said again.

"Never the less men, please excuse me for being late. Now the task was for each of you to bring me six names you thought would be good for this hop. Half you start and after he's done, #3 you go then 4 followed by 5. The floor is yours #2." CJ said as he put his feet up on the table.

As Half began to speak, with each name he mentioned, their face and small caption of their qualifications appeared on the small screens . . . I've selected for my squad, Woll Ackermen, Henry Wallace, Derrick Marshall, Allen DePaul and Greg Weaver. DePaul and Weaver are my heavy drew serve weapon carriers and the others are all Path Finder's and Ranger qualified." He said.

"For my squad, I've chosen, Aalen Richards, Chris Jett, Brian Prindal, Michel Vines and Tommy Brown. On this hop since we're going to more than likely attack a Head quarters building, I've chosen all mortar men. The third will supply the indirect placement support fire for the mission." Dusty said.

"I've drawn the demolitions detail on this hop. All of mine are demo and engineers. They are Montelongo, Martinez, Petermen, Tillman and Cheeks." Big Dog said.

"I've chosen Aanbrocio, McLemore, Daniels, Scott and tmas. The fifth squad will be composed of some of our former Delta force and Navy Seal team members. The Shadow doesn't stand a chance against us #1." Sandman said with a touch of pride in his voice.

"Very good men, Half your squad will storm the Shadow's HQ directly after the third softens them up with indirect fire. Big dog, your squad will team up with Sandman's squad. By the time Half and dusty reach the Shadow's HQs, I want their front door to have already been blown off of its hinges with the Fifth engaged in room clearing fire. I'm the lead element on this hop and I've selected, Swango, Blake, Dixon, Surles and the Sarge to make up the first squad. Half you'll take the second wave in on chopper two and #3 keep in mind that once you get dropped off, they'll only be minutes for you to have the first rounds in the air on its way down range. Lastly men, we'll be flying into China and once the birds are in the air, you'll proceed straight to the Shadow's HQs, Bob and his son has the correct locations already locked into their flight computers on board their choppers."

"#1 what time is the exact hop assembly time set for?" Sandman asked.

"Good question, I'm glad that you asked because I had totally forgotten to tell you all. The assembly time is set for 4:15PM and tells your people that that plane has a takeoff time of 5:00PM sharp, so they need to have all of their gear with them by the set time of assembly. That's it men this meeting is at an end and please men get some rest. Take the time to hug your kids' good bye for those of you that have them and for the others, give your girl friends a kiss and tell her that you'll be back." He said as he and the other leaders stood to their feet and exited the room.

While they did that, Tracy called down the hallway to CJ as he and Aaron walked toward control.

"Chris, Dee-Dee said that you need to come up stairs and eat because you hardly ate anything at breakfast. You know that you don't want her to come down looking for you." She said.

"Half, we'll see you at Kennedy later on. I better get upstairs before she starts trippen. Come on Sarge." He said as he and Aaron turned and walked down the long hallway toward the elevator.

Once the hallway was cleared, Tracy walked into control then closed the door behind her. There she saw Pope who sat with his back to the door and had a pair of head phones covering his ears. She walked up behind him and caressed his neck and chin with her baby soft hand to gain his attention. The touch startled him at first, but once he recognized the familiar touch and looked into her gentle brown eyes, which looked blue under the lights of the control center, he removed his head phones and smiled as he said . . . "What do you want Tracy? I learned from the last time you were down here and conned me into giving you some information I shouldn't have." He said with anger in his voice.

"Now baby, why can't I have just come down here for some of your good Texas loving?" She asked through a fake smile.

"Bitch, you really do think I'm stupid. After we fucked and I gave you the disk with CJ battle plans on it, you dogged me out saying that your thumb did a better job and was even bigger than my dick." He shouted as he jumped to his feet and looked her square in her eyes.

"Wow Popie, I know I wasn't very nice to you, but I was only doing what my big sister Dee-Dee told me to do." She said in an 'I'm so innocent voice'.

"That right huh? Well tell Dee-Dee that after CJ and the boys leave, I'm gonna put my foot up her big ass!" He said with conviction in his voice.

"But baby if you do that, then I can't give you this," She said as she reached into strap of her skin tight pink cat suit which ran only to the upper middle of her thighs and pulled out from her left breast . . . "Jamaican weed straight off of the plane." She said as she waved the bag around his face and watched him follow it with his nose.

Pope was not a very tall man. He only stood an even five feet, seven inches in height and was built like a slim basket ball player. His eyes were dark drown and slightly blood shot from his constant weed smoking and in his hair through the smooth out waves, he had his initials of CL with the word smooth. Dress in his black Infiltrate uniform, his eyes closely followed the bag of weed as she waved it from side to side.

After a few waves back and forth, she stopped as she placed the bag in her palm and made sure that he had her in full view. She wanted him to see all of her shapely curves in her skin tight Cat suit and leaned forward slightly to give him a better view of her plentiful cleavage. Tracy stood a curvy five feet, nine inches in height, but wore a size 34DD bra size. Her skin was very light completed as her face bared the high cheek bones of her native American heritage, while she wore her hair down over her shoulder as it showed her corn silk waves which were natural.

Once Pope focused on her palm, he tried to grab the small plastic bag, but as he moved forward, she pushed him back down into the seat and said . . . "Hold on now mother fucker, cause if you want what's in this bag Niggah, you gonna have to give me some lip and tongue service." she said she placed her white six inch pump onto his chest then pulled down her white fish net nylon panty hose, to expose herself to him.

A smile jerked across his face immediately as he laid his eyes on her vertical lips but, was wiped away by her next comment.

"Yeah home boy, you left me hanging last time. This time I'll make sure that I get mines before I put your ass to sleep." She said as she cupped the back of his head and pulled his face into her warm juiciness.

As he began to taste her womanhood, she leaned her head back against the wall of screen and moaned with pleasure. He went on and on until her lips quivered and her body trembled with ecstasy! As he licked and sucked, Tracy's moans got louder and louder until finally she couldn't stand anymore and exclaimed in a violent orgasm.

She pushed his face from between her legs and had tears in her eyes from Cumming so hard. She looked at him seriously as she wiped tear soaked cheeks and said . . . "Before I go to work, I'm going to need the map of North Korea and the grid coordinates of the Shadow's HQs." She demanded. Once he handed the map and computer disk with necessary information to her, she grabbed him out of the chair, and then threw him onto the floor with a wild look in her eyes.

"Yeah mother fucker, you done stirred up some shit up inside of me. You're in for one hell of a wild ride." She said as she tore him out of his uniform and hop on top of his already erect shaft.

While the control center down stairs heated up below ground, ten minutes later upstairs in CJ's and Dee-Dee's loft, the phone rang as Dee-Dee, CJ and Aaron all sat at the huge green glass dining table. Dee-Dee sprang to her feet soon as she heard the phone's first ring and told CJ that she'd answer it because she was sure that it would be for her.

As she went to the other side of the building and answered the phone, CJ yelled to her as he told her to tell Chipmunk to shut the hell up in a laughing voice! Once she picked up the phone, she heard Tracy's voice and quickly asked her . . . "Did he give it to you, do you have everything?" She demanded.

"Damn girl, I'm fine and doing well thanks for asking. And you know this fool gave the maps and the disk to me." She answered with a bold cocky tone in her voice.

"Good! But damn sis, I hope you didn't have to do too much with that little troll. I remember you telling me about the last time and him being a three minute man and all with a little dick." She said.

"Oh no not this time girl, he lasted a whole seven minutes this time. For a second, I thought that I was loosing my touch, but once I flexed my shit, he was done, but you better believe that I got mines this time! I put my shit on a plate and told him to have a lick or nibble as long as I was satisfied after he finished his meal, things would be all good." She said through laughing voice.

"Damn sis, you're crazy girl, but where is the little troll? Did he run off after his short performance or did you send him away after you talked about his thumb sized wiener?" She playfully asked.

"He's here on the floor sleeping like a baby. You see he lasted for seven minutes but he took three minutes to fall sleep this time. When I hang up with you, I'm going to kick his feet and wake him up so I can dog his ass out. I know its wrong sis but, hey I had to get mine before he did his few pumps routine and drifted off into la-la land! Oh shit he's coming to. I'll talk to you later after your hubby and the boys pull out alright Sis?" She said.

"Alright sis, I'll talk to you later. I'm about to go get me some from Chris before he leaves. Hey do me a favor. Come up stairs in about five minutes and keep the Sarge Company. I'd really feel bad just leaving him alone while I get me some."

"Alright sis, I'll be up there, I've got to go." She said as she hangs up the phone.

Dee-Dee placed the receiver back on the hook, then walked back around to the other side of the loft where CJ and Aaron still sat at the table. As she walked toward them, she made sure to catch CJ's eye with her own as he knew that look all to well. She came back then reseated herself, just as he thought she would, where Dee-Dee said . . . "Baby, I have something that I need to give to you before you leave. It's of a personal nature so if you would come with me into the bedroom, I'd be able to give it to you; You coming baby?" She asked.

"Hell yeah, um Sarge, sorry to be so rude, but my baby's got something for me into the bedroom. We've got satellite TV on the other side of the loft." He said as Dee-Dee pulled him out of the seat by his hand and hurried into their bedroom.

"It's all good CJ, I'll be alright out here, and you just go and handle your business!" He shouted as the master bedroom doors closed.

In the room, in front of the huge pure Ivory framed King sized bed, Dee-Dee rapped her arms around his neck, then looked into his deep brown eyes as she said . . . "Why Mr. Johnson, have I told you that I love you very much today? If I missed the chance then please let me do so right now baby. I love you Chris Johnson, very deeply with all of my heart and with all of my soul." She said as she genially kissed him on the lips.

"And my love for you is as strong for you now as it was on that fateful day of June 23rd. 1993, when I took your hand in marriage. You're just as beautiful as the day when I first laid eyes on you, behind that counter in Macy's and if I come back for no other reason, is just so I may lay yet another night in your arms and gaze into those hazel eyes that have me under your spell." He said with compassion in his voice.

He barely finished his statement when she pushed him down onto the bed, then pulled off his black leather shoes, yanked down his brown slacks and toasted them onto the thick, plush blue carpet, as she began to kiss his passionately. She popped the buttons of his pink preacher collar shirt off one by one as she genially kissed and felt his chest. After she pulled his silk green boxers off and removed his black dress socks, he sprang up and pulled down her white tights then ripped off her tang top.

CJ slowly rubbed his hands up and down her smooth, light completed back as he admired her shapely, 5FT, 71n body and removed the clips which held her shoulder length corn silk hair in a bun. He remover her sports bra, which held her 38DDD cup chest in place and kissed from her belly button down as he grabbed her red silk panties and pulled them down to the carpet, where she stepped out of them and laid back onto the bed.

As he climbed atop her, he moved his body into a position to where they both pleasured each other with their mouths. He licked the inner and outer lips of her woman hook and clit until she couldn't stand any more, which caused her to exclaim out his name in joy! As her body twitched with orgasmic rhythms she pushed him from atop herself and grabbed him by the hair, then pulled him to her, to where there was only an inch that separated their faces.

She gritted her teeth as she looked deep into his eyes and said . . . "I don't want to be made love to! Since there is a remote chance that you might not come back, I want you to fuck me! Chris I want you to fuck me like you've never fucked me before! Show me baby; show me why this is your pussy!" She shouted.

He smiled as he positioned himself in between her legs as she wrapped them around the bottom of his legs. He maneuvered his waist into position and grabbed her legs by her knees, then draped them over his shoulders as he said . . . "I'm going to show you why I'm the brother who can work it out and when I'm done, there'll be no doubt." He said as he entered her and began to thrust wildly.

As they went at it in the master bedroom, thirty minutes later, in the living room, Aaron spoke to Tracy. From the bedroom, they both heard Dee-Dee voice as she shouted, you go boy, this is CJ's pussy!!

"Oh brother, those two are really going at it huh, Tracy?" He asked her.

"Don't pay them any mind, CJ just left the door cracked because he knew that you were out here. Trust me; Chris does crazy shit like that from time to time. In fact, the last time he did something like this was when all of the group leaders were up here watching the Super Bowl when my sister got horny for some reason. We all ended up leaving after about an hour of her and his moans and screams." She explained.

Well I hate to sound like a prick but, I hope that he handles his business in the next hour because that's what he has left before it's time for us to pull out for Kennedy." He said.

"Tell me something Sarge. Now you can tell me to shut the hell up but, why are you going through all of this just to save a white woman? I mean most white girls don't even like to stand by a brother when the going gets rough so my real question is; is she the exception to what I've mostly seen?" She asked.

"Tracy let me tell you she's not like any woman that I've ever met before. Damn it's hard to explain. Laura is my night and bright sun shinny day that always knows just how to make me feel special. I've been all over the world and I'll tell you I've never met a more special person than her. I've loved, made love to and been in love with many other women and I'll tell you nothing compares to her. Not to mention, the Shadow. The main reason that I need to get her back is because, she's mixed up in this because of my past, so I must see to it that my Laura makes it back to upstate NY alive and well. I have to do this or else, I'm always going to be In the Hands of the Shadow." He said with metal in his voice.

"Damn," She said as tears ran down the sides of her cheeks, "You really do love her. That's so beautiful. I hope that you do get your love back safe and sound because I to have never been in love but, I hope that I may find that special man of my own on day. You hold on to your love with both hands when you find her."

"Thank you Tracy but you're still young and Love will find you one day you just watch. When you're not even expecting it, it gonna hit you and before you know it you'll be head over heels in love. Hell if it could happen to a former Dog like CJ then it could happen to anyone, trust me!!

"Yes that what Dee-Dee tells me all the time. Funny thing is, I was there when she met Chris through our first cousin Anthony, You know Half? Those 2 have been joined at the hip ever since and I've in some ways been a bit jealous of them and their love but that because when they met I was 16 and Dee-Dee was my Big sis and my world!! I've never told her this though and you need not say anything either Sarge!"

"My lips are sealed Tracy. I'd never mention anything like this to CJ for any reason because something like this would hurt your sisters feeling and kind of cause a bit of family problems if it were to get out. Now I know secrets can be dangerous. Laura learned of something that I let happen in my stupidity and trust me, when someone you love finds out about something you really didn't want them to, the guilt can reach the point where it just about kills you. Hey Tracy tell me something, how long do CJ and your sister usually go at it?"

"Well Sarge, Infiltrate has an SP time of 4:00PM which is just under two hours from now, but CJ has on several occasions almost missed his own pre-hop roll call meeting because he was fooling around with

Dee-Dee. She has told me that he can on some days go at it for three to four hours straight. In the mean time Sarge, have you been fitted with a radio and weapons from our arms room?" She asked.

"CJ said that he'd hook me up with those things just before we left."

"Tell you what; I'll leave CJ a note right here telling him where I've taken you. Instead of us just waiting here doing nothing while those two fuck each other's brains out, how about you follow me downstairs into Infiltrate HQs so we can get you your gear and the proper cloths." She said as she began to write on a yellow stick'em pad.

Aaron walked into the guest bedroom and changed back into his old Shadow uniform and strapped his huge sniper rifle across his back and once he rejoined Tracy in the living room, she led him out of the loft to the elevator. There he noticed as she reached into her shirt as she pulled out an exact copy of the odd shaped key had had seen CJ use earlier.

After they boarded the elevator car and the doors closed, he asked about the key . . .

"Hey Tracy, what's the deal with that funny shaped key? I ask only because I saw CJ with an exact copy of it and asked him about it, but he never did get around to telling me about it."

"Oh this, it's an electronically coded key that signals the computer once you plug it into its hole. Only the most trusted members of

Infiltrate have one and then we have to leave it here if we intend to leave the Infiltrate headquarters or street Foundation buildings. With this key, if you were to find the right entrance, all of Infiltrate becomes an open book, that's why CJ imposes such harsh restrictions on the handling of them." She explained carefully.

After she finished explaining the keys to him, the elevator reached the sublevels where Infiltrate HQs Lied. They walked down the dimly lit hallway until they reached the arms room, where on the inside of this room he saw every type of weapon from hand held to crew serve. He saw everything from 25 auto hand guns to fully automatic eight bard mini-guns. His eyes grew as wide as half dollars as he felt as if he was a kid in a candy store after his mother handed him a twenty dollar bill and told him to spend it all. The Sarge began to stutter for a few seconds until he regained his composure and asked . . . "Did CJ say what kind of hardware he wanted to bring along on this hop?"

"Whatever you want Sarge, but you did attend the leaders meeting and hear what every ones function was didn't you? And beside what more do you really need with that monster you have strapped across your back.' She asked.

"This is my sniper rifle. I'll use this only if I get a clear shot from about two miles away but, if we get into a close quarters fire fight, I'll need something like this MP 5 10mm. sub machine gun. If possibly, I'd like to take about ten clips of ammo, because you never know when the shit hits the fan how long it might last." HE said.

Tracy fitted him with his weapon and radio in the lower reaches of the building and as she did, slowly one by one, the other members of the strike team began to filter into the arms room. CJ and Dee-Dee joined the group as everyone grabbed their gear and weapons. Once everyone was thought to have been there, CJ had them all pile into the truck for departure. Dee-Dee kissed him one last time before he shut the door and told her that he'd be back safe and sound in one piece.

After the last of the good buys were done, Half called Pope in the control center and told him to open the Kennedy airport tunnel and disarm the defense grids for their passage. Once he heard the go ahead from control, he threw the truck into gear; then began the slow, tight drive along the narrow corridor. Behind the huge five ton truck, Sandman and Dusty followed closely in two heavily armed Range Rovers.

The mood was definitely different from the last time he was in the tunnels, Aaron thought to himself as he noticed the looks of deep concentration on all of their faces. He thought back to his Desert Storm Days and the looks of his men before they had gone into battle. This is a good look he told himself, they're not worried; they're only concentrating on the coming task. No words were spoken during the ride, any laughter or smiles. Even the Sarge himself has some thoughts of the pending battle.

The ride was smooth but long and once Half drove up the ramp into the sewers, he looked across at Aaron and told him that there was only a short while before they would be in the hanger. In the Sewer tunnel, Aaron saw that it was twice as wide as the underground old subway tunnel and almost three times as tall. In the distance, he saw an eighteen wheeler which waited with its engine running and its tail gate down. By the ramp, they all saw the Big dog as he stood by the ramp of the larger truck.

Half drove past him and stopped as Sandman and Dusty drove their smaller trucks onto the rear of the rig. Dusty had so much as stepped on the breaks, to stop the truck when Big dog lifted the ramp and slid it into the bottom of the truck, then closed the door behind them. Once he climbed into the cab of the truck, he radioed to Half and told him that the two gun trucks were secured for outside travel; CJ nodded to Half, then watched as he shifted into gear and resumed their journey as Big dog followed closely behind.

Thirty minutes later after the brief stop off, Half drove out of the tunnels and onto the service street which led to Kennedy Airport's back entrance. They drove for a short while until they arrived at a large hanger which had Chinese writings on it and once the trucks stopped, CJ hopped out of the truck, then banged on the door. After the echoes in the metal subsided, the huge doors began to slide open.

When they were fully opened, before their eyes, they all saw the Russian transport called the Condor. CJ waved his hand forward as he walked toward a distant figure of a man who appeared to be working on the plane.

As he rode into the hangar in the truck, Aaron over looked the plane as they approached it from its side. He had never seen anything other than a carrier quite that size. He thought back to the days when the Russian government first proclaimed that they had the largest plane in the world. Now as this huge beast filled the trucks windshield, he still couldn't believe it's awesome size.

In a dimly lit corner of the hanger, Aaron also saw a white leer jet as it sat with its door open and its stairs down. As they drove around to the front ramp of the transport plane, he watched CJ slowly walk over to the jet, which caused him to ask Half who was in that jet in the corner. Half told him that it was probably Stevens in it waiting for their arrival and after he heard who was in the jet, as soon as the truck stopped moving, he jumped out and ran toward the darkened corner.

When he reached the jet, he climbed up the stairs and stepped in where he saw CJ and five other people seated. He recognized Topher Stevens immediately who sat at the rear of the plane with a small Chinese girl laid across his lap. This entire seen struck Aaron as odd being that CJ and the others present, watched on in silence as Stevens snorted white cocaine from between the woman's cleavage. Having seen enough after only a few seconds, the Sarge stepped two steps closer and cleared his throat loud enough for all on board the small jet to hear and once the silence was broken, everyone including Stevens, placed all eyes on him.

"Oh shit, the Sarge is here, Hey woman, go get cleaned up in the back and if you can, don't let too much of that go to waste. Now CJ, Sarge all of your arrangements have been made. I must admit though, when Tracy contacted my office and explained everything, I wasn't sure if I'd be able to help any, but after several phone calls and some

old favors owed, your arrival and border across points are locked in."
Stevens said.

"Well Stevens, I see you've finally reached your position in life
where you can give back to your fellow brothers. That was what you
said you were trying to do when I last saw you." Aaron said.

"Those days are long done now and besides, yes I was an asshole
back then and I did step on a lot of toes on my way up, that why you
and my now good friend CJ were ordered to kill me. I was young back
then, I've completely made a 360 degree turn for the better. Not to
mention, I do owe my life to you, after all, you were the one who told
CJ to let me go." He said.

"Ok, alright, I hate to break up this reunion but I have a hop roll
call to conduct and over see the final travel preparations. Stevens
are you certain you've not forgotten to mention anything? I only ask
because the last hit you paid us for, you forgot to mention that he had
a small armed force of guards around his mansion. Now is the time to
tell us Stevens." CJ said.

"I haven't gotten any Intel from that region as yet, but as soon as I
get any information, I'll be sure to send it to my people on the ground
for you in China. For now though, all that you know is all that I know"
He answered.

After hearing his reply, Aaron walked toward Stevens and
extended his hand in a gesture of thanks. He looked him dead in his
eyes and told him that Laura was the world to him and he'd give up

everything just to have her back. Stevens nodded his head and said that he understood, then again told them both that he would do what he could.

When they were done inside the smaller plane, CJ and Aaron walked back across the hanger where the group leaders had their men assembled by squad. CJ walked over to Half and took hold of the clip board then began to call off names.

After he called out a name, each man said here Number 1 and once he was through, he walked up onto the ramp of the plane for a few steps, and then turned to face his men. He cleared his throat and took in a deep breath before he began to speak as he said . . .

"We have a long journey ahead of us men. I suggest you all take time to clear your minds of all that you love or care about here in this world and focus on the mission at hand. I have two goals for this hop going into North Korea my men. I hope that every one of you shares these in common goals with me. The first is to bring back the Sarge's girl Laura Hinkley alive and well. The second is to bring back all of you my men alive and well. Don't get me wrong on this one men, for the mission is not more important than you are to me. To me, I think of the mission and my men. Everything else, all other considerations are secondary in my eyes. I want you all to board this aircraft with an inner confidence knowing that his buddy has got his back. That's all that I can say men. You all know the risks. All who are with me and the Sarge on this one follow me." He said as he turned and walked into the plane.

After his speech this time, there were no cheers from the men. There were no smiles or jumping up and down in joy. They all only collected their things and boarded the plane behind CJ. When he saw every one strapped in and set for the long flight, he went to the cock pit and told the pilots that they were all set.

The Chinese crewmen double checked all of the choppers and truck tie downs and ensured that they were all secured for flight. Young Chinese flight attendants saw to all of the men before the pilot told them over the plane's PA system in Chinese to prepare for takeoff.

Stevens and his small group, waved as the world's largest type of aircraft rolled out of the hanger and made its way up to the taxi way. As the plane rolled out of sight, Stevens heard the phone inside his plane ring and dipped his head to one of his body guards, signaling for him to go answer the phone. While he went into the plane, Stevens and the other walked to the door of the hanger and watched as the bird with Infiltrate in it soared into the heavens and out of sight.

As soon as the plane was out of view, the body guard jumped out of the jet then ran over to Stevens at his top speed. He spoke in Chinese but, he told him that he had just received word from a South Korean contact who told him that the Shadow was moving Laura across the border to one of their whore houses.

Stevens gasped at the news and began to try and think of how he could get word to CJ the fastest way. He looked up at his body guard as he told him to get Tracy on the phone and minutes later he was on the phone with her as he told her . . . "Tracy, its Stevens listen to me;

you've got to get word to CJ. I've just received vital information about Laura Hinkley." He stuttered.

"Stevens calm down, I've never heard you sound so worried like this. Now what's the information so I can pass it on to #1?" She asked.

"Laura Hinkley is being moved to South Korea within the next several hours. My contact in country says that she's being taken to a whore house across the border."

"Damn Stevens Pope just told me our satellite communication system is down. He says he can have it operational in about six hours."

"Tracy if you don't get word to CJ soon, he'll be taking his group into a trap. There has to be a way for you to contact CJ." He demanded.

"There is only one way Stevens. Dee-Dee and I were going to come to you in a few hours, because she and I were planning to go over there on our own mission. Now that things have changed Stevens, let me ask you something, how fast is your jet?"

"Chipmunk forget it. I can't let you take this jet because I have to see after it at all times. Sorry there has to be some other way." He said flatly.

"You listen to me Stevens! MY sister, Big T and I are on our way to that damn hanger where you are! If that jet can fly and you have to be with it, then you're just gonna have to be with us because we're going over to South Korea, then to the North. Now we'll be there in thirty minutes and I expect you to have the arrangements made by the time we get there! You got me Stevens!" She shouted into the phone.

"Damn Trace, I'm going to regret this but yeah everything will be ready when you arrive. I owe the Sarge my life and I can't even count how much I owe to CJ."

As soon as she hangs up the receiver, she jumped to her feet and ran out of the control center. She yelled to Pope as she ran into the hall, telling him to call her sister upstairs and tell her that she was needed in the leader's room. Once in the hallway, she ran up to the steel door and opened it as she called to Big T and told him to come to the leader's room.

Five minutes later, when Dee-Dee stepped into the room, Tracy had her take a seat at the table as she told what the situation was and what the stakes were. The look of shock and worry jerked across her face as she received the news of the new developments and CJ possibly walking into a trap. Tracy went on to explain what the new plan was and who was going to be with them on this mission going into South Korea. When she finished explaining, neither Big T nor Dee-Dee had much to say.

They all went into the arms room and gathered their gear. Both girls took MP 5 10mm along with a hundred clips of ammo while Big T opted to carry his specially made, silent firing GE mini-gun with a two thousand round back pack. After they all grabbed their gear, Pope had one of the Infiltrate members drive them to the airport through the tunnels under the city.

The jeep pulled up in front of the hanger twenty minutes after Tracy's conversation with Stevens over the phone. In the hanger, the jet sat with its engines running and taxi lights flashing. Before the jeep pulled off the Infiltrate member wished them good luck, then drove off into the evening.

Tracy, Dee-Dee and Big T boarded the aircraft and took their seats. Stevens then called up to his pilots and told them, that they were ready for takeoff. He looked at Dee-Dee with a reassuring look on his face since the look of worry showed across her face. Tracy called across the plane to Stevens and asked if he was ready to get dirty as he answered hell yeah!

The pilot taxied onto the runway and awaited their turn to take off and when it was up for then, the captain called back to Stevens and told him that they were about to be air born. Stevens looked at the three of them and told them to lean back and get comfortable, because they had a long flight ahead of themselves. He told them that they'd make good time, but he knew as well as they all did deep down inside, that time wasn't on their side.

The pilot brought the plane to speed, and then pulled off of the runway, as he turned the nose of the plane toward the west coast. Dee-Dee thought of CJ as she looked over the New York City sky line as they pulled away in the air. The captain then pulled back on his yoke and flew off into the skies bound for South Korea.

CHAPTER V

⌒⌒∿∿⌒⌒

THE MOON WAS full over New York City at 2:50AM, Thursday morning as Pope worked feverishly on his equipment. He had promised Tracy and Dee-Dee that he'd have communications back on line in six hours, but he was already an hour and fifty minutes over that time line as it was. He worked and worked until his fingers began to bleed because he was to be damned if he'd let his group down.

Pope had a small team of workers in the control center with him, working as hard as he was. They pulled out the entire console with the communications equipment and went over each component, along with their connections between each other. One of the workers unhooked the satellite relay junction box and found the problem. As she did, she called over to Pope who had his hack turned toward her and told him to hurry over to her. Once he did, he knelt down beside her and saw what the problem was then laughed out loud.

"A mouse; You gotta be kidding me, a fucking mouse! Millions of dollars worth of computerized equipment and we're shut down by a mouse. How bad is the damage Stacy?" He asked.

"This isn't good Pope. I'll have to go over to the warehouse and replace this and most of the other parts in the console. We'd really be better off if we did things that way because, all of the satellite equipment was inner connected and if this relay was burned out or shorted, the rest of the components may have burned out as well. If you call Iassac and tell him what I need, I can be back in about three hours or less." She said.

"Ok, everybody listen to me. Stacy has found the problem. What I need now is for everyone to help pull out all of the satellite components. Stacy, the faster we get this system up, the faster I will be able to save CJ and the group." He said as he placed his hand on her shoulder.

"Getting there and back won't he the problem, it's dealing with Iassac that will be a bitch of a problem. Every time I go over there he gives me a hard time. The two bit hustler, drug dealer. I still can't figure out why CJ deals with Iassac when he knows as well as you and I do how he makes his money. Telling you the truth Pope, I really feel that Infiltrate should exterminate people like him." She said

"That's not for us to decide. Look, I to share some of those same feelings, but he is our supplier of arms and owns the warehouse where we store our equipment. But look here, we don't have time for this discussion right now. That bird with Infiltrate will make its final landing in four hours. Dee-Dee and Tracy will be on the ground in Soul, South Korea in less than one hour. Our communications gear must be up and running by the time infiltrate lands or else all is lost. Go now, I'll speak to you later and tell Iassac I said what's up." Fe said as she turned and headed for the door.

As she ran down the hail, Pope had the other personnel in the control center go over every other component for any signs of further damage. While that happened, Stacy jumped into her Grand Jeep Cherokee which was parked in the Infiltrate underground parking complex, then started it up. After she shifted into gear, she pulled off toward the up ramp and without even looking, through pure instincts, reached up and pressed the button of her specially coded garage door opener.

Once she pressed the button, a signal was sent which caused the wall to slide over at the top of the ramp where she drove into the Street Pound.3tion's underground parking complex. She stopped her truck just short of the toll gate and looked at the guard in the both as he knotted his head then raised the gate to let her pass. After she cleared the ramp and turned onto the street, she turned her truck toward Manhattan and headed into the traffic.

As she made her way toward their warehouse and Pope along with his crew of technicians checked and double checked the control center electronic components, in the air just off the Chinese cost, across the International Date Line, Dee-Dee, Tracy and Big I prepared themselves and the others as they all checked their gear, weapons and equipment. As they all did, the jet began its final decent into Sour South Korea.

"Stevens," Tracy said," are you sure your people on the ground will be able to take us to where the Sarge's girl has been taken?"

"Not only that Stevens but if and when we do get to where ever it is that we're going, are you mentally prepared just in case we have to lay down some rounds." Dee-Dee asked

"My people in Soul are waiting on our arrival. They'll take 'is to the whore house Laura Hinkley has been taken to and they've assured me that there would be a fire fight to get her out of their hands. To answer your question Dee-Dee, I started training in battle tactics after CJ and the Sarge allowed me to live those few years ago. I don't believe that I'm on their level, but I do know how to fight and I am ready to do so if it comes to that." He said as he looked Dee-Dee in her eyes with the look of intensity in his own.

As they continued to speak amongst themselves and prepare their gear, the pilot of the let radioed to the air field tower and received clearance to land. Ten minutes later, they touched down onto a quiet air field just outside the city limits of Soul and after the jet completed it landing, it taxied over to a small terminal, where a grey Range Rover sat parked with a lone figure in its driver's seat.

As the let rolled over to the truck, the man inside it lit a cigarette then opened the door of the truck as he stepped out and waited. As soon as the jet stopped moving and it side door opened and Stevens stepped out, the man walked over to him and said . . . "Mr. Stevens, I am Mr. Sann and I have been ordered to take you and your group to where ever you need to go. I have been briefed on your situation and now the locations of the shadow's whore houses. Please if you and your group would get in, I could take you to where they are."

"Mr. Sann how far are these houses and how many of them are we talking about?" Asked Stevens as he stepped into the truck and handed his gun to the rear. "They're all near the city of Chinchow. One is right inside the square of the city while the other two are closer to the US ARMY base, camp Garry Owen. Mr. Stevens I don't know what you and your group here were expecting, but this isn't going to be easy. From what I've been able to gather, the shadow has sent several of their men to al-l three of the houses for security and I tell you now so this won't come as surprise later. I don't know which house Laura Hinkley in being held in." He said in a flat voice.

"That's a big fuck'en problem! If we hit the wrong house, the other two will be alerted. There's no two ways about this, if we can't find out which house has Laura in ft then I don't think we should even fuck with this shit!" Big T said

"That's not an option Big T neither is failure. Think about it, if we leave the Sarge's girl here in this country and hit the shadow's HQ, she'll he killed for sure, but if we hit either of those whore houses, the shadow may be distracted just enough for CJ and the Sarge to slip through their trap. There no way around it Big T, if we don't hit them now our people will he lost in the hands of the shadow forever." Dee-Dee said with compassion in her voice.

"Then it's settled, Mr. Sann, please take us to the shadow's whore house near camp Garry Owen. Hopefully we'll get lucky, if not then we'll just have to do things the old fashion way. That being, blast our way in and shot our way out. "Tracy said as Mr. Sann started the truck, shifted into gear and pulled off toward the city of Chinchow

As they pulled onto the dirt road and made tracks across the land, in the air over the Pacific Ocean, Infiltrate along with Aaron Williamson soared patiently through the skies as they made their way toward China. Everyone on the plane to this point had been extremely quiet and in fact only the constant hum of the plane's four huge turbo jets broke the silence in the cabin. After hours of this Half had finally had enough of the long faces around him, so he decided to lighten thing up a bit.

"Ok everybody listen up," He said as all eyes in the cabin focused in on him "Check out this joke. President Clinton, Mrs. Clinton and Chelsea were on a plane flying toward Bermuda and crashed. Everyone on the plane died and went to heaven as God spoke to them all. He asked Bill, who are yon and what have you gone good in your life my son? And the president answered, I'm Bill Clinton and I was the President of a nation which helped millions all over the world. So God turned to Chelsea who was in the middle of the two and asked the same question, who are you and what have you gone good in life? And she answered, Cod sir. I was just a kid, but I always said my preys and went to church every Sunday. So God said, very well my child then turned to Hillary and asked; who are you and what have you done good in life my child? And she answered, my name is Hillary-Rodham Clinton and I believe you're in my seat." Half finished as all the men in the cabin laughed out loud.

"You all know something; it's been a long time since we've cracked on one another. I'll start it off, Yo Big dog, your new girlfriend is so ugly, it looks like she's been chasing parked cars" Sand man said as all the men in the cabin laughed and said ooh.

"Oh yeah well that piece of shit you call a house is so small, both the rats and roaches are humped backed." He replied as the men all went into a frenzy of laughter

"Hey half," Dusty called out," Yo I heard that when you were younger in your house, when someone stepped on a cigarette on your floor, they put out your central heat." He said to a few snickers and giggles." "Well I personally know that your family was so poor and fucked up, your older brother wore hand-me ups. Old sorry ass family: One time I went into his apartment and a rat tapped me on the foot and asked me who I was and what I was doing in his house." half said as everybody burst into laughter.

While the men all past put down jokes back and forth between themselves, CJ and Aaron spoke to one another in the forward of the cabin as they said . . . "You know Sarge, I have finally come to understand that look on your face. All those many times when we were on alert on the Demilitarized zone in South Korea and on the battle lines in Desert Storm, I never understood what that look meant. Now I understand what it is like when you have another person depending on your leadership for their survival, It is hard to sent someone to their death, especially when their your closest friend." CJ said.

"You're damn right it's hard, but that's not the only hard part about things, do you hear your men behind us? I don't know about you, but I can hear the fear of death in their voices as they try to hide it behind laughter. At the very least, your men have a strong leader; I sense your inner strength and love for your man, that's why this entire situation is even harder on me. If not for me, neither you nor your men would be going into possibly the worst thing they've ever faced before. If you're anything like me, you'd wish some time that you were made of stone, so you wouldn't have feelings." He said.

"I do hear the fears of my men in their attempts to hide it and I have on several occasion wished that I was stone. One time in particular comes to my mind, when Dee-Dee went on a mission with me into Rockwell international maximum security installation in Nevada. We made it into the main building and had the plans to the back then new stealth fighter, FII7A. without any problems, but when someone in big dog's squad tripped a light beam sensor on the floor. Needless to say Sarge, the shit hit the fan quickly, but thanks to all of our training, we made it out of there without any loses. Ever since then Dee-Dee and Tracy have always asked to join us on our hopes and missions. We made it out of that one but not without some very close calls. Thanks in large part to the fact that we laid down the fire and kept it on until the last man was on the chopper. I can't even imagine my life without Dee-Dee in it, that's why I say I hear what's in my men's hearts, but most of all, I even feel what's in your heart and the pain that you're in." He said

"Old friend, I assure you that the pain Alex Kim Jr. has caused me will be nothing compared to what I will do to him and the shadow. CJ I fully intend to make damn certain he and they don't ever cause this kind of hurt to anyone else ever again and you know that's only one way to ensure this." He said with Iron in his voice.

"I know Sarge, I know and neither I nor my men would have it any other way. We're going to take him down, burn them down and make sure that they stay down for the final count. That way we might wash our hands of the shadow and be out of theirs. Check it Sarge, there's only about two hours or so before we have to out on our game faces, how about we join in on this snap section behind us and share a laugh or two with the men?" He said as he and Aaron undid their seat belts and turned onto their knees in their seats.

"Oh yeah" shouted sand man toward one of the men in the rear of the cabin, well your mother is the only woman I know who drags her knuckles when she walks." After the crowd went into their series of oh, OOOs and laughter, Aaron stood on his seat and said . . . "Yo Half, I heard that your mother is so fat, that she can sit on a nickel and squeeze out five pennies." Half of the men burst into laughter while the other half all looked over at #2 with their mouths hung open in shock.

CJ himself even thought to himself, if he had been white his cheeks would have turned blush pink. Half himself only shook his head and waited for the slightest moment of quiet. Once the moment was at hand, he struck back with a lighting quick snap and said . . . "Sarge I know you ain't talk'en about mothers because yo mamma is so ugly, the bitch tried to become a mud wrestler, but they told her no thanks, we already have the mud." And as the cabin rumbled from the men's laughter, Aaron looked over to Half then smiled as it to tell him that he had gotten him with a good one.

As the snaps and jokes continued to fly across the cabin of the huge aircraft, the pilot of the bird spoke over the PA system in Chinese to the flight attendants and after they had heard what the captain had told them, the head attendant walked to the forward of the cabin and told CJ that they were on final approach to the air field. After he heard this, his face switched as if he had a switch in his pocket. His smile disappeared along with the bright twinkle in his eyes and was replaced by the look of deep concentration and hardness in his them.

He stood on his chair then raised his hand as the men all quieted themselves and gave him their undivided attention and once he saw that all eyes were on him, he began to speak as he said . . . "Men we're about 80 minutes out on final approach to touch down. This is it my men, time to put on our game faces. Whatever it is that gets you through the tough time, whatever your motivation is, I suggest you all concentrate on it for the next 79+ minutes, because in 81 minutes, Infiltrate will go into high gear and kick some Shadow ass." He said as he turned and slid back into his chair.

While all who were seated in the cabin took the time to think of their love ones, girlfriends, families and friends, back across the international dateline in New York City, Stacy searched for the components she needed for the control center. She had made good time in getting into Manhattan on a drive which usually took well over 90 minutes from Infiltrate HQs only took 45 on this day due to the light traffic. She looked and looked for the satellite components she needed, which were placed on high shelves in this warehouse.

The reason she had to look so hard for what she needed was because; Iassac had fallen back asleep after he had spoken with Pope over the phone. Iassac who stood a slender 185LBS at 5', 10" had on his brown silk shirt and pants set. The clean cut 33 year old wore several expensive rings and around his neck sat his trade mark Herring bone gold necklace with the word' HUSTLER' spelled out in diamonds with gold trim.

"God dam it Iassac, you were suppose to have the satellite components out and ready for me. Now it's taken me all of this time to find what I've found and I still have to find a hell of a lot more!" She shouted.

"Hold up a minute gal. All I have to do is hold yall's shit here in my warehouse, according to our contract. It doesn't say anything about me having to listen to some bitch that's on her rag. Now I want you to remember this statement because it fits this entire situation all too well. A lack of preparation on your part doesn't constitute an emergency on mine. Tell you what though, since CJ is my boy and all, soon as one of my men gets in here, I'll have him help you out what looking for your stuff. How's that sound?" He said with a smile on his face.

"Well how soon will that be Iassac, I've got lives depending on this system getting back on line?" "Not long, the first of them should be in arriving, oh around nine this morning. I know that's three and a half hours from now, but hell with what Pope told me you all needed to get your system back on line you by your self will he here by the time nine AM rolls around anyways. HA, HA, HA, HA." He said laughing as he turned and walked away from her.

The rage and hatred Stacy felt toward Iassac and his laughing, churned her stomach as she continued to place the satellite components she needed on her rolling cart and as she pushed on in her search, she began to wonder if she make it back to HQs before it was too late for CJ and the Sarge. She knew the time was running out and that if she wasn't back in a timely manner, the group would be in serious trouble with little hope of any means out. Even Pope back in the control center began to worry if she'd make it back in time to save the group.

While he and his crew worked to put the components back in place, Pope would from time to time glance at the phone on the wall and contemplate calling Stacy on her personal cellular phone, but decided to continue working instead. As he along with his crew toiled in the Infiltrate Control center, over in South Korea, Dee-Dee and her group readied themselves for their attack.

"Alright people, this is it. "Dee-Dee said as she pulled out the floor plans of the whore house and showed everyone it's lay out on the hood of the Range Rover. There are only two floors as you all can see, so there will be no need for any of us to go in from the top as well as the bottom. Big T, I want you to take Stevens and one of his muscle men and take the front. Tracy and I will go in through the back and take the rear staircase. Be sure to check your targets every one, because I only want members of the Shadow killed, no civilian's deaths." She said.

"Dee-Dee we're going to need at least one gun on the front door. Mr. Sann, would it be safe to assume that you're handy with some steel in your hands?" Tracy asked.

"I am highly trained in operations such as these. If you need another gun, I can post a few hundred meters off the front entrance once I've dropped you all off." He said flatly.

"Good we can have you on the front just in case some way, somehow, they manage to slip past Big T's group. Listen close everyone, this is what's going to happen from this point on. Once we're back in the truck, Tracy Lee-Ho and I will exit the truck three miles away from the target house. At that point, Mr. Sann, I'm going to need you to take to the rice patties and off of the road the rest of the way there. Give us no longer than 15 minutes before you begin your attack Big T, I'll give you a push over the net once we're act in position. Leave no stone unturned, no room cleared. In and out with what we've come for, the Infiltrate way. Let's move!" Dee-Dee instructed as they all jumped back into the truck and pulled off down the road.

As they drove, they all saw the rice fields and marsh lands which seemed to extend both left and right to the horizon. All was quiet in the cab of the truck; only the sounds of clicking metal could be heard as all in the truck checked their weapons except for Mr. Sann. Once he reached the three mile point, he stopped the truck as he jumped out and ran to the back and pulled the tail gate open.

Dee-Dee, Lee-Ho and Tracy wasted no time exiting the truck as they quickly ran off of the side of the road and began their trek through the rice fields. Seeing them on their way, Mr. Sann closed the gate, hoped back into the driver's seat then steered off of the road to the left. Although the ride was a rough and rugged one, the Range

Rover made quick work of the rice fields and shallow marsh thanks to its sturdy construction and dependable four wheel drive.

After five minutes of off road driving, Mr. Sann brought the truck to a stop some 300 meters away from the front of the whore house where Big T, Stevens and his other body guard Wan Sin-way exited the truck. They moved through the marsh land, stelthfully but quickly and set themselves all but 100 meters away from the front of the house. There they waited until Dee-Dee called them over their radio and told them that they were set and ready for attack.

After ten long minutes of waiting, Big I finally received the go ahead signal form Dee-Dee and with weapons in hand and determination in their eyes, both groups stormed into the whore house like a wool wind sweeping across the land. Big I's group reached the house first with him kicking in the front door and Stevens and Wan scanning about the front room of the house.

Inside they all saw several women along with several men, both Korean and American. Big I at first was surprised that neither of the two with him let off any shots as they entered the room. He knew right off that the Americans men in the house were more than likely US soldiers looking for a quick good time with a hooker, but wasn't sure about the Korean men though.

From the corner of Steven's left eye, he saw a sudden movement. Turning in its direction, he saw a long haired Korean man drawing what to him looked like a small submachine gun and in one fluidic motion aimed and let off a three round burst from his MP 10 submachine gun which struck the man center mass in his face. After those first few shots broke the silence which lingered in the air, from every direction, they all heard the sounds of women screaming and saw weapons being pulled out on them.

Big T spoke into his head set as he fired across the room and killed another Korean man who was trying to pull his gun out of his pants. T called Dee-Dee who along with Tracy and Lee-Ho were still running across the rice field and informed her of his situation. "Mother 1, mother 1, we're in a fire fight with the shadow. American soldiers and Korean women all around, take caution, they heading down the hall toward the back door!" He shouted into his head set as Dee-Dee and the other two with her heard machine gun fire and women screams of fear in the back ground.

Reaching their position outside the rear exit Dee-Dee, Tracy and Lee-Ho rushed in with their guns to bear, but before she even had the chance to give any instructions to her sister or Lee-Ho, a Korean man wearing a Shadow uniform began to fire at them with a 45 Cal. hand gun. The first shot he fired, struck into the wooden wall near Dee-Dee's head, the second by her shoulder, but before he could pull the trigger for a third shot, Tracy fired a four shot round burst at the Shadow member.

The rounds hit the Korean man in a straight line, starting at his forehead down to his stomach. Down the hall they all saw the American GIs and women running away from the firing in the front room of the house and Big T' as group enter into the first room. Dee-Dee hated this house's setup and the way they had gone in for this extraction.

She told herself, next time we'll go in through the roof and fight our way down.

In the mist of all the screaming and shouting, Tracy looked over at her sister and saw that she was in never-never land and had a thousand yard stair in her eyes. Tracy hopped over to her, placed her hand on her shoulder and asked if she was alright. Dee-Dee looked up with a slight look of embarrassment in her eyes then began to speak as she said . . ." Sorry sis, I was just thinking about the way we came into this place. I know I thought of the attack plan, but I just realized that I fucked up. Come on Lee-Ho, we still have a second floor to clear." She said as she pulled out one of her concussion grenades, pulled the pin and threw it up the stairs.

The second group braced themselves for the flash and bang which was forth coming and readied them to rush up the stairs as soon as the blast subsided. When it broke, Dee-Dee spoke into her mike, telling Tracy and Lee-Ho to move up the stairs . . . "Keep alert up here; we all know the people up here heard what was going on down stairs on the first floor." She said as she stood to the top of the staircase with her back to the wall. She nodded her head at Tracy, giving her the signal to reach around her and throw another concussion grenade.

Tracy pulled the pin, reached around Dee-Dee then threw it away from them; then ducked her head down onto the staircase. After the blast, Dee-Dee turned the corner to find another member of the shadow standing in a doorway to the first room on the second floor. The brown haired Korean man had an AK4J in his left hand, but had his right hand over his eyes. No doubt he was feeling the effects of that grenade Tracy had just thrown, Dee-Dee thought to herself.

Before the Then ever had the chance to regain his eye sight, Dee-Dee let loose with a four round burst from her machine gun which dropped the shadow member where he stood, both teams made short work of clearing the floors, going through each room, throwing a concussion grenade in before they would enter a given room. The case was the garlic in each room they cleared, no Laura.

"Mother 1 its chipmunk, other than a couple of hookers and embarrassed US G.I.s up here, our target isn't here. I think we should high tail it back to our transport and rethink our situation." She said as she walked out of the last room on the second floor.

"You're right Chipmunk; this entire operation is a bust. Attention all units on this net, this is mother 1. Break off and regroup on our land transport. Rally time, 03 minutes, move people!" She said as her group ran down the stairs then out of the building.

Big T waved his hand in the air in a circular motion, signaling to his group to break off and regroup at the truck, but before they had the chance to leave the house, an older Korean woman who was the madam of the whore house, began to shout at them in Korean, saying nigger and white trash go home. Big T would never have guessed what happened next, in a million years, because in a blink of an eye, the older woman pulled out a large meat cleaver and reared back as if she was going to throw it at them.

Stevens saw this cleaver and without hesitation fired off a burst from his machine gun which killed her where she stood. He fired three four shot bursts and was about to let loose with another one, but before he was able to pull his trigger, Big T grabbed his by his arm and said . . . "Cease fire man, she's dead. Come on we're moving out Stevens let's go!" He shouted as he pulled Stevens by the arm out of the house.

Big T's group regrouped with the others shortly after they ran across the rice field back to the truck where Mr. Sann was waiting along with Dee-Dee, Tracy and Lee-Ho. They all jumped back into the Rover after which Dee-Dee instructed Mr. Sann to move on to the other whore house, but before he shifted into gear, he turned to Dee-Dee and asked . . . "Which house do you wish me to drive you to?" He asked with a serious look on his face.

After the question, she immediately turned to Tracy with a puzzled look on her face but, before she ever had the chance to say a word, as Tracy interjected with . . . "Now don't you even fix your mouth to ask me what to do? You're the head honcho on this mission and you know it." She said in a stern voice with an equally stern look in her eyes.

"Damn it I just wish CJ was here because he'd know what to do right about now. It's bad enough not having communications with the main group, but this situation is really above my head. Being that Chinchow is the second largest city in South Korea and the shadow's whore house is right in the square, it sounds like the next best place to strike, but this time around we're going to do things different. Please Mr. Sann, to the city of Chinchow at all speeds possible. After

I rethink things, I'll let you all know what we're going to do different in the coming extraction." she said as she closed her eyes and leaned back into her seat.

After she completed her instructions to the group and Mr. Sann, Big T removed his headset and laid his weapon on the floor of the truck then grabbed Stevens by his shirt and pushed him against the left side rear door. Big T gritted his teeth as he looked deep into his eyes and began to speak saying . . . "Now that we're cleared form the battle site and I have your undivided attention, I thought I'd ask you what the fuck was going through your mind as you opened fire on that old woman just as we were indexing." He shouted as he pressed his fist into Steven's chest and looked at him with a glare of intensity.

"Get the fuck off of me," He shouted as he brought his hands up knocking Big T's hands away from his body. "That old bitch was about to throw that meat cleaver at one of us and at that distance it would have killed whoever it would have struck. And besides, she was a madam for the shadow. She damn sure wouldn't have given a damn about us if she would have had the drop on us, so I took her out because I didn't give a fuck about her. Any other questions Mr. Big T." Stevens asked with a touch of sarcasm in his voice.

"You listen to me Mr. Stevens, this all may seem real cool and all to you who sits behind a desk all day long pushing a couple of pencils along with a few phone calls, but this is serious shit we're doing. If you ever go overboard on a kill like that while you're with me on this mission, I'll run you through with my blade personally. I don't give a damn how much of a corporate kiss ass white collar boy you are because out here, a man is measured by his actions, not what kind of cell phone and services he uses. Do you understand me?" He shouted as Dee-Dee and Tracy both placed their hands on his shoulders in an effort to calm him down.

After his outburst of emotions, everyone quieted themselves as Mr. Sann turned onto the major though fare leading to the city of Chinchow. As he drove down the highway toward the next whore house owned by the shadow, CJ and Aaron along with infiltrate touched down on a desolate airfield just outside the small Chinese city of Antung.

Once the plane was on the ground, the pilot taxied into a large hanger near the end of the runway, then brought the bird to a halt. Once it came to a standstill, the men of Infiltrate went down into the cargo hold of the bird's belly and slowly unhooked both choppers as trucks while the group leaders stayed upstairs and spoke of their pending mission.

"I just wanna say CJ," Half said as the other group leaders focused in on him from their seats. "1 really don't think it's such a good idea for you to take the first squad out ahead of everyone else." He said as Dusty cut off his statement short.

"I feel the same way CJ. I really think you'd be making a mistake if you divide the force. Think about this CJ, if you and your squad come into contact with some enemy force, we won't be able to help you until our first bird is up and running." He said."

"CJ you know I'm the last one to tell anybody about not being a team player, but this time I think the entire team should storm the Shadow's HQ's when the first chopper is air worthy." Big dog said

"I hear and understand all of your concerns, but I've made the decision. Men the first bird won't he airborne for another four hours. That's the fastest bob and his son along with their crew can work. By truck, it's roughly seven to eight hours drive. By the time we make it there, chopper I should touch down at the same time. I mean really think about things now, what sense would it make for all of us to stay here in this hanger for the next six hours waiting until the first bird is operational ." CJ said with conviction in his voice.

"CJ's right boys, it doesn't make any sense for everybody to sit and wait around here, but CJ I don't think you should go with the advanced party. And in case none of you have tried, the satellite cellular communication system isn't operational so my concerns now become, what happens if the advanced party takes on fire?" Sand man said as he saw the faces of the other group leaders go blank.

"Shit CJ, with this system down our head sets will only have a maximum range of only 5 miles. We can't conduct operations without commo." Half said as he pounded his fist into his palm.

"No matter the circumstances men, I'm taking the first squad along with the Sarge ahead while you all stay here and help Bob and his son along with their crews get those birds airborne. The cell phones outage is serious, but not enough to scrub this hop, especially since we're already on the ground in China, across the Pacific Ocean only a few hours away from the Shadow's HQ. This is serious shit we're dealing with here and if we don't put an end to the Shadow once and for all it will only be a matter of time before they come through you all to get to me, so our hands are tied on this one men, we have to end this here and now, once and for all. So let's move." CJ said after which, he stood as the other group leaders stood to their feet and made their way down into the belly of the plane where the rest of the group worked on the choppers.

When they walked down the stairs CJ call to his squad of men and told them to lump into one of the armed Range Rovers. After they collected their gear and hopped in, CJ drove out of the rear of the plane, and then drove up onto an eighteen wheeler where two Korean men were waiting as they closed the doors to the trailer. After they locked the doors, both men jumped into the cab of the rig, shifted into gear them pulled off and headed for the border.

Once the huge blue and white truck was under way, the driver of the truck flipped a switch on the dash board, which turned on the lights inside the trailer. As soon as his eyes were fully adjusted to the light going from total darkness, CJ turned and looked Aaron in his eyes and said . . . "Rest up and get comfortable Sarge because in seven hours all hell breaks loose."

After Aaron heard what CJ had to say, he leaned back in his seat then closed his eyes as he thought about Laura. He thought about her smile as well as her beautiful hazel colored eyes. He restated the oath he had made to himself in his head about rescuing Laura and making the Shadow pay. He also thought about Alex Kim Jr and his dark Beatty little eyes and his annoying smirk which was always on his face. Aaron envisioned himself and Alex Jr. in a final hand to hand battle with him knocking all of his teeth out of his mouth. After a few moments he decided to clear his head of all thoughts so he would have a clear mind for when the time arose.

With the truck on its way toward the north Korean border and the other members of infiltrate working to get their choppers airborne, Tracy, Dee-Dee and company crept through the south Korean city of Chinchow. Going from roof top to roof top, they finally reached the shadow's whore house in the center square of the city.

They kept their heads low and out of sight being that this house had armed guards on its roof walking around pulling security on the building. As Dee-Dee looked through a pair of binoculars, she saw Laura through the window on the third floor of the four story building. Her eyes were blind folded, but Dee-Dee saw that her lips had been busted and the side of her face which was turned toward the window was swollen probably from a hit from one of the shadow members in the house. She also saw several well armed men walking through the halls on the third and fourth floor as the whores who had the worked on the first and second.

She tried to think of a way they would go about getting Laura out of that house alive and without any of her group killed, but was at her wits end. She turned over on her butt, placing her back against the side of the short brick wall of the roof and began to whisper to the other members of her group who all had saw the same as she had on the whore house as well.

"If anyone has an idea of how we're going to go about this, I'd really love to hear it right about now." Dee-Dee said with frustration in her voice.

"On the fourth floor alone, I counted thirty armed Shadow members. There are just as many on the third as there were on the forth. To worsen matters, it's a brick building we're talking about, not a wooden one, so blowing a hole through the roof is going to take a hell of a blast not to mention that she's on the third floor and not the top one. The further we go into this impromptu mission, the more and more it seems to be turning into a one way trip!" Stevens shouted as Tracy placed her hand over his mouth in an effort to silence him.

After his short outburst, a hush fell over the entire group as they all looked at each other as if they were waiting for someone to come up with an idea. As the silence among thickened, Big T sat up as the others watched his eyes and face light up as he began to speak. "I've got it, choppers and two 50 pounds satchel charges. Think about it Dee-Dee, if you all were to lay down covering fire for me, with the two charges and a small shape charge, I'll be in and out in a matter of seconds with Laura alive." He said

"First things first Big T, where the hell are we going to come up with a helicopter not to mention the rope we'd need nor the C4 charges. Unless you know someone in country whom you're close to, I can't for see us coming up with necessary equipment required for what you're talking about." Tracy said with a matter of fact tone in her voice.

"Well Mrs. Tracy, I just happen to have a brother stationed at a helicopter airbase depot just on the other side of this city. As far as the charges, I know I'll be able to pick them up from one of the black market dealers in this city. The only question left now is; am I making this quick drive over there and will be given the necessary time I need to get all this stuff Dee-Dee?" He asked as the other members all focused in on her.

Dee-Dee took a moment to look into every single pair of eyes that looked at her and met their questioning stairs with a look of reassurance and confidence. She knew just what her answer had to be if they were going to complete their mission. After she arranged the words just right in her mind, she bowed her head then cleared her throat before she began to speak.

"Mr. Sann, if you would be so kind, please take Big T' where he needs to go. Tracy, Stevens, I'd like you to go with them back to the truck and bring back the sniper rifles. If my memory severs me correctly, Mr. Sann you have 5 M24 Simi-automatic rifles with X10 scopes on them?" She asked

"Your memory severs you correct Mr. Johnson. Each rifle has six, eight round magazines with them. That's not a hell of a lot of amino to get into an extended fire fight with, but for what you're talking about, what I have in the Rover should do. "He answered

"There we have it then, Tracy go with Sann back to the truck along with Big T and Stevens and bring back those guns. Wan and Lee-Ho, I'd like you two to stay up here with me and keep eyes on that building. Let's get moving and keep in mind; Infiltrate is on the ground already and more than likely CJ and the Sarge along with an advance party are on their way into a trap. It's up to us; we're their only hope unless the satellite system comes back on line. Good luck Big T and be careful. "She said with conviction in her voice and a powerful look in her eyes as the members of her group made their way to the truck.

Within a matter of minutes, Big T, Stevens and Tracy reached the truck and unloaded the rifles along with their magazines. After which T and Mr. Sann screeched off toward the outskirts of town, but in that short span of time, once Tracy and Stevens regrouped with the others, their plans slightly altered.

Making their way back onto the roof, Tracy and Stevens saw Lee-Ho and Dee-Dee still watching the house through their binos but noticed that Wan was nowhere in sight. Tracy laid the rifles down then turned toward her sister with a puzzled look on her face as she began to ask . . . "Where the hell is Wan and what is going on sis? I know that look in your eyes and you know I hate it when you get those looks because it most always means trouble for me." She said after the asked the question.

"Here take these and see for yourself," Dee-Dee said as she handed Tracy a pair of binos then said . . . "We saw a member of the shadow walking down an ally away from the whore house who was about Wan's size. That's when an Idea came to me" She said smiling as Tracy cut her off.

"Dee-Dee, don't tell me you sent Wan after that shadow guy, hoping he'd come back with a uniform and a possible way into the upper levels of the house. Sis did you stop to think maybe they have some type of secret hand shake or pass word of the day. I'm sure that an organization as large as the one CJ told us about keeps some sort of security measures in effect for just the type of stunt you're thinking of pulling." She said.

"I don't think so Tracy," Lee-Ho interjected, "Really think about the situation over there in that building. Whores all over the place along with Korean men and US GI's with them in there. I believe Wan who is fluent in Korean will be able to slip in during the confusion and made the extraction smoothly and quietly with the least amount of danger posed on Laura."

You know that he's not going to be happy about this entire situation. In fact, I'll even go as far as to say, he's probably going to kick your ass as soon as he hits the ground." She said with a smirk and a slight laugh in her voice.

"I'll cross that bridge when I get to it, but this is the best and safest way to accomplish this mission, so it must be done this way, hell if your little toad boyfriend Pope and his staff of fuckups had their shit right, we wouldn't even need to be here right now. I would have just called CJ and told him the new development. He would have known what to do and how to get his hop completed." She said as she pulled out a picture of CJ tied to a string around her neck and kissed it.

"Don't worry Dee-Dee; I'm sure CJ wouldn't have placed a total idiot in charge of the Infiltrate nerve center. From my conversations with him over the phone, I feel confident that Pope will push his people and have that satellite system back up and on line in time." Stevens said.

Even as Stevens had spoke of him and his confidence in him, Pope and his crew waited down in the control center of Infiltrate's HQ as they waited for Stacy to return with the necessary component to the satellite relay. Pope sat with his back to the wall of screens as he said a silent prey to himself, hoping that she would return in a timely fashion. Minutes later, his prayers were answered.

On an instrument panel behind him a signal sound chimed as all present in the center looked up to the monitor. They all released a sigh of relief as they saw Stacy drive into the Street Foundation parking complex and without even looking; Pope reached down and pressed a button, which opened the sliding wall to the Infiltrate underground complex. When he saw her drive her truck through the second entrance, he turned to the other four in the room with him and told them to go assist her in carrying the components down into the control center.

As the other four men ran out to help her, Pope sat staring at the wall clock. His look extended far beyond the wall and the clock which ticked away, but reached the region where CJ and the group moved about. He thought on the time it would take to get the first bird airborne as well as the time line involving a drive to the Shadow's HQ by truck. No matter how he tried to work things out and rework them, he reached the exact conclusion every time, they were out of time

He continued with his hundred mile stair until the trance was broken by the sound of Stacy's voice . . . "Hello, Earth to pope, come in Pope" She said smiling.

"Stacy, four fuck'en hours, four fuck'en hours don't even tell me, you got stuck in traffic. God Stacy, Infiltrate is already on the ground and more than likely they have an advance party in route to the shadow's HQ for observation. We have to have this system up in less than an hour. Their lives are in our hands at this point and it's up to us to ensure that they don't end up in the hands of the shadow, now let's move!" HE shouted as they all went to work on reconnecting all of the components together in the satellite console.

Fifty eight minutes later Pope sat back into his seat in front of the wall of screens pressing buttons in every direction. After they listened to the clicks and chirps of the satellite gear activating, they all saw the section of the screens light up with the ready blue color.

After another few seconds of silence, Pope then entered the access codes to the network of satellites in orbit above the earth. Two of the screens flashed up timers count down with white letters, saying time till maximum area operation. The first screen read four hours thirty minutes till NA. 0 and the second one read, only two hours and ten minutes out from the area of operation near the Far East region. Once he read those numbers, he punched up the second screen's access number as it displayed the Korean region on both screens.

Although communications were two hours and some minutes out of his reach, the satellite was close enough to give him the exact locations of all the members of Infiltrate in both North and South Korea. He was able to track them through a location tracking device installed inside the headsets each member wore.

Inside North Korea, he saw six red dots traveling slowly down a highway toward the city of Kaesong. Pope thought to himself, things are going to be very close because they were only about two and a half to three hours out form the city and walking into the Shadow's trap. He wasn't sure who it was heading toward that city, but he knew they were finished if they reached that city before he or Dee-Dee and Tracy could stop them.

While the left screen displayed North Korea and the advanced party's movements, on the other screen to the right of it, he saw the location signal of the smaller group in South Korea. The signals were spread out across the city of Chinchow as one of them appeared to be flying over the city close to the buildings. He saw a concentration of three signals which appeared to be on a roof while a single one moving about in a building a few roof tops away from them.

All of those signals all over that city caused him to start wondering what was going on over there. He held the highest confidence in Dee-Dee and Tracy, but seeing what he saw, caused him to become very worried. For the life in him, he couldn't fathom what they could have been doing with so many signals spread in that manner. He knew it had to have something to do with Laura, but exactly what he just didn't know.

As they all watched the two hour timer countdown till communications were possible and both screens of the two different regions with the headset signals moving, Dee-Dee and her group watched a black hawk helicopter fly close over the building in the distance, while Tracy, Stevens and Lee-Ho loaded and cocked their rifles.

For a while they had been on pin and needles watching Wan go after that member of the shadow for his uniform form atop the roof. They all knew if He wasn't successful, the shadow would be alerted to their presence before the proper time causing the entire mission to be in jeopardy. Luckily enough for them, Wan was able to attack and kill the shadow member quickly and quietly enough not to drew any attention to himself.

From the roof top, they all watched on as he made his way back to the whore house and in without any problems. Through the windows facing them, they even saw him enter into in of the room on the second floor and pass time with one of the many Korean prostitutes moving about the first and second floors.

As soon as he entered the room, Dee-Dee and the others knew just what he was planning to do. They figured he'd use the confusion of the pending fire fight to conceal his movement around the third floor as he would go in and rescue Laura. Since none of them knew if there was a certain hand shake or pass word involved with going up on the third and fourth floors which were full of shadow members, it seemed like a good idea for him to go about things in that manner.

When the black hawk finally reached the whore house, Dee-Dee hand signaled the others to the ready position with their rifles then said. "Don't fire just yet; I'm going to need those guards on the roof snipped off first. After that give them everything we've got. Wait, wait, and wait, just a little longer. Not until Big T's on the rope with his charges."

"We don't have that long sis, look; the look-outs are about to fire on him. It's now or never Dee-Dee." Tracy said as she placed the cross hairs of her scoop on one of the four guards.

Dee-Dee never had the chance to give the command to fire due to the fact; Tracy opened fire and killed the guard with one shot. Before the other guards on the whore house even had the chance to react to their fallen comrade or the approaching chopper, soon as the first shot was fired, the others including Dee-Dee opened fire on them.

As the bullets flew and killed the men on the roof, other shadow members tied to go up on the roof, but every time one of them stepped into the door way and showed himself, he was shot dead where he stood. And while all of the shooting was going on, Bit T hovered over head in the chopper, dropping out glass jars with grenades in them.

He made sure to pull the pins in all of the baseball sized grenades before he placed them into the jars. Big T was careful not to allow the spoon on the explosive to flip off, for he knew that it that were to happen there was a three second timer in motion before it exploded. From the height they hovered at, the grenades would have gone off before they would have reached the roof.

As the shooting continued, everybody redirected their firing to the windows of the house. Some of the shadow members managed to let of a few burst of automatic fire at them. They made sure none of the rounds were shot in vain because every time one of Dee-Dee's group pulled the trigger of their rifle, they killed a man either through the window or trying to made it onto the roof.

The entire situation began to worsen for the shadow as the grenade exploitations began to weaken the roof and as the battle thickened, more and more members of the shadow tried to storm the roof top. At one point, a wall of men purred onto the roof some being shot and killed, most making it taking up defensive positions and returning fire.

They quickly discovered though, that there was no defense against a falling jar and that exploding grenades had no prejudices. For once the other group of jars were dropped, the band of about fifty or so shadow members died as the roof fell in onto the third floor.

Through all of the shooting and exploitations going on all around the building, Wan slipped into the room where Laura was at without any resistance. In the white panted room, there were only two guards with her and they were both shooting their submachine guns out of the windows. Wan quickly shot both of those men in their backs once he was fully in the room. In fact, just as the roof had fallen in on the fourth floor was when Wan had shot the two shadow in the room.

He turned to Laura who was bounded and gagged at the mouth, with a blind fold over her eyes so she couldn't see anything around herself. All of the explosions going off around her made her jump and struggle to get free every time they went off. Wan walked over to her and removed her blind fold first before he had began to speak to her . . . "Listen to me closely Mrs. Hinkley, my name is Wan and I am not with the shadow. I've been sent in here to bring you back to Mr. Williamson and CJ. As soon as I finish getting these ropes off of you, you will do exactly what I say, when I say and move when I tell you to and not question me. Do you understand me?" He asked as he removed her gag

"Yes, I understand." She said in a very timid voice.

As Wan undid her bonds he thought all was going to go well. He had removed all of the ropes but, once she was freed from her bounds, she quickly kicked him in his face. She watched him fall on his back as she jumped to her feet and in a lighting fast motion, stomped him square in the groin. The shooting pain caused him to cringe up into a ball. Quickly as he lay on the floor in pain, she jumped on top of him and pulled out his 45 handgun from his pants and said . . . "Sorry Shadow asshole, but I'm not in the mood to hear any more of your lies. God damn it you asshole, you didn't chamber a round. No matter though because that won't save you."

But before she had the chance to pull the slide back to chamber the round, Wan rolled her from atop him and threw her to the floor. He was still in obvious pain, but still had the sense about him to knock the gun out of her hand. He quickly slapped her twice to make sure he had her undivided attention as he said . . . "Mrs. Hinkley, I understand you ye been through a lot over the past few days, so I'll let that balls shot go, but for future reference, don't ever fuck'en do it again! I know I'm in this shadow uniform, but I had to kill a man to get it to get close to you. Hear all of that shooting out there; well those are my comrades out there. We're all risking our asses just to save your sorry ass, now come on, this roof is about to collapse." He said as he pulled her by the shirt and placed his and her back to the wall.

He stuck his head out into the hall to make sure that the coast was clear and as soon as he saw that the hall was empty, he pulled her by the hand and ran down the hall to the staircase. Two minutes later, they were both running down the street toward the building where the group was set atop.

As the shooting and exploding grenades continued, Dee-Dee realized that Laura was no longer in sight. Through all of the confusion of combat she realized she had completely lost all track of her and Wan's movement throughout the building. She pressed the button on her radio box and began to speak into her mike . . . "Wan this is Mother 1, what's your location and sitrep, over?" She asked.

"Mother 1, it's Wan. Extraction has been completed and as far as my location, turn around." He answered as she and the others turned around and saw him standing there holding Laura by her wrist.

"I don't believe it. How long have you been standing there just watching us provide cover fire for you? I mean hell; we've only been raising enough hell up here to wake up the dead!" Stevens shouted as Tracy cut him off.

"Lee-Ho, keep her head down while we get back to the truck. Mrs. Hinkley, my name is Tracy and this woman going crazy with her machine gun is my older sister Dee-Dee. I am the woman Aaron spoke with over the phone when he called the Street Foundation. I can't even imagine what's going through your mind right about now, but if you just trust me and the others, we'll see to it that you and the Sarge, that being Aaron make it back to up state NY safe and sound." She said.

"Please call me Laura and is Aaron with you or is he up there in that helicopter? I just want to see him please?" She pleaded.

"That's a long story Laura, one that I'm going to have to tell you on our way into Worth Korea, where we will meet up with the main group of Infiltrate, but for now though I have to speak with my sister right now." She said as she leaned over to Dee-Dee, who was still firing shots into the windows of the house trying to hit some of the running member of the shadow.

"Sis what about Big T; we have Laura now, so the question is how do we get past the border and up to the Shadow's HQs?" She asked.

"Remember that's Mr. Sann and Mr., Steven's part in this mission. They're the ones with the connection in this region and as for Big T, let me handle that right now. T this is Mother 1, come in over." She said as she heard his voice come in over her head set.

"This is Big T! What the fuck is going on Mother 1! Is that our target I see down there with you and the others on that roof while I'm up here hanging from a rope being shot at by men in black pajamas?" Re shouted over the net as Tracy and the others all laughed out loud.

"The only thing I can say Big T is that things changed along with tactics. I made a decision and that's all there is to it. Now I need you down here so we can make our next move, how copy."

"I'll give them the hand signal after I drop both of these satchel charges. In the condition that building is in, things will be over real quick."

"I don't, those Hookers on the first and second floors won't survive that cave in. I said that only shadow members were to be killed. I mean it Big T, only members of the shadow, Over!" she shouted in to her mike to no avail.

From the roof top, they all watched the chopper rise slowly into the air and the two satchel charges fall onto the roof. As they simultaneously exploded, Dee-Dee screamed the word No into her mike at the top of her lungs, but Big T told her not to worry about those hookers and the other people in the building's lower floors.

After the explosion, everyone watched on as they saw the two upper floors of the building explode away into dust. In their ears, they all heard Big T explain how he knew that those two charges weren't powerful enough to demolish the entire building. Dee-Dee, who was obviously upset, looked up at Big T as she stood up and said . . . "Big T get your ass down here now, time is wasting and we still have another part to this mission! Oh yes and Big T; I do have some choice words for you when you get down here." She said as he gave the pilot of the chopper his hand signal to set him down.

Moments afterward, the group started to make their way down to the Rover when Dee-Dee took hold of Big T's arm and told him to hold up for a few seconds.

"Big T we've know each other for a long time, but, with that said, I don't ever want to see you do such a stupid thing like that last stunt again! You're not God, so you shouldn't and won't take chances like that with innocent people's lives!" She shouted

"Innocent, innocent, get a fucking grip Dee-Dee! Those were whores and johns looking for a quick fuck! There were no innocent people in that building and like I said over the net, I knew those charges weren't going to demolish the entire building. The shadow members are all dead, we have Laura Hinkley and we still have an entire battle group to save which is made up of mostly friends of mine, so if we're finished here, it's time to hit the road!" He replied forcefully.

She gritted her teeth as she looked him in his eyes, but decided it was best if she let the situation pass. They soon joined the others in the truck; after which, Mr. Sann pulled off toward the highway which lad back to Soul.

Tracy feeling that they weren't heading toward North Korea began to ask questions . . . "Where the hell are we going? This is the road that goes back into Soul. We need to be going in the other direction. Mr. Sann, Stevens, what the fuck is the deal?" She said as Mr. Sann spoke up quickly.

"Look Tracy. I know what the mission is and where you need to go next. The fastest and safest way to reach the Shadow's HQ in Kaesong, North Korea is by airdrop out of a fruit plane bound for China. There is no other way for you to get into that country, so if you don't mind, just sit back, enjoy the ride and shut the fuck up alright!"

After his statement, the others in the truck all looked around at each other as they burst into laughter as Tracy simply gritted her teeth and remained quiet. As they drove down the lonely highway toward Soul, back at Infiltrate HQs, across the international dateline, Pope sat in the control center waiting.

He sat in front of the wall of screens watching the location beacons in the head sets move about. He saw the group of signals moving toward Soul South Korea. On the other screen he counted six signals moving down a highway toward the city of Kaesong, North Korea. After taping on the computer keyboard for a few seconds, he then extended the screen's view of the map to include the region of China where the airfield was located.

There in China near its border with North Korea, He also saw the main concentration of signals and as he continued to monitor the region, he noticed a lone signal break off from the main group of Infiltrate. The red dot moved across the map at a much higher rate of speed than any of the other signals. As he saw it move across the North Korean border to the south, he thought to himself, it had to be one of the choppers in route to meet up with the advanced party.

He watched the speed of the chopper and used his computer to calculate it's time of arrival in Kaesong. The figures of ninety minutes read across the screen as he thought to himself again, that chopper might be high enough to try and signal with the communications system in a few minutes.

As he sat and waited for the satellite in orbit to get closer to the region, he then thought, oh my god, is time standing still? In his mind, things seemed to be moving in slow motion as he watched the advanced party move closer to Kaesong. He wondered what and who was in the party of men as the dot flashed and moved along steadily.

While he watched and waited thinking of the personal in the party, little to his knowledge did he know that CJ and the Sarge were the ones traveling toward the trap. In fact as the truck drove down the highway, in its cab, the group of six men spoke to one another.

"Sarge, you mean to tell me that you didn't tell Laura about your past until Yung Lee was in her face?" CJ asked "I mean what the hell Sarge, were you going to wait until your wedding night to tell her?"

"I knew that one day; I was going to have to tell her about my past, I just didn't know how I was going to do it though. Yung Lee fucked everything up with that bullshit she pulled. I swear CJ, the look on Laura's face seemed like her heart had been ripped out. Then not to mention that shit with the needle and that knockout drug, making it look as if I had fucked her" He said.

"Sarge, I hate to say it, but I did tell you all those many years ago not to fall in love with that crazy Korean bitch in the first place. Look at me man, what was my motto whenever one of those Korean women would try and put the whip appeal on me?" He asked

"I know, I remember, fuck them hoes, you always use to say."

"Yeah, that's right, fuck those hoes man! If you had been saying that from the first start Sarge, most of this shit wouldn't even be necessary. To really tell you the truth though, I think you should double tap that bitch Yung Lee and take your son back to up state NY. That's the only way you and Laura are ever going to have any peace in your life." He said

Before Aaron ever had the chance to respond to CJ's wild comment, they all heard the driver of the trucks, voice come over the speaker in the trailer and tell them that they were 30 minutes out from their drop off point. After he heard that, CJ turned and looked at his men in the rear of the small truck as if he was telling them to prepare themselves to move out.

Once the truck stopped, the driver ran around to the back of the truck then yanked open the double doors of the trailer. As soon as the doors cracked open to let the night light into the box, the upright ramp slammed down to the ground as CJ threw the smaller truck into gear and roared out into night.

When the armed, primer black Land Rover, Defender hit the ground and cleared the ramp, CJ stomped on the break and shifted into first gear. He along with the others in with him, all held up the thumbs up sign as they passed by the Chinese driver on the highway.

The dark night clouds loomed low over the landscape as they partially blocked the light form the half moon and as they moved about the highway in complete darkness with their headlights off. CJ had to rely totally on his memory of the lay of the land and the highway's land marks to reach their destination. As they speeded down the road at 95MPH with their traffic radar jammer activated, Aaron turned to CJ and said that it was payback time.

While he drove, he looked over for a second and saw the Sarge opening his sniper rifle case, piecing it together section by section and said . . . "Not much longer now Sarge, not much longer."

"Once we reach the outer limits of the city, find a high point so I can use the long range scope on my rifle to scan over my place and the Shadow's HQ." He said as CJ noticed something different in his voice.

He had heard him talk with that certain something in his voice before when they both use to work for the shadow. CJ thought to himself, if I could only see his eyes, I'd recognize the look in them because he had seen it all to many times before. The look of strength! The look of hardness! The look of determination!

After a few short minutes of driving, CJ exited the highway, and then drove off of the paved road onto a short hill which over looked the city of Kaesong. When he stopped the truck, Aaron stood to his feet and used his night scope to look over the shadow's HQ as well as his mansion.

In his scope, he saw the different rooms in which the shadow members moved about and tried to locate Alex Kim Jr. but couldn't find him in his sight. He knew that at the range that he was sitting at form the HQ, it would have been an easy one shot kill to take him out.

Over at his mansion, he saw that the lights were on, but most of the curtains and drapes were pulled closed. In the back of his mind he had a feeling Yung Lee at his place, but wasn't certain if it was her or not other member of the Shadow laying in wait for him. When he was done looking over the two places, he began to look over the rest of the Kaesong.

As he scanned, he came across the cemetery where he had remembered Mrs. Kim had been buried in. Next to her pointed headstone, he also saw a larger one to its left and two other smaller ones to the right of Mrs. Kim's as well.

He tried to think of who it would be buried next to her under the other headstones beside her husband. CJ and the others, in the truck all looked up at him as they saw him dropped back down into his seat and say . . . "CJ, I need you to go and clear my mansion for me. I know it may sound crazy, but I've got to go over to that cemetery and pay my last respects to Alex and his wife."

"Sarge what the fuck are you thinking? This is Kaesong, North Korea. What are you going to do, just walk through the city with your sniper rifle across your back and your MP 10 on your shoulder?" CJ asked.

"Well Chris, I'm not going to walk, I'm going to run and as far as this city goes. You know as well as I do that it is 1:30 in the morning, Kaesong is asleep. You know that this is something I have to do before everything kicks off. Really CJ, please, I'll only be there for a short while."

"Alright Sarge, I know this is important to you. Even though I couldn't give a fuck about Kim or his wife, I do remember how close you were to them. You just watch your ass while you're over there Sarge, we'll have that mansion cleared in no time. In fact, by the time you get there, I'll have my feet up on your coffee table the way I use to do, that would always drive you crazy." He said with a smile.

Once their words were completed between each other, Aaron jumped out of the truck and began running toward the cemetery as CJ shifted into gear and drove back onto the road. During the short drive over to the Kaesong city park, CJ told his men to prepare themselves because, once he had stopped the truck, the action was going to be coming at them fast and furious.

Before they reached the park, Santiago, Swango, Blake, Dixon and Surles loaded and checked their weapons as they listened to CJ give them their instructions, telling Swango and Blake to go in through the back and begin their clearing. He told Dixon and Surles they would be going in with him through the front door.

They all nodded their heads as they heard and understood what he was saying to them and when they reached the city park, which was only a mile and a half away from the mansion, CJ and the rest of his squad, hoped out of the truck and made their mad dash across the city. CJ made sure that he pulled into a set of bushes, which hid and covered his gun truck from plane sight and as he ran with his men: (he and them all dressed in black with ninja masks covering theft faces), he loaded and checked his MP 10 before they reached the streets of the city.

Since the mansion was only one and a half miles away from the park, they made it to there and were all set in their attack positions in just under seven minutes. Once Swango radioed that he and Blake were set and ready, CJ looked at the two who were with him, as if to ask if they were prepared, they both held up their thumbs up sign, telling him that they were ready. After he saw that, he radioed team two then told them to move in as he waved his hand forward telling him team to move out.

Once they all stood to their feet and ran at full speed toward the front door, when they reached it, CJ stopped just short of it as Dixon and Surles placed their backs against the walls on either sides of the door. In his mind, CJ knew since most of the lights in the mansion appeared to be on, this was the only way to be safe about going into this huge place.

This way being an all out frontal and rear speed assault; which was what it was as he kicked in the front door and held his gun out in front of himself, as Dixon and Surles swung around to the left and right of him and began to scan the front room for any movements. They heard over their headsets the other group tell them that the first rear room had been cleared and once he heard this, he motioned with his hands telling the other two with him to move into the other room to the left.

In front of them upon entering the main front room, CJ and the other two saw the huge double rap around staircase in the circular front area. As they moved over the grey marble floor, Surles Dixon and Santiago all looked at the letters on the floor which were centered in the room that said AW, and when CJ saw what they were looking at, he said as they stood by the door of the next room . . . "I know what you're all thinking and to answer your questions, yes those letters are real 14 karat gold. They're seven feet long, 4 inches thick and totally solid, through and through. The Sarge never liked them though, Yung Lee had them put in on his birthday as a gift for him."

After the short explanation of the letters, CJ stood just short of the door in the front room, just as he had done with the front door and for the life in him, he couldn't remember if the room they were about to enter was the study or the library. As he looked at Surles, Dixon and Santiago with their backs to the wall on either side of the door and thought to himself; I better check with the other two and see how they're doing before we go any further.

"This is 1, come in 3 and 4. What is your sitrep over?" He asked (Sitrep stands for, situation report.)

"This is 3 #1; we've just cleared the library off the back den. We're about to head into another room. We've received no contact as yet; will keep you informed of our progress, over." Swango said.

"That's a roger 3, we're about to enter our second room, no contact as yet over and out." He said as he stepped forward and kicked in the door.

Once the door was fully opened, Surles and Dixon, swung around, one high the other low with Santiago just off the right shoulder of Surles. With their weapons to bear, CJ himself stood in the center with his gun cocked ready to fire with his finger on its trigger. In the bottom of his sight, CJ saw and recognized Yung Lee sitting on a love seat just off the center of the room. She looked up with her eyes to meet with CJ she was startled again by the far side room door flying open with a thud against the wall. There in the other doorway, CJ and the others with him saw Swango and Blake burst into the room with their weapons to bear as well as Young Lee looked at 3 and 4, then turned in her seat to look at CJ with obvious surprise on her face then said . . . "I don't know who's house you all thought you were trying to rob, but I assure you all of just one thing and that is, you picked the wrong mansion to jack tonight!" She said as she looked at CJ's group with venom in her eyes.

CJ yanked off his mask and smiled as he said. "I see that you still have your vicious temper like I remember. If you've forgotten me, I'm CJ, Aaron's friend from the old days."

"Oh my God, CJ it's been years since I've seen you. Please come in and have a seat. Who the hell are these men with you and why are they still holding their guns on me? I mean them no harm." She said as she stood up and held out her hands, motioning him to come over to the seat with her.

"Team, I want you all to secure the rest of this mansion and give me a push over our net once you've finished. #5 and 4, you finish out the first floor and 3, 6 and 7, I want you all to start clearing the second floor. I'll monitor your progress over my headset." He told them as they moved out into the rest of the house while he sat with Yung Lee on the love seat.

"CJ, why did you send your men through the rest of the house? I'm the only adult in the house and Aaron Jr. is sleeping in his room. In fact, CJ, if you feel your men just have to go through the mansion, please tell them not to wake up my son because, he's just like his father when he gets woken up." She said.

CJ smiled at her as he placed his hand on his radio box unit, but before he began to transmit his message to his men, he asked her which room Aaron Jr. was in as she replied . . . "It's the only room upstairs whose door is closed. Tell them not to make a lot of noise either, because he's a light sleeper just like his father. Thank you CJ." She said with as ear to ear grin as she tapped him on his arm.

"3, 6 and 7 this is #1, hold down any noise up there while you're searching the second floor and stay away from the room that has it door closed, #1 out.

"That's very considerate of you CJ, thank you. So tell me Chris, what have you been up to since you left the shadow?" She asked with a flat look in her eyes.

CJ leaned back into the seat as he placed both of his hands behind his head and interlocked his fingers and began to tell her what it was that he did. While he spoke to her in the study and his men went through the rest of the mansion, over at the cemetery, Aaron knelt down in front of Alex Kim's tomb stone.

It had surprised him that he could still read the Korean symbol writings. He saw the date at which Alex had died along with his epitaph and walked over to his right and read Mrs. Kim's tomb stone and her epitaph as well. With yet another step to his right, he read their youngest son's stone and saw the other stone next to it, to its right then walked over to it. This stone he noticed was different from the others. In fact it had another type of writing on it all together.

Chinese he thought to himself as he tried to remember which symbol meant what in the Chinese alphabet and after a few seconds of staring and thinking, the meanings of what the symbols up and down the tomb stone meant, finally hit him like a ton of bricks. Alex Kim Jr. he read to himself as he also read its epitaph. Here lies the bastard for a son, of a good man and woman. What he read before his eyes, upset him so much, it caused him to begin to talk to himself.

"Wang and Lee thought that they were coming after ne for the Shadow master. If Alex Jr. had been here dead two days after his father's death, than that means; oh good, lord help them!" He shouted as he turned and ran at his top speed toward the mansion.

Meanwhile as he gritted his teeth and ran back toward his place, CJ and Yung Lee continued to talk in the study. They both laughed as they talked of the old days from his days as a member of the shadow. In a short break in their conversation, Yung Lee took the time to ask him a direct question . . ." Yeah CJ, it sure is good to see you again, but what I really want to know is, where is Aaron at? I know he wouldn't have just sent you to do his dirty work for him." She asked with a fake smile.

"Always straight to the point as I remembered you, Yung Lee. To tell you the truth, Aaron went over to the cemetery to pay his last respects to your father and mother. You remember how close he was to them both? He'll be here in just a few minutes. He's not very pleased with you though, he told me something about you sticking him with some kind of needle with a sedative in it. I think that he going to break your ass when he gets here because whatever you did, really upset Laura." He said after he answered her question.

"That bitch will get over it. You know how I am anyways right CJ? To tell you the truth, she's not really cut out for this type of life. She's too delicate a person to be the woman or especially the wife of an assassin. As far as Aaron goes, I'm sure that once he sees his son up stairs sleeping so peacefully, he'll melt like butter in the palm of my hand." She said with a smile.

"Well now that you've mentioned him again, would it be alright if I looked in on little Aaron Jr. before his daddy get here? I'm sorry, but Yung Lee, I just can't imagine you as a mother with the apron, baking a cake & cookies and the whole nine yards. Still though, I would like to see little Aaron Jr. before the Sarge gets here, so I can fuck with him, telling him that his son get his good looks from his mother." He said through a laughing voice.

"Fuck you CJ, come on, I'll show you to his room." She said as she took him by the hand and stood up.

As they walked out of the study and headed toward the staircase back at Infiltrate headquarters, Pope's timer finally flashed, telling him that the satellite was in range for limited communications and when he saw this, he reached for his mike and pressed its button to activate it. On the view screen only the ten digit number for chopper 2 read across in bold white numbers and after he tapped out those numbers, he spoke into the mike as he said . . . "Chopper 2 this is control, can you read me? What is you crew and sitrep over?" He asked

"This is Rick with Co-pilot Jason, crew chief and four door gunners. We're in route to location the Sarge's mansion for the advanced party pick up, over."

"The Shadow had set a trap in that mansion, I repeat; the shadow knew that they were coming. Stay clear of that location, I repeat, stay clear, over" He shouted with the sound of urgency in his voice.

"Control, we're just over the city now, and I can see someone running up the long drive way toward the mansion. He looks like one of ours and I'm going to land just in front of him to stop him from going into the location. How copy control?" He asked

"That's a roger, chopper 2, keep me informed, control out." He said as he terminated his transmission.

Rick dipped the nose of his bird, then swooped down over the mansion's drive way. Since he had his rotor blade sound dampening system engaged Aaron never knew that the chopper in the area until it landed some one hundred feet in front of him. Through his headset, Aaron heard Rick radio him and tell him to get into the bird quickly and once he saw the rear ramp drop open, he ran into the rear of the bird and kept on going toward the cockpit.

As he spoke with Rick and his copilot, inside CJ was only steps away from Aaron Jr.'s door. Before he placed his hand on the door knob to open it, something struck him as odd. My men he thought to himself as he looked down into Yung Lee's jet black eyes. He pressed the button on the box of his radio belt and spoke into his mike as he watched Yung's face go blank.

"All units this net, this is 1 with a commo check. How copy over?" He said to a clear communications net.

"Maybe it's something in the walls or this floor that's preventing their transmissions from reaching your radio." She said with yet another fake smile.

"I don't think so Yung. I'll take a quick peak in on Little Aaron, and then go check on my men." He said as he placed his hand on the door knob and turned it open.

As he opened the door to the room, before he had the chance to notice anything, Yung Lee diverted his attention with this question . . . "So you said that Aaron went over to the cemetery on the other side of the city, huh?"

He turned and looked at her as he answered her strange question . . . "Yeah Yung." He said as he began to turn around as he continued to speak . . . "I told you that he would be here in; . . . Uh my God! What the Fuck is that Yung! I thought you said your son was in this room?" He shouted as the look of shock and disbelieve flashed across his face.

As he stood there just in the inside of the room, he saw not a crib with a baby or a bed with a child in it, but instead he saw in the center of the room, a clear glass container with what looked like the fetus of an unborn child in water. After seeing this, the only thought that ran through his mind, was for him to get the fuck out of that room, but when he took the first step backwards, he felt a sharp pain in his left cheek and jumped forward to one knee.

After the needle's sticking sensation, he turned and looked up at Yung Lee who he saw holding a needle in her hand with a mile wide smile on her face. She walked over him as he stumbled and tried to make it back to his feet, but was unable due to the fact that he was beginning to lose consciousness.

"Oh that's right CJ, you to have fallen victim of my trusty little needle with sedative in it. You see, when you left the shadow, something in and about Aaron changed, and once he disappeared two years after you did along with the constant stress of my brothers harping, it caused me to lose my baby which Aaron didn't know about in the first place. When I lost it, the doctors told me that it was a boy, so I took it from them and kept it here in this room, waiting for the day when I could show both you and Aaron what you did to me and my baby. You'll get off lucky CJ, I'll only kill you once your usefulness is done, but as for Aaron and his white bitch, they'll pay with torture until they both beg for their deaths!" She said as CJ losing consciousness saw the book case on the wall slide open and several Korean men in Shadow uniforms come out and walk toward him.

He tried to make one last fight and stand to his feet, but the sedative was too strong to be resisted. He was no match for the six Shadow members who walked over to him and carried him away into the night.

As this happened on the inside, on the outside, just off the front steps, Rick and Aaron tried to make out a strategy but, as they talked one of the gunners in the back yelled forward and said . . . "Enemy choppers coming in at our six. It looks like they're heavy gunships!"

In a flash of instincts, Rick grabbed the thrust control stick and yanked up as he moved his joystick to the left. As the bird rose into the air, a rocket hit the ground and missed them by only a fraction of a second. He completed his cork screw maneuver he had learned from his dad, to come around to a full view of four Havoc attack helicopters still coming toward them.

During the sudden lift off, Aaron had been thrown against the side wall of the chopper, where he stayed due to centrifugal force. Once the bird was still for a moment, he fell down into a seat below him, where he strapped himself in for the rough and bumpy ride he knew he was in for.

After he cinched himself in, he clicked his headset to the choppers internal frequency as he began to speak to Rick . . . "Can we lose them Rick?" He asked with the sound of concern in his voice.

"All I have to go by are these maps which are about thirty years old but, if they're still accurate, I'll be able to lose them in the mountains not far away from here. It's not going to be easy, but I think that I can handle it. If I had my dad here, I would feel a hell of a lot more confident but, you have to work with what you've got. Hold on back there Sarge, we're at the first peak and I'm going in!" He said as he rolled the chopper over and dipped down into the darkness of the mountain range.

CHAPTER VI

THE SITUATION LOOKED dim in the skies over North Korea as four heavily armed and armored Havoc attack helicopters closed in pursuit with their guns and rockets blazing. As Rick trembled in his pilot's seat as he entered the mountains near the North, South Korea border, he began to wonder if he would live to see his 18th birthday.

As the scenery wizen by and rockets impacted against the mountain rock face, Aaron said a silent prey to himself as he thought, I've always hated to travel by helicopters and now my life is in the hands of this kid, who is was only seventeen years old. He tried to clear him mind of Rick's age and lack of experience and tried to steady his stomach as he felt the chopper go into a hard jerk to the right then drop for some five seconds. He wasn't sure of what was going on with the attack choppers behind them, but he knew that Rick was going something right, because he was still alive.

In the darkness of the mountain tops, Rick pushed his chopper to its limits. He was certain, he didn't have to worry about any high tension wires being in his way Because of the fact that they were so high up. His crew chief, who looked through the rear small window of the bird, told him that one of the Havoc's had slammed into a rock face and that there were only three still in pursuit.

The only guide that Rick had to go by was Jason, his co-pilot who told him, either hard right or hard left as he constantly talked and told him what was coming up next. He knew as well as Rick did, that the only chance they had against those Havocs, was to out maneuver them, because they were just as fast as they were and had more armament to throw at them.

In fact, every time that one of the Havocs pilots got a clear look at the fast moving bird they were chasing, they would shot off a rocket and let a couple of bullets fly from their chain gun. It was tricky for them to hit the Chinook though, because of the fact that they were a single person chopper and it was up to them to both fly and gun at the same time and in that mountain range that wasn't easy.

In the back of the Chinook, the crew chief jumped to his left as he saw the lead Havoc open up with its chain gun and hit the rear ramp which poked holes through it. He keep in constant contact with Rick and Jason, telling them what the position of the enemy birds was and what the type of formation was that they were in.

As Jason told Rick hard right, the chief watched as the second attack bird slammed into another mountain face and exploded into a bright ball of frames. He then told them both that there were only two birds left as he felt the chopper go into a hard roll to its right and narrowly escape a servo of rockets form the lead Havoc.

Jason looked down at his map and saw something that they could use to their advantage in the darkness . . . "Rick just ahead I want you to air break then turn to the right and max elevate with our broad side toward the enemy birds. You know what I'm talking about?" He asked as they both heard the chief in the back yell into his headset . . . "Hard left, hard left!"

After he rolled the bird to the left then up, Jason saw a long trail of glowing bullets wiz by his right side window. Rick kept his eyes forward as he spoke to him and answered his question.

"You're talking about aerodynamic breaking against a mountain aren't you? Just begin to count down from twenty to when it's time for me to execute the maneuver. I can't see shit with this night vision scope on; it sucks. Never mind if I can do it or not because if I fuck this up, none of us will be around to notice anyways."

Jason's face drew blank for a moment as he listened to what Rick had said and then took in a deep breath—looked down at his map and began his count down from twenty. In the rear, Aaron and the other crew members all listened as they knew what was coming up next.

His stomach was already churning from the constant banking and rolling to the left and right and wasn't looking forward to what was yet to come. When he heard Jason's count get down to eight, he thought to himself as he gritted his teeth, oh shit, I'm going to throw up.

"4-3-2-break now Rick." He shouted as he felt the chopper jerk over to its left and roll over on its side in mid air and keep travelling forward.

In knowing what was about to happen, Rick lowered the landing wheels which touched the mountain face just as the aerodynamic forces of the blade stopped the helicopter in mid air. With an almost bungee cord effect from the stop, Rick worked the controls and elevated the chopper up as he rolled the chopper away from the mountain face with his broad side toward the enemy birds.

Jason's gamble paid off as both of the door gunners on the left side zeroed in on the Havocs as they struggled to climb away from the Mountain without hitting it. With a bright cascade of lights, the rear and front guns opened fire on the helpless Havocs as their under sides were exposed to their full wraith of fire from the GE mini-Guns of the Door gunner. Once both gunners fully opened up the 8 rotating barrel fully automatic machine guns, it appeared as if there were waterfalls of glowing bullets dancing away from the Chinook. As they continued to pump more and more rounds into the under bellies of the Havocs, they burst into huge balls of fire.

Once the light from their explosions lit up the skies, Rick stopped the chopper from elevating, dip its noise then preceded back toward Kaesong.

"Pilot to crew, crew check over. Sound off." He said.

"Gunner 1 up."
"Gunner 2 Up."
"Gunner 3 up."
"Gunner 4 up."

"Crew chief up, all's well in back." He said as Aaron cut in and said . . . "Somebody get me another air sickness bag god damn it, I'm gonna lose it again—Blaw . . ." He said as he threw up again into a near full air sickness bag.

Shortly afterwards, once he recovered from his air sickness, he told Rick to fly over the river which flowed into and through Kaesong~ He took one of the inflatable one man rafts that were in the emergency kits then told Rick to drop the rear ramp once they were over the river.

He was certain that he didn't have to tell Rick he needed to decrease his speed in order for him to jump out safely and just before he was ready to go, he took off his sniper rifle then placed it into the hands of the crew chief and asked him his name . . . "You can call me Johnny, Sarge." He quickly snapped with a smile as he grasped the rifle with both hands.

"Well Johnny, I'm handing you me second woman and since the Shadow HQ is right on the river and has an access point under it on the river, I'm going to need her to stay here safe and dry in good hands. She's very temperamental and hates the water. When she's unhappy,

I'm unhappy—and when I'm unhappy Johnny, I'm not a very nice to the person who has made her or ME unhappy." He said as he looked him in his eyes

"Say no more Sarge. I'll guard your second lady with my life. Hey Sarge, Rick has just told me to tell you, we're here so get ready, he's about to drop the ramp. Good luck Sarge, you just make sure that you watch your ass so I'll be able to hand you your second lady in person and not lay it across your body bag, ok"

As the chopper slowed and the rear ramp dropped open, Aaron winked his eye at Johnny as he noted his head and inflated the raft. With it in his left hand and a paddle in his right, and his black MP 10 with silencer along with his black pack filled with clips, he hopped out and placed the raft under himself as he splashed down onto the calm running river.

While he paddled silently up the river and Rick flew over to a field just outside to city limits and set down, high above in the skies over Kaesong, a midsized C141 opened its rear ramp. Inside the plane Dee-Dee's along with her group waited with parachutes strapped to their backs.

Mr. San stood by the ramp and wished them good luck on the next phase of their mission, since he had already explained to them before they had even left, that he wouldn't be jumping with them. As the red light turned to yellow Dee-Dee checked Laura's chute one last time and when the light turned to green, signaling them that they were over the drop zone Big T along with most of the group jumped out into the dark skies.

Dee-Dee didn't like the idea of Laura having just been rescued, being taken right back into the Shadow's HQs, but she knew she had no choice. She knew that once the plane landed, it would he searched from top to bottom by the North Korean customs agents; not to mention the fact that Laura didn't even know how to use an MP 1O until she showed her how to. With all of the others already on their way down, Dee-Dee gave one last tug on Laura's shoulder straps the slapped her across her ass. She looked into Laura's eyes where she asked her if she was ready for all of what was coming up.

Laura swallowed in a deep breath and nodded her head and as she did Dee-Dee took her by the hand then jumped out of the plane into the darkened skies over Kaesong. Their chutes opened quickly and after hers was fully deployed, Dee-Dee used her radio to call the other members of her group as they quickly descended upon their targets. Everyone came back quickly over the net without any prolonged chatter since they had been in contact with Infiltrate HQ and the main group in china which was still on the ground.

They all knew going in that CJ and four of his men in his squad had been captured and that they may have been listening in on their transmissions as they descended. On the way down, Bit T used his night scope where he zoomed in on the roof of the Shadow's HQ building. When he saw four look outs posted in the roof with weapons, he slid his gun into position and began to fire off his silenced MP1O.

He only let go six rounds as he saw the four men drop dead where they stood. Since he was directly above those men, they never knew what hit them as he sent them to heaven or hell.

Once Big T landed, he quickly gathered his chute and scanned the roof top with is weapon for any enemy movement and as he did that, the other members of the group landed while Dee-Dee brought up the rear. After they all gathered their chutes, she had them assemble around her as she pulled out a floor plan of the huge building they were standing on.

As Big I look at the strip map, he thought to himself, damn, this entire building is just one huge warehouse that has been turned into a three story office building with storage space. We'll never make it out of this alive. He was careful so he didn't show any facial expressions, as he cared about Dee-Dee too much to let her know just what he thought about her plans.

Just as they made their plans on the roof, at that exact moment on the waters of the river just below them, Aaron paddled his raft onto the banks just under the pier of the building. As he waded through the water effortlessly without making a single ripple, he saw that there were only two Shadow members guarding the pier entrance.

He stepped out of the water under the pier where heard one of the men walk down to the end of it as the man began to take a piss in the river. When he heard the men's urine splashing down into the water, he quickly ran toward the building to a point where he could jump onto the pier with ease.

With catlike speed and agility, he hopped onto the pier and shot the Shadow member who stood by the door, then whipped around with blinding speed and threw one of his knifes dead center in the back of the neck of the one who was still urinating. As the man's body fell towards the water, he made his way into the building before the dead man's body hit the water.

Only one thought ran through his mind as he quickly moved down the hallway of the basement, and that was to knock out the power to the entire building and send it into darkness before daylight hit. Once he reached the hall with which the generator room was located, he saw yet another group of Shadow members walking toward him from the corner of his eyes.

He wasted no time as he raised his weapon and span in their direction while he let off a burst of shots. The six rounds hit the men sending them all to their deaths before they knew what had hit them as their lives slipped away into eternity.

He tried to think to himself as he entered the room, what room CJ and his men may have been held in the building and which route would get him the fastest. The second floor, he thought as he cut of the wires to the generators and broke off the switch. He remembered there being a holding room down from the Shadow master but he also remembered that the only way to it was to reach the main staircase by going through the cargo hold down the hall from the room he was in.

This presented a problem for Aaron. He remembered there was always many Shadow personnel in the cargo hold at all times. As he stood in the doorway of the generator room trying to decide whether or not if he should go through the cargo hold, he heard about four or five men stumbling down the hallway as they spoke to each other in Korean. He listened to them as they drew closer and closer as he heard and understood what they were saying.

He raised his gun to the ready as he heard one of them say; the damn thing must have blown again. In his mind, he knew he'd never let them have a chance to Find out. Once they were all in range, judging from the sounds of their voices, as they drew closer, he span into the pitch black hallway and opened fire on all of them standing there.

He caught them all completely by surprise as he watched through his night sights, as they tried to turn and run once the first of the rounds lit up the darkness. He fired two seven rounds burst out of his weapon before he saw all five of them drop to their deaths as their blood stained the floor and walls.

After he blew down the hole of his barrel, he slipped off his night sights, took in a deep breath, then thought to himself, fuck it, if I'm walking into a trap then I'll walk into it with my ears as my guide. That's the only way I stand any chance of holding out until reinforcements get here.

As he stepped over the dead bodies on the floor, he ran using light foot steps down the hall toward the cargo hold door. Since his destination was down a few halls with a couple of turns to make, he paced himself as he went along and as he made his way through the darkened building, moments earlier, as he was just reaching the pier on his raft, in a room on the second floor, CJ came too in a room with his men.

His eye sight was still slightly blurred from the effects he was still feeling from the drug, Young Lee had stuck him with, but once he heard a familiar rough and scratchy Korean voice speak, he snapped right out of his daze . . . "I never thought see you again Mr. Johnson. Even my father knew that you hated this place, so now my question is why have you come back?" The Shadow master complete in glass mask and all said.

"Untie my hands and feet and I'll show you why I've come back. Where the Sarge's woman at you fagot!" He shouted as he jerked violently at his chains.

"Why Mr. Johnson, I hardly think that you're in any position to demand answers from me. In fact, since you're in my Head Quarters, that simple fact alone will ensure that Williamson comes to me on my terms and when he does, he's mine."

"Be careful of what you wish for Alex Jr.! Hell we both know that you might get you wish and that one on one, he'd mop the floor with you! That's why I'm chained and bound by the feet; you're a bitch with his clit in a bind." He said with raw emotion and venom in his eyes.

After his statement, the Shadow master jumped to his feet then walked over to him as he pulled out his gun, and placed it against CJ's nostril as he said . . . "I always knew that niggers were stupid, but I guess that you think that I need you alive since I want Williamson to

come after you. Here's a news flash, I don't need you or any of your
men that you brought with you. I'd be happy and more than obliged to
show you what I mean Johnson." he said as CJ and the others watched
as he pointed his gun toward Surles and pulled its hammer back.

Just as the gun's hammer reached its locking position and Surles's
eyes met with the one eyed stair of the 357's barrel, the lights in the
office and building went out. Surles let off a sigh of relief as he thought
this new development had saved his life, but just as he and the others
started to breathe easy, they all heard and saw the gun go off as the
shadow master said . . . "What makes you all think just because the
lights are out, your lives are saved. This just prolongs what's in store
for you, that's all. CJ your life will end as soon as Aaron Williamson's
eye meets your own. Then I'll kill him as well." He said as he let go of
CJ's jaw with his left hand and stepped back into the darkened room.
CJ tried to use his ears to pick up any signs of movements in the room,
besides that of his men, but as he did, he felt a gag go around his
mouth as the Shadow master slapped duck tape over his eyes.

Meanwhile as that transpired in the Shadow Master's office on the
second floor, down on the first floor, Aaron made him way toward the
cargo hold. As he increased his speed, he sensed the huge double doors
as he drew near them and stopped just before he reached them.

He reached into his belt, grabbed another clip of ammo as he pop
out the used one and slapped in the new one into place as he cocked
it to the ready. His heart raced as he felt the sudden rush of adrenalin
kick start his body. After he took in a deep and calming breath, he

said to himself, this is it, I live or I die as he opened one of the doors without making a sound and stepped into the huge cargo hold area.

Before he ever had the chance to set his back against the wall next to the doors, he felt as he saw, several bright lights click on him which blinded his eyes sight. Through pure instinct alone just before his eyes sight went white, through the corner of his eye, he saw a number of tall, wooden cargo boxes by the wall and with cat like agility; he sprang over to them as he noticed that there was enough space for him to fit between the boxes and the wall.

Once he landed though, before he rolled back to his feet, to get a gage on what it was he was dealing with, he heard a familiar female voice shot out in Korean; End of the line Williamson; your time has come. Only one name flashed across his mind's eye as his sight slowly returned to him. Lyn Ty, that bitch, daughter of Kim Li Snag, the dictator of this god forsaken country and never one of his biggest fans. After his eyes were fully back, he stood up from behind the boxes to see just who that bitch has with her.

Jesus Christ he exclaimed in his mind as he counted at least one hundred Shadow members and saw Lyn Ty standing on a small stand with a spot light trained on him. He looked about the room as only one question rang across his mind, which was, how the fuck am I going to get out of this one?

"Look about Williamson; you're out gunned, one hundred to one. Come out from behind those boxes and stand before me like a man!" She shouted over a bull horn

"Lyn Ty, did Young Lee send you in her place for this foot I intend to put in her ass, because if she did, then let me tell you something, ass kick'ens are on special today in my book, kick one bitch in her ass, kick the other one for free." He said through a shit eating grin.

"Always the smart ass just as I've remembered you. You know something Williamson, I never understood just what Yung Lee my Nuna ever saw in you, but I'm not telling you anything that you didn't already know, right Williamson?" She asked condescendingly

"Hell, you don't and didn't ever have to tell me that you didn't understand what Yung and I had. I knew that just because of the simple fact that you ate more cunt than a little bit, ya fuck'en dike. Anyways Lyn what do you want out of my life?"

"I want your life you bastard American nigger. All those many years ago, my father told my uncle; Yung Lee's father that he didn't think it was a good idea to allow non-Koreans into the Shadow because you couldn't be trusted. He was right, your friend left first, and then you betrayed us as well. All of you Americans are the same way, you use some one until their usefulness is at an end, and then you dump them like garbage. I'll not allow for you to get away with it though Williamson, do you hear me; I will not! If you will not come back to the Shadow, then you and all of your friends will surely die this very day. The choice is yours Williamson.

As Aaron had listened to her ramble on he noticed some movement in the window of the third floor which looked in high over the cargo hold area. He remembered that all of the three floor in the building had different staircases which all led to the cargo hold and as he looked at Lyn, he used his top vision to see if he could make out who or what it was that was up there.

Once he stepped from behind the boxes and began to walk toward Lyn Ty, on the third floor, Dee-Dee and her group watched and wondered as Laura had to be held back as she saw him walk forward with his hands in the air. Big T told her that if she was to alert them down there of their presents up here, it would seriously jeopardize his life at that point in time. He told her to calm down as he too watched Aaron stop and begin to speak as he noticed what he thought was eye contact with Aaron.

Big T let go of Laura, and stepped over to Dee-Dee and Tracy, who were both standing on the chests of two dead Shadow members they had just shot and killed as they reached the windows. With a twinkle in his eyes, he told them that if they struck hard and quick, they'd be able to kill most of the Shadow members in the cargo hold before they would have the chance to harm the Sarge.

After she heard this, Dee-Dee looked at her sister, then down at Laura as she saw her looking down at Aaron with tears of fear in her eyes and asked him what he was thinking of. He told her that if they split the group and sent down three of their group with guns and left the other three on the third, that they would cover most of the room with a confusing blanket fire.

Once she heard what he had to say, she told Tracy and Lee Ho to go with him and to do just what he told them to do. T told her that he would give her a push over their net once they were set in position as he and the other two headed for the staircase leading to the cargo hold.

As the left, Dee-Dee stepped off of the dead man and walked over to Laura then put her arm around her shoulder and looked softly into her eyes as she began to speak to her . . . "Hey Laura don't you worry, we're going to get him out of this yet. I can't even imagine what is running through your mind considering all that you've been through in the past few days, but what I need to know is, are you going to be able to fire your weapon when the time comes?" She asked in a very soft and delicate voice.

"I know I shouldn't feel this way, but I can't help feeling somewhat responsible for getting him into this situation he's in down there. If it wasn't for me, he would have never come back to this country. Sorry Dee-Dee, I know that I'm rambling. I will be able to help with Aaron down there as well as be there for you as we get CJ out of this mess alive and well." She said with both compassion and conviction in her voice as she looked Dee-Dee straight in her eyes.

While Dee-Dee looked at her with the look of appreciation in her eyes, Big T's voice came across her headset and told her that they were set and ready. After she heard that, she turned to the rest of her group and told them to get their guns ready and in position to start shooting through the windows.

Two floors below on the cargo hold floor as Aaron listened to Lyn Ty shout at him as she put her final demand across to him; Pledge your loyalties and devotion to the Shadow and my father right here and now or die this very morning Williamson, that's what is left for you.

He took a second to look around the room as if he was truly thinking about what she had just said to him, but in reality, he was trying to see who it was moving around in the window on the third floor. While he let his eyes wander, he heard the bolts being pulled back into firing position by the Shadow members as he made eye contact with Laura through the window. He saw Dee-Dee and Stevens as well as the Chinese body guard he remembered seeing on board Stevens white jet. He saw Laura signal for him to get out of the way as she held up her MP 10 and pointed her finger at it.

After he saw this, he looked back at Lyn Ty with a huge smile on his face as he said . . . "Now hear this you fucking slope dyke! I'll NEVER pledge but Hatred towards you or your father! I ALWAYS hated you & Yo Daddy! Oh Yeah one more thing; kiss my big black Mandingo ass!!"

Just as he said the word ass, he jumped back into a flip and continued to flip until he was back behind the huge cargo boxes by the wall. Right as he went into his motion, everything seemed as if it was going in slow motion to him as he saw the glass window on the third floor burst into chards with tracer rounds of automatic fire spray out from behind them.

He watched as the first stream of bullets hit their targets as the men of the Shadow fell to their death. Once he saw Stevens walking his rounds toward the lights, he pulled out his night scopes and prepared for the darkness as the search lights were shot out.

Once the darkness covered the cargo hold, he saw some tracer rounds fly up from the floor up to the third floor window, but as soon as that happened, he saw a flood of glowing rounds fly in from the door in the corner of the cargo hold and hit the Shadow men as they tried to fire back. With the entire floor in full view under his night vision sights, he saw most of the men of the Shadow fall as he noticed Lyn Ty heading for the staircase which led to the second floor and the Shadow master's office.

He put on his headset, clicked it on, and then told Dee-Dee that he was going after Lyn Ty. After she heard what he had to say, Dee-Dee saw Laura strap her weapon across her shoulder and make a dash for the staircase. She yelled into her mike, as she tried to tell her to stay out until all of the men in the cargo hold were dead, but she heard no answer.

Laura ran past Big T, Tracy and Lee ho as they stopped firing and followed along with her. They shot men at random as they all ran from box to box and in a bold move. Suddenly though without warning, Laura jump out from behind her box and light up the entire room as she Chris crossed the room with automatic fire.

Big T looked as Tracy and said . . . "God damn, that girl is bad. I thought you and Dee-Dee said that she didn't know how to fight."

"I know hell I thought she didn't either! Now come on let's keep up with her before she gets too far ahead for us to watch her back!" She said as she pulled him by his arm and ran after her.

"Tracy this is Mother 1, we're on our way down. I'll meet up with you on the second floor. How copy?" She asked as Tracy listened over her headset.

"That's a roger Mother. Hurry up! This white girl is going cold Rambo all over the place down here. Trace out."

After she terminated her transmission, she and Big T jumped from behind the boxes and held their guns to the ready as they followed Laura onto the staircase. As they turned the corner and looked up the long flight of stairs, they all saw several dead Shadow members laid out on the staircase.

Tracy counted the bodies to herself as she climbed the stairs. Damn, there were fifteen men laying in wait for someone to turn that corner but, they didn't make it. As they reached the top of the staircase, Laura ran out into the hallway without bothering to look left or right as Tracy who was only a few steps behind her keyed her radio and told her to watch herself as she went into the different rooms and hallways.

Once she reached the doorway at the top of the staircase, she looked left to see Laura then right just in time to see two members of the Shadow jump down from the support beams in the rafters. She quickly opened up on them with her gun in automatic fire without hesitation, but not before one of them managed to let loose with a burst from his submachine gun himself.

The glowing rounds struck the wall just barely missing Tracy as she lit up the hallway. Laura heard the blasts from the shadow member's weapon and jumped to the floor, and quickly rolled over to see what was behind her, but when she looked down the hall, all she saw was two dead bodies on the floor as Big T, Tracy and Lee ho ran over them toward her.

Tracy leaned over her once she reached her where she told Laura that she owed her one for saving her life. After that, they picked her up as they heard Dee-Dee come across their headset and tell them that she and her group was on the staircase in route to their location. When she reached them, she pulled out her layout of the building in hopes of finding the Shadow master's main office, but as she knelt down with Big T flashing a red light on her papers, Tracy saw a movement down the hallway behind her sister.

Without warning, she dove at Dee-Dee and knocked her back against the wall, while the others all looked up just as they saw a bullet fly over Tracy's airborne legs and strike Lee Ho square in the center of his chest. Big T, Stevens and Wan all hit the floor as Lee Ho's body fell to the floor with them as they all looked down the hall to see Lyn Ty light up the hallway with another shot from her 44 magnum revolver. Dee-Dee kissed her sister when her back hit the wall once she saw Tracy had saved her from certain death.

Five or more shots flew down the hall as most of them hit the walls, while a few of them struck the floor just in front of Big T's face as it kicked up floor debris in his eyes. After hearing all six rounds go off, Dee-Dee whispered into Tracy's ear as she told her, "how about we kill that ugly slope bitch". After she heard that, Tracy rolled off of her sister, then fired a short burst in Lyn Ty's direction to keep her off balance as Dee-Dee jumped to her feet and took after her down the hall. As Tracy flipped to her feet, she yelled back at Big T and the others as she told them to find the Sarge while she took after her sister.

Big T yelled into his mike as he told them both to watch their asses as he made his way back onto his feet then turned around to see Laura already running away from them. He looked down at Stevens as he leaned over Lee Ho's lifeless body with a deep look of regret in his eyes while Wan knelt down on the other side of the body. Stevens looked up at Big T and said . . . "He was only 22 years" . . . He stammered as Big T quickly cut him off . . . "We don't have time for this shit right now Stevens. We have to keep up with the Sarge's girl"

He reached down and grabbed Stevens by his arm, then picked him up as he started down the hallway after Laura. As all of this happened down the hall, up the very same hallway, Laura ran in full stride as she ripped her way through the darkness with her night vision sights on, she didn't bother to scan to the left or right as she approached a T at the end of the hallway.

Once she stepped into the hallway intersection and planted her foot to make the cut down the new hallway to the left, she felt something hit her and as it took her off her feet. Just as she hit the floor, she ripped her night vision sights off to see Aaron staring at her in disbelieve.

The very second their eyes met through the darkness, she reached up, and threw her arms around his neck, then pulled his face toward hers with all of her might as she showered him with kiss after kiss. In-between each kiss, all she could say was I love you; I love you as tears of joy flowed down the sides of her cheeks.

"I love you too baby and I'll never allow anything like this to happen to you ever again. I swear, honey, I swear." He said as he slipped his hands over her mouth and shushed her with his other finger.

Just as that happened, the two of them heard loud running footsteps coming toward them, as he wasted no time in flipping back to his feet while he drew his 44 auto handgun and put his night vision back on.

As he looked down the sight post of his gun, he saw and recognized just in the nick of time, Big T and Stevens along with Wan advancing toward their position. Laura quickly placed her arm on his as she looked through her night sights and told him that they were with her. After he lowered his gun, he looked down at her and said . . . "I want you to keep by my side Ms Laura. I'm not taking my eye off of you. Are you with me?" He asked as he took hold of her hand.

"For the rest of your life Williamson, you're stuck with me." She stated with pure conviction in her voice.

"That's it then isn't it Sarge? Let's go and put an end to this shit once and for all!" Big T shouted as he pulled the blot back on his weapon and let it snap forward.

"And we'll end it together, me and you hand in hand. Come on, I think they're in the Shadow master's main office just around the corner. Oh yeah and Stevens, I owe you big time for all of your help in saving her man. I mean it!"

"We're even Sarge. If you remember, I still owed my very life to you and your compassion for a crying young upstart who got into some shit that was way over his head. This was the very least that I could do." He said as he placed his left hand on Aaron's right shoulder and smiled from ear to ear.

"Look you two, I hate to break up this little love feast along with walk down memory lane, but CJ and the others aren't out of this yet. So let's go kick some more Shadow ass."

With Big T having said those words, Aaron turned and kept hold of Laura's hand as he began to run down the hallway. As T, Stevens and Wan followed him closely, in another section of the second floor, Dee-Dee closed in on Lyn Ty's heals. In her haste to make it back to the staircase, she made a wrong turn into a short dead end hallway and just as she tried to change direction, Dee-Dee tackled her as she hit Lyn Ty in the center of her back with her shoulder. Lyn felt a sharp and sudden pain as she saw the floor rush up to meet her face with a brilliance flash of light, followed by even more pain.

Dee-Dee quickly sprang to her feet after she tackled Lyn Ty, and then kicked her for a few more times square in her ribs with a thud. Kick after kick, with each punt, she spoke in-between each one as she said . . . "You can (KICK), talk your ass (KICK) off because, (KICK) I'm gonna, (KICK) Break my foot off up it, (KICK) you Korean bitch!" she said with yet another kick in her ribs.

All in all, she kicked her about 20 times before she heard her sister's voice in the distance. When she began to hear Tracy's footsteps drawing closer, she stepped back away from Lyn, to allow Tracy space to deliver a few blows herself, but in that split second of time, in one blink of an eye, Dee-Dee saw the bottom of a foot sweep around as it struck her straight across the eyes.

Once Tracy rounded the corner she made it just in time to see her sister falling to the floor with her hands covering her face and Lyn Ty recovering from a spinning round house kick. She quickly reached into her belt and slipped her fingers into her brass knuckles as she ran toward Lyn Ty and said . . . "Here bitch, try this on for size!" She said just as she landed her punch flush against Lyn Ty's jaw bone.

The power of the blow multiplied with her forward momentum, sent Lyn Ty off of her feet to land some three to four feet further down the hall. To her surprise, Lyn jumped to her feet then shook her head as she cleared away the cobwebs created by the blow, then slowly walked toward her as she smiled maniacally. Dee-Dee quickly made her way back onto her feet to stand beside her sister as they both watched and listened as Lyn Ty said . . . "So ladies, shall we dance."

With said, she jumped into a flying kick which struck Tracy in her chest just as Dee-Dee came across the top of her still out stretched leg with a right cross punch to her jaw. Once Lyn hit the floor, she whipped her leg into a spinning kick and took Dee-Dee's legs out from underneath her as Tracy hopped back onto her feet.

She tried to jump at Lyn, but her feet proved to be too quick to handle as she carried her spinning kick around into a jumping round house kick, which hit her in her stomach. After Tracy hit the wall with a thud, Dee-Dee flipped back to her feet and yelled, come on at the top of her lungs as she got into her defensive stance.

In the blink of an eye, Lyn span around as she extended her arm and clenched her fist and with pin point accuracy, lined it up with the bridge of Dee-Dee's noise. To her surprise, she caught her blow in her right hand, and then flipped her over her back onto the hard wooden floor with a thud.

She tried to gather herself as she laid on her back, while sharp spurts of pain shot through her back as she saw Tracy step into her field of vision. With her shocked with pain and slowed by exhaustion, the only thing that she could do, was look and listen as Tracy said . . . "In case you didn't know, sister girls from Brooklyn won't ever lose a two on one fight. And you can take that one to the bank, bitch!" she said as she stomped her foot across Lyn Ty's forehead.

Once they saw that she was out for the count, they preceded to tie her hands and feet together, using industrial plastic draw ties and after they were done, they gave each other Hi fives as they tried to contact the others. After a few seconds of listening to static over their headsets, they finally decided to try and rejoin the others by the Shadow master's main office.

After they made that decision and began to run back toward the office, down around a few corners on the very same floor, Aaron and the others closed in on the main office of the Shadow master. When they arrived at the office door, Aaron told Laura to stay put while he and the others cleared the room.

He motioned Big T, Stevens and Wan forward as he steadied himself against the wall next to the office and just before Big T raised his foot to kick in the door, the building lights clicked back on as Aaron thought to himself, there must still be Shadow members alive that they had missed.

They all yanked off their night scopes as they waited for their eye sight to return to them from the blinding effects the white light had on their night scope. After he saw that they were ready, he nodded his head at Big T, giving him the signal to kick in the door as the others all fanned around into the doorway to clear the room.

My sector clear, each one of them said one after another as they all saw no signs of any resistance in the room. Aaron quickly turned his attention toward CJ as he ran over to him, where he was tied to a hook on the wall.

CJ's mouth was bounded by duck tape as he hung on a meat hook and went frantic as he saw Aaron walk into the room, kicking his feet out and about while he also made moaning noises as loud as he could as Aaron approached him. Aaron placed his arms around his waist as He tried to lift him off of the hook and set his feet on the floor, but CJ kicked him away as he moaned even louder.

Aaron looked at him and asked what was wrong as he tried once again to lift him off of the hook but, this time from across the room, Big T and the others saw a bright red dot flash against the Sarge's head as T yelled at him telling him to move as he himself looked up to see the Shadow master in the rafters of the office preparing to fire a hand gun with a laser scope.

As Aaron tried to dive to his right, he felt a bullet pass through his left shoulder and leave a burning sensation behind. I'm hit, I'm hit he screamed before he hit the floor as Big T opened fire on the shadow master from the floor.

In the blink of an eye, they all saw the Shadow master, flip out of the rafters away from the stream of tracer rounds and land on the desk and without any hesitation, three shots were fired from the Shadow masters gun as he watched Big T, Stevens and Wan fall to the floor with gun shots wounds in their legs.

Aaron quickly rolled over as he threw one of his knives and knocked the gun out of the shadow master's hand. Aaron threw another knife at him; Laura stepped into the office as she saw the shaded glass mask shatter from the impact of the knife throw.

Once all in the office saw and recognized the face behind the mask, all of their mouths dropped open in disbelief. Yung Lee Kim, Aaron thought, and she was behind all of this from the very start. None of what was happening made any sense to him so in a futile attempt to make sense of the whole thing, he asked . . . "Why Yung Lee, why did you go through all of this trouble to lure me back into this country?"

"You were the light in my father's eyes Aaron and when you left, things fell apart for him, He died of a broken heart because of Alex Kim Jr.'s death. It was too much for him to handle I guess, but my brother found out that I was pregnant and had a miscarriage and was threading to tell father. I couldn't have that, so I had no other choice other than to kill him. Things could have been so good between us Aaron with you as you were before you left, but no I guess things will never be the same since you have her in your life" She said as she sneered at Laura.

"So, is that why you did what you did to me in my office that day with the needle and my cloths? Did you really think that such a bulshit stunt would make me come back to you? Life just doesn't work like that Yung, it just doesn't."

As the brief exchange of words continued, CJ tapped his feet and legs against the wall in hopes of catching Laura's attention and once she looked over at him, she saw him jerking his head while he tried to moan the words, come over here. When she walked over to him, she ripped the tape away from his mouth so she could hear him speak.

Just as she did that, they both heard Yung Lee stamp her foot down against the floor as she said . . . "Damn it Aaron, we could have been so good together; you me and our son Aaron Jr."

"Don't listen to her Sarge, that bitch is crazy! There ain't any Aaron Jr.; it's a clump of blood and guts in a jar of water in your mansion! She's fucked up man!" He shouted out as Laura tried to lift him off of the hook.

Yung took a second to look at Laura as she lowered CJ to his feet and went to work on freeing his hands and legs. She looked back at Aaron as she noticed his attentions had been diverted toward Laura's direction for a moment, then back on her as she made a movement forward toward him.

"I had hoped that you would have come back to your old life here with the Shadow and with me, but I see that she's has taken a great hold in your life. I don't like it Aaron Williamson and I'll tell you; if I can't have you then no will, especially that white bitch over there!"

Without any warning, she lunged at Aaron and kicked him in his right shoulder where he had just been shot. CJ managed to pull Laura down out of the way as Yung Lee fired off two shots in her direction and missed.

Although he was severely stricken with pain from her kick, he managed to flip back onto his feet and kick the gun out of her hands as she whipped around to face him. She jumped back into her defensive stance as they eyed each other in a long moment of silence so thick, anyone in the room could have cut through said silence with a knife.

While his eyes were locked on hers, he thought to himself, Yung Lee wasn't like the others bums he had faced, because she had many skills. In thinking on further, he thought, she got skills, but still; I'm better!

With a quick shuffle of his feet, he turned in a circular motion toward her as he whipped his leg up into the air and struck her across the face as she blinked. In that same spin, he also smacked her across the mouth with the back side of his left fist and sent her down hard to the floor.

Since she wasn't one to be taken lightly, he began to stomp against her ribs as he grunted with each blow. Just as he lifted his foot off of her after only five good stomps, she swept his legs out from underneath him and flipped onto her feet.

While those two squared off in the center of the office, Laura continued to remove the ropes and duck tape from around CJ's wrists and ankles. He kept telling her to hurry up and get his hands and feet freed because he knew that the Sarge wasn't a match for Yung's Kung fu with his wounded shoulder.

As soon as he was freed, they both heard a loud thunderous thud on the floor as they saw Aaron's back slam against it after having been flipped across Yung Lee's shoulders.

Everyone present in the room seemed to be dumbstruck with aw as they were all frozen in place, while the action occurred before their eyes. Back and forth the battle went, move after move until Yung Lee stepped toward the desk, placed her left foot on its edge and went into a high back double kick which struck him in his wounded shoulder and chest.

Already fatigued from the combination of the thirty minute fight with Young Lee as well as the high movement fighting he had gone through prior to this fight, Aaron struggled to recover from this vicious blow dealt to him by Yung Lee. He tried to flip back onto his feet, but no sooner than steadied himself once he was up right, when Yung whipped her leg around and struck him square on his top lip and sent him flying back down to the floor, flat on his back.

Still watching as all of this happened, Laura jumped in her place as she gasped in a deep breath of air of shock. When she moved, she felt something poke her on her leg that she hadn't even noticed was there before. As her eyes saw Yung Lee reach into her belt and pull out a switch blade and open it, she thought to herself; oh my God, it's the 44 auto hand gun. He must have slipped it on my belt when we were on the floor out in the hallway.

Once she pulled it out of her belt, she cocked it immediately and raised it up next to her head as she almost hit CJ in his face with it. Yung Lee was already atop Aaron and had his arms pinned under her legs as she reared back with the knife, ready to strike as Laura quickly ran over and grabbed her wrist out of the air as she placed the end of the gun's barrel against Yung's head

She bared down on Yung with a look of burning intensity as she pulled the guns hammer into firing position, but before she had the chance to pull the trigger, Yung used her own force against her as she threw her over Aaron's head, where she landed flat on her back. In mid air as she was flipped, she lost grip of the gun that she was holding as it landed in the far corner of the office and discharged a shot.

The stray round struck CJ in the center of his right thigh, where he dropped immediately as he clutched his leg and screamed out in agony. Yung Lee herself, dove at Laura, but was tripped up before she reached her as Aaron grabbed he by the ankle. He positioned himself in a way to twist her leg in an attempt to injure her, but she used her other leg and foot and kicked his hand away, as she lunged forward and pounded Laura on the forehead with her fist.

She sat on her knees with Laura's head in-between them on the floor as she felt a sharp pain in the small of her back as Aaron tackled her away from Laura. In the split second of air time that they were both in from the tackle, she had managed to twist her body to where she was on top of him just before their impact against the floor.

Once his back landed with thud, he tried to swing a wild, mistimed punch in her direction, but was quickly blocked and countered with a vicious double back fist strike that rocked his eyes sight. From the corner of her eye, she saw a movement coming toward her and when she looked up to see what it was that was flying at her, she saw an electric pencil sharpener coming straight for her face.

After she ducked in the nick of time to Laura's dismay, she saw Yung Lee jump to her feet and look at her with the look of pure evil in her eyes as she started toward her. And when she reached her, Laura tried to hit her with a closed fist, but was quickly caught by Yung as she wrapped her arm up in a submission hold which put pressure against her elbow.

With a lighting fast punch to her face and a knee to her gut, Yung released her arm as she bent over and grabbed Laura in a cross body hold as she prepared to body slam Laura across the desk. As she threw her, Laura grabbed two fists full of Yung's long jet black hair and held on with all of her might. Since this was in the heat of battle, she hadn't even noticed that Laura had her by her hair when she threw her across the desk, once she landed with her stomach coming down on the edge of it; she pulled with all of her might as she saw Yung's face smash down hard against the hard wooden desk.

While her head was still down, Aaron who had managed to make his way back onto his feet, grabbed her by the head then slammed it against it again and again. Using her leg, she reached back and kicked up with all of her strength where the kick landed right against in the center of his crotch!

His body went numb with pain as Yung grabbed him by the left shoulder and punched him in his wound on his right shoulder. As she continuously hit him with explosive force again and again with clinched teeth along with a deranged look in her eyes, Laura looked around for something to throw at her But, when she finally got tired of looking, she jumped across the desk where she grabbed her by the hair once again as she pulled her away from Aaron, then slammed her head back down to the desk.

Laura released her fists full of hair and tried to pound Yung in her face, but she again proved to be too quick for her as she caught her by the wrist in mid swing and after she knocked her hand away, in the same motion, reached back and kicked Laura in her chest, sending her flying into the wall. With her head turned, she never saw Aaron coming as he grabbed her by the legs and arm and threw her half way across the office into the near wall with a loud bang. In his great rage, he never took the chance to consider where he was throwing her or what was in the area of her impact when he did it.

As she slid down the wall and hit the floor on her butt, they both saw her 357 handgun at the same time. His eye sight, along with everyone else's in the office went to tunnel vision as they all focused in on that gun and watched as she sifted her weight and moved toward it. Just before her hand reached it though, a foot came out of nowhere and stomped down on her hand with a loud thud.

Her entire body was stretched out as she lifted her head up and eyes to see Laura standing over her, as she held the Desert Eagle 44 auto hand gun on her. As she gritted her teeth and bore down on her hand with her foot, she looked into Yung Lee's black colorless eyes as she said; while she pulled the guns hammer back . . . "Remember a few days ago when you told me that the only reason I was still alive, was because you allowed me to be? Remember when you made me thank you for allowing me to live? Well they'll be no need for thanks from you to me Yung Lee Kim, because I'll not allow you to live past this minute!"

Even though everyone was watching as she pulled the trigger, it still didn't stop them from jumping as the powerful gun went off and lit up the side of the office. After seeing the side of Yung's head explode, Laura still wasn't satisfied as she fired again and again as she yelled at the top of her lungs . . . "Come on bitch," BANG! "Talk shit now!" BANG! "Don't bitch up now!" Bang!

By her third shot, Aaron grabbed the gun out of her hand, and then embraced her in a hug as he tried to calm her down as he said . . . "Its ok honey, she's dead now and she won't hurt us anymore. That's it now baby, I've got you now and I'll never leave your side ever again."

"Aaron is it really over now? I mean really over? I love you so much, please don't let me go." She said as she hugged him even tighter.

"I love you too honey, I love you so much." He answered with tears in his eyes

As they embraced one another neither one of them heard anything else around them that was going on, as Dee-Dee and Tracy stormed into the office with their weapons drawn.

"What the hell is going on in here? We heard several shots and came running . . . Oh my god, CJ baby you've been shot. I'm coming baby; momma will take care of you." Dee-Dee shouted

"God damn it Sarge, what the hall happened in here? You along with everyone else in here look like you've been drug through hell and back." she said with a slight laugh.

"We were Tracy, we were, but it's over now. My question is where the hell have you two been? I really could have used you both in here!" He blurted out with anger in his voice.

"When the lights went back on after we tired that other Korean bitch up, we went to check it out. I don't know how you did it, but you missed about 15 members of the Shadow. Don't worry though, we took care of them all, they won't he bothering anyone ever again." She answered with the sound of cockiness in her voice.

"You mentioned the other Korean woman, that being Lyn Ty I take it yes? Well you did leave her knocked out didn't you?" He asked with obvious concern in his tone

"No we just left her tied with industrial plastic draw ties. Those things will cut her skin if she tries to struggle in them. Why." Tracy Asked

"Laura, honey stay here and help with the wounded. I have to go make sure that Lyn Ty is still there or else her father will send more men after me. Tracy, Dee-Dee you all get these men down to the pier, I'll be right back. Love you honey." He said with a kiss as he turned and ran for the door.

"I love you too Aaron and be careful." She shouted at his back.

In the hallway, as he made his way down each of the corridor, he heard a chopper come in over head and landed on the ground just in front of the main entrance as deep in the back of his mind; somehow he knew that it was her trying to make her way back to her father. He headed down the staircase as he spoke into his headset as he contacted Rick over their net and told him to make a meet with him on the roof of the building as he himself ran across the cargo hold and headed up the stairs toward the third floor.

Once he reached the roof, he saw Lyn Ty's white chopper pulling off in the near distance as Rick circled in over the roof just seconds after he had reached the top and when the rear ramp dropped open, he ran on and grabbed his rifle case. As he assembled his weapon, he spoke to Rick again as he told him to elevate to about 10, 000 FT and hold her steady for him when he was ready to fire. One minute later, after his rifle was all together completed, by-pod and all, he told Rick he was ready and set for him to take off.

Rick himself pulled up on his thrust control stick as Aaron felt the bird raise steadily as the crew chief told Rick that all was well since he had the rear ramp opened during flight as he himself watched on while Aaron a fixed his laser range finder, 20X10 sight scope to the top of his rifle. Once they reached 10,000FT in the air, Aaron looked through his powerful scope as he picked up a sight picture of Lyn Ty's fleeing chopper. After he pressed a red button on the side of his scope, he saw the exact distance of his intended target in small red numbers as they showed up in the bottom of his scope picture.

2100 meters and growing he thought to himself as he breathed in a deep breath and steadied himself for the shot. Being that he was firing at a Jet Bell Ranger helicopter, he knew that he had to place the cross hairs of his scope right on the butt end of the Chopper's cab and in one smooth motion, he squeezed the trigger as his rifle fired one tracer lit round.

Only seconds passed by as he saw the round strike the chopper's rear end and pierced its fuel tank, sending it into flames in mid air. After he saw the explosion before his eyes, he said to himself, one shot one kill, that's the only way to do it.

He told Rick to set the ramp down on the pier and to wait for him and the others to get there and once the ramp touched the wood of the pier, he jumped out then ran inside as he left his rifle inside the chopper. Once he rounded the corners, he arrived back at the cargo hold where he saw Laura, Dee-Dee and Tracy as they helped the wounded men walk long through the huge room. Not a word Sarge, CJ said with his arm around his wife's shoulder for support as he gazed met with Aaron's eyes.

Just as the group as a whole began to move as one toward the doorway that led back to the pier, they were all startled as the roof of the cargo hold exploded in with a loud boom. Luckily they weren't in the center of the room and were totally clear as they all saw the huge fragments of the roof crash down onto the floor in front of them. They all watched on as they saw four ropes string down into the room as Half, Big dog, dusty and Sand man repel down into the hold.

As they were closely followed by the other men of Infiltrate, they looked around the room as Half walked over to CJ and the others by the doorway as they were covered in dust and wood debris. The other group leaders all held their positions as Half walked up to CJ and asked . . ." #1 what the hell happened to you? Did you all leave any of them for us?"

"Na man, you missed the party and it was all that-too man."

"Well since everything is already done in here, what's our next move #1?" He asked as he took hold of his other arm and helped along with carrying him.

"I say we blow this mother up as we head back to China. What do you say Sarge?" He said with a touch of enthusiasm in his voice.

"I've got my lady by my side and the Shadow is no more, old friend, anything sounds good to me right about now." He said as he hugged Laura with his good arm.

Half call to the others telling them to come and help with the wounded as they all made their way back into the two choppers and headed back toward China Aaron and Laura never left each other's side all during the long ride back across the border nor did they part as they sat next one another on the plane hack to the U.S.

At one point during the long ride and—slow ride back, as the men of Infiltrate joked and laughed amongst themselves. Laura looked into Aaron's eyes and asked . . . "Honey is there anything else that I should know before anything like this happens to me again?"

"That's everything baby, that's everything. Life might get real interesting once we're back upstate in New York. The shadow left quite the mess in our building not to mention what they did to the Rock Palace. As far as my past, all of that is dead now and behind me. There's only us now baby. I only hope that through everything you can find it in your heart to forgive me for lying to you in the first place?" He asked as he took her by the hand.

"What, after all that I've been through, shit you're into me big time after this Mr. Williamson. I think that we can start off by you giving me a bath and doing my toe nails afterward. No I'm just playing babe. Now that I have a full understanding of what it was that you wanted to protect me from, I can see where I might forgive you. I just might see it." She said as she kissed him genially on the lips. "You just might huh? You know, I've never loved a woman like the way that I love you. I can't even imagine my life without you in it, I just can't." He said as he embraced her with a look of tenderness on his face.

"Oh come on now baby, I told you, you're stuck with me hopefully, for the rest of our long lives. Now baby I have a question that I've always wanted to ask you, but never had the chance." She said as she looked up at him with a devilish grin on her face.

"Ok, and that question is?"

"Are you a member of the mile high club" She asked through an ear to ear smile.

"What the hell is that, I've never heard of it before honey." H answered with a puzzled look on his face.

"Well Mr. Williamson, since you've never heard of it, I think it's a club that we should both join while we're both on this flight."

"And how do we join this club my dear and what must we do to join it?"

"Follow me into the bathroom and I'm sure that once we land back in the USA, we'll have what it takes to be members of the club, several times over." She answered with a devilish smile on her face as she stood up and Ted him by the hand into the bathroom toward the rear of the plane.

They made love in the bathroom some five miles above the earth as the pilot of the plane flew back into the night as he took the world's largest cargo plane back across the International Date Line. As they chased the night some slept as others joked and carried on during the entire flight, but one thing was to be certain, no matter if it was them making love in the bathroom, or them just holding each other in their seats, Aaron never let go of Laura nor did she let go of him for in the end the love they shared was strong enough to endure all that the mean world had to thrown at them; this time. The plane flew on into the night as the darkness fell over the Pacific Ocean and the West Coast of the United States.

THE END